Praise for *New York Times* Bestselling Author

HEATHER GRAHAM

"Graham plays the story's supernatural angle
for both chills and chuckles…. Ringo is the
best ghost to come along in ages."
—*RT Book Reviews* on *Nightwalker*

"Romantic flourishes enhance this bewitching blend
of Native American lore, ghostly shenanigans and
modern-day chicanery."
—*Publishers Weekly* on *Nightwalker*

"Mystery, sex, paranormal events. What's not to love?"
—*Kirkus Reviews* on *The Death Dealer*

"Graham peoples her novel with genuine,
endearing characters."
—*Publishers Weekly* on *The Séance*

"Graham's latest is an entertaining vampire yarn."
—*Publishers Weekly* on *Blood Red*

"The intense, unexpected conclusion will leave readers
well satisfied."
—*Publishers Weekly* on *The Dead Room*

"Even though this ghostly thriller is not a romance…
[Graham] introduce[s] delicious romantic interludes.
She also brings a fresh perspective to New York's
mysterious underground city."
—*Booklist* on *The Dead Room*

New York Times bestselling author Heather Graham has written more than a hundred novels, many of which have been featured by the Doubleday Book Club and the Literary Guild. An avid scuba diver, ballroom dancer and mother of five, she still enjoys her south Florida home, but loves to travel as well, from locations such as Cairo, Egypt, to her own backyard, the Florida Keys. Reading, however, is the pastime she still loves best, and she is a member of many writing groups. She's currently vice president of the Horror Writers' Association, and she's also an active member of International Thriller Writers. She is very proud to be a Killerette in the Killer Thriller Band, along with many fellow novelists she greatly admires. For more information, check out her Web site, theoriginalheathergraham.com.

HEATHER GRAHAM

THE KEEPERS

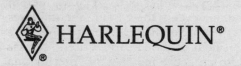

HARLEQUIN®

TORONTO • NEW YORK • LONDON
AMSTERDAM • PARIS • SYDNEY • HAMBURG
STOCKHOLM • ATHENS • TOKYO • MILAN • MADRID
PRAGUE • WARSAW • BUDAPEST • AUCKLAND

Recycling programs
for this product may
not exist in your area.

ISBN-13: 978-0-373-61844-6

THE KEEPERS

Copyright © 2010 by Heather Graham Pozzessere

Dear Reader,

First, thank you for reading this! There's nothing in the world to me like the pleasure of telling a story—unless it's getting to do so with friends.

Alex Sokoloff is the author of the second book in this series. I met Alex when we were both called to be in the Thriller Killer Band—and it felt immediately as if I had known her all my life. We share a love of adventures—in the water, on land and in our great cities. Every year I do a Labor Day benefit in New Orleans, and Alex has been there, helping, teaching screenwriting and giving her all.

Deborah LeBlanc is another amazing woman. She's from Louisiana, and has done brilliant things for me and on her own to support reading, our youth—and New Orleans. Deb is president of Horror Writers of America, teaches a boot camp called Pen to Press and has attended many an autopsy!

For the three of us to come together—as we were able to do several times, luckily, in the planning of this series—and work on a project has been sheer joy. And, of course, since we all love New Orleans so much, when we began to think of a world where paranormal beings might just blend in…well, New Orleans popped right into all our heads. Seriously—where else would you hide in plain sight if you were a bit different from others?

My admiration for these two wonderful authors is absolute, and I hope you'll enjoy our combined venture, that you'll enjoy The Keepers—our three sisters charged with keeping the balance in the underworld.

Please look for their books in the months to come!

Best,

Heather Graham

To Connie Perry, my extremely dear friend and cohort in many an endeavor. Thank you for all you do—and especially for New Orleans!

Also, for Daena Moller and Larry Montz and the ISPR. Thank you for some great adventures, too!

Prologue

When the world as we know it was created, it wasn't quite *actually* as we know it.

That's because so much was lost in the mists of time, and the collective memory of the human race often chooses what it will hold and what it will discard.

But once the world held no skyscrapers, rockets did not go to the moon—in fact, the wheel had barely been invented, and families lived together and depended upon one another. The denizens of the world knew better the beauty of waterfalls, of hills and vales, sun and sunset, shadows—and magic.

In a time when the earth was young, giants roamed, gnomes grumbled about in the forests and many a creature—malignant, sadly, as well as benign—was known to exist. Human beings might not have liked these creatures, they might have feared them—for a predator is a predator—but they knew of their existence, and as man has always learned to deal with predators, so he did then. Conversely, there were the creatures he loved, cherished as friends and often turned to when alliances needed to be formed. Humankind learned to exist by guidelines and rules, and thus the world went on, day after day, and man survived. Now, all men were not good, nor were all men bad, and so it was also with the giants, leprechauns, dwarfs, ghosts, pixies, pookas, vampires and other such beings.

Man was above them all, by his nature, and he prospered through centuries and then millennia, and learned to send rockets to the moon—and use rockets of another kind against his fellow man.

When the earth was young, and there were those creatures considered to be of light and goodness, and others who were considered to be, shall we say, more destructive, there was among them a certain form of being who was human and yet not human. Or perhaps human, but with special powers. They were the Keepers, and it was their lot in life not only to enjoy the world as other beings did, but they were also charged with the duty of maintaining balance. When certain creatures got out of hand, the Keepers were to bring them back under control. Some, in various centuries, thought of them as witches or wiccans. But in certain centuries that was not a healthy identity to maintain. Besides, they were not exactly the witches of a Papal Bull or evil in the way the devil in Dante's Inferno, nor were they the gentle women of pagan times who learned to heal with herbs and a gentle touch.

They were themselves and themselves alone. The Keepers.

As time went by, anything that was not purely *logical*

was no longer accepted, was relegated to superstition, except in distant, fog-shrouded hills or the realm of Celtic imagination, which was filled with Celtic spirits other than those of which we speak. But some of the beliefs of the past were not accepted even there. Man himself is, of course, a predator, but man learned to live by rules and logic, or destroy all the creatures upon which he might prey. Too late for some, for man did hunt certain creatures to extinction, and he sought to drive others to the same fate. But those other creatures learned a survival technique that served them well: hide. Hide in plain sight, if you will, but hide.

As human populations grew, as people learned to read, as electricity reigned, and the telephone and computer put the world in touch, the earth became entrenched in a place where there were things that were accepted and others that were not. Oh, it's true that the older generations in Ireland knew that the banshees still wailed at night. In Hungary and the Baltic states, men and women knew that the tales of wolfmen in the forests were more than stories for a scary night. And there were other such pockets of belief around the globe. But few men living in the logical and technological world believed in myths and legends, which was good, because man was ever fond of destroying that which he feared.

All creatures, great and small, wish to survive. We all know what humans are like—far too quick to hunt down, kill or make war on those they didn't fully understand. Many people are trying, as they have tried for centuries, to see the light, to put away their prejudices. But that's a long journey, longer than the world has lasted so far.

Even so, those who were not quite human found various special places of strange tolerance to live their lives quietly and normally, without anyone paying them too much attention. Places where everyone was accustomed to the bizarre and, frankly, walked right by it most of the time.

Places like New Orleans, Louisiana.

Since there were plenty of people already living there who *thought* they were, or *claimed* to be, vampires, it seemed an eminently logical place for a well-behaved and politically correct vampire society to thrive, as well.

As a result, that is where several Keepers, charged with maintaining the balance between the otherworldly, under-the-radar societies of *beings* who flocked there, came as the twenty-first century rolled along.

And thus it was that the MacDonald sisters lived there, working, partying—this was New Orleans, after all—and, of course, keeping the balance of justice in a world that seldom collided with the world most people thought of as real, as the only world.

Seldom.

But not never.

There were exceptions.

Such as the September morning when Detective Jagger DeFarge got the call to come to the cemetery.

And there, stretched out on top of a tomb in the long defunct Grigsby family mausoleum, was the woman in white. Porcelain and beautiful, if it hadn't been for the delicate silk and gauze fabric that spread around her, she might have been a piece of funerary art, a statue, frozen in marble.

Because she, too, was white, as white as her dress, as white as the marble, because every last drop of blood had been drained from her body.

Chapter 1

"Sweet Jesus!" Detective Tony Miro said, crossing himself as he stared at the corpse.

The cemetery itself had already been closed off, yellow crime tape surrounding the area around the mausoleum. Jagger DeFarge had been assigned as lead detective on the case, and he knew he should have been complimented, but in reality he just felt weary—and deeply concerned.

Beyond the concern one felt over any victim of murder or violent crime.

This was far worse. This threatened a rising body count to come.

Gus Parissi, a young uniformed cop, stuck his head inside the mausoleum. The light was muted, streaks of sunlight that filtered in through the ironwork filigree at the top end of the little house within the "city of the dead."

Gus stared at the dead woman.

"Sweet Jesus," he echoed, and also crossed himself.

Jagger winced, looking away for a moment, waiting. He wanted to be alone with the victim, but he had a partner. Being alone wasn't going to be easy.

"Thank you, Parissi," Jagger said. "The crime-scene crew can have the place in ten minutes. Hey, Miro, go on out and see who's on the job today, will you?"

Miro was still just staring.

"And get another interview with Tom Cooley, too. He's the guide who saw her and called it in, right?" Jagger asked.

"Uh—yeah, yeah," Tony said, closing his mouth at last, turning and following Gus out.

Alone at last, my poor, poor dear, Jagger thought.

The dust of the ages seemed to have settled within the burial chamber, on the floor, on the stone and concrete walls, on the plaques that identified the dead within the vault. In contrast, the young woman on the tomb was somehow especially beautiful and pristine, a vision in white, like an angel. Sighing, Jagger walked over to the body. To all appearances, she was sleeping like a heavenly being in her pure perfection.

He pulled out his pocket flashlight to look for the bite marks that had to exist. He gently and carefully moved her hair, but there were no marks on her neck. He searched her thighs, then her arms, his eyes quick but thorough.

At last he found what he sought. He doubted that the medical examiner—even with the most up-to-date technology available—would ever find the tiny pinpricks located in the crease at her elbow.

He swore out loud just as Tony returned.

His partner was a young cop. A good cop, and not a squeamish one. Most of the crimes taking place these days had to do with a sudden flare of temper and, as always, drugs. Tony had worked a homicide with him just outside the Quarter in which a kid the size of a pro linebacker had taken a shotgun blast in the face. Tony had been calm and professional throughout the grisly first inspection, then handled the player's mother with gentle care.

Today, however, he seemed freaked.

"What?" Tony asked.

Jagger shook his head. "No blood here at all, no signs of violence. No lividity, but she's still in rigor....Is the M.E. here?"

Tony nodded.

"Send him in," Jagger said. "Have you interviewed the guide yet?"

Tony, staring at the body, shook his head. "One of the uniforms went to find him."

"He can't have gone far. Stay out there until they find him and interview him. And anyone who was with him. Then meet me back at the station, and we'll get her picture out in the media. I want uniforms raking the neighborhood, the dumpsters, you name it, looking for a purse, clothing, anything they can find."

Tony nodded and left.

The M.E. the Coroner's Office had sent out that morning was Craig Dewey. Dewey looked like anything but the general conception of what a medical examiner should: he was tall, blond, about thirty-five. Basically, until they found out what he did for a living, most women considered him a heartthrob.

Like the others, he paused in the door. But Dewey

didn't stand there stunned and frozen as Tony and Gus had done. He *did* stare, but Jagger could see that his keen blue eyes were taking in the scene, top to bottom, before he approached the corpse. Finally that stare focused on the victim. He looked at her for a long while, then turned to Jagger.

"Well, here's one for the books," he said, his tone matter-of-fact. "On initial inspection, without even touching her, I'd say she's been entirely drained of blood." He looked around. "And it wasn't done here."

"No. I'd say not," Jagger agreed with what appeared to be obvious.

"Such a pity, and so strange. Murder is never beautiful, and yet…she *is* beautiful," Dewey commented.

"Dewey, give me something that isn't in plain sight," Jagger said.

Dewey went to work. He was efficient and methodical. He had his camera out, the flash going as he shot the body from every conceivable angle. Then he approached the woman, checked for liver temperature and shook his head. "She's still in rigor. Other than the fact that she's about bloodless, I have no idea what's going on here. I'll need to get her into the morgue to figure out how and why she died. I can't find anything to show how it might have happened. Odd, really odd. A body without blood wouldn't shock me—we seem to attract wackos to this city all the time—but I can't find so much as a pinprick to explain what happened. Hell, like I said, I've got to get her out of here to check further. Lord knows, enough people around here *think* they're vampires."

"Right, I know," Jagger said. "When did she die? I was estimating late last night or early this morning."

"Then you're right on," Dewey told him. "She died

sometime between midnight and two in the morning, but give me fifteen minutes either side."

"I want everything you get as quickly as you get it," Jagger said.

"I have two shooting deaths, a motorcycle accident, a possible vehicular homicide—not to mention that the D.A.'s determined to harass an octogenarian over her husband's death, even though he's been suffering from cancer for years—" Dewey broke off, seeing the set expression on Jagger's face. "Sure, Lafarge. I'll put a rush on it. This is the kind of thing you've got to get a handle on quickly, God knows. We get enough sensationalist media coverage around here. I don't want to see a frenzy start."

"Thanks," Jagger told him.

He looked around the Grigsby family tomb one more time. It was what he *didn't* see that he noted. No fingerprints in the dust. No footprints. No sign whatsoever of how the girl had come to lie, bloodless and beautiful, upon the dusty tomb of a long dead patriarch.

He wanted the CSUs, Tony and the uniforms all busy here. He had some investigating to do that he needed to tackle on his own.

He lowered his sunglasses from the top of his head to his eyes and walked back out into the brilliant light of the early fall morning.

The sky was cloudless and brilliantly blue. The air was pleasant, without the dead heat of summer.

It seemed to be a day when the world was vibrant. Positively *pulsing* with life.

"Hey, Detective DeFarge!"

It was Celia Larson, forty, scrubbed, the no-nonsense

head of the crime-scene unit that had been assigned. "Can we go on in? I've had my folks working the area, around the entry, around the tomb…but, hey, with the cemeteries around here being such tourist hangouts, folks had been tramping around for an hour before we got the call. We've collected every possible sample we could, but we really need to get inside."

"It's all yours, Celia. And good luck."

She leaned into the mausoleum and said accusingly, "You and Dewey have tramped all over the footprints."

"There were no footprints."

"There had to be footprints," she said flatly, as if he was the worst kind of fool.

He shrugged and smiled.

"None, but, hey, you're the expert. You'll see what we missed, right?" he asked pleasantly. Celia wasn't his favorite civil servant with whom to work. She considered every police officer, from beat cop right on up to detective, to be an oaf with nothing better to do than mess up her crime scene. She didn't seem to understand the concept of teamwork—or that she was the technician, and the detectives used her information to put the pieces together, find the suspect and make the arrest. Celia had seen way too many CSI-type shows and had it in her head that she was going to be the detective who solved every case. Still, he did his best to be level-tempered and professional, if not pleasant. He did have to work with the woman.

"Get me a good picture of the face, Celia. We'll get her image out to the media."

She waved a hand dismissively, and he walked on.

This wasn't going to be an ordinary case. And he

wasn't going to be able to investigate in any of the customary ways.

He made it as far as the sidewalk.

Then he saw real trouble.

He groaned inwardly. Of course she would show up. Of course—despite the fact that he'd only just seen the corpse himself, word had traveled.

She didn't look like trouble. Oddly enough, she came with a smile that was pure charm, and she was, in fact, stunning. She was tall and slim and lithe, mercurial in her graceful movements.

Her eyes were blue. They could be almost as aqua as the sea, as light as a summer sky, as piercing as midnight.

Naturally she was a blonde. Not that brunettes couldn't be just as beautiful, just as angelic looking—or just as manipulative.

She had long blond hair. Like her eyes, it seemed to change. It could appear golden in the sun, platinum in moonlight and always as smooth and soft as silk as it curled over her shoulders. She had a fringe of bangs that were both waiflike and the height of fashion.

And naturally she was here.

Sunglasses shaded her eyes, as they did his. The Southern Louisiana sun could be brutal. Most people walked around during the day with shades on.

"Well, hello, Miss MacDonald," he said, heading for his car. Officers had blocked the entry to the cemetery and the borders of the scene itself with crime-scene tape. But the sidewalk was fair game. The news crews had arrived and staked it out, and the gawkers were lining up, as well.

Before Fiona MacDonald could reply, one of the

local network news reporters saw him and charged over, calling, "Detective! Detective DeFarge!" It was Andrea "Andy" Larkin. She was a primped and proper young woman who had recently been transferred from her network's Ohio affiliate. She was a fish out of water down here.

She was followed by her cameraman, and he was followed by a pack of other reporters. The local cable stations and newspapers were all present. And yes, there came the other network newscasters.

He stopped. Might as well handle the press now, he thought, though the department's community rep really should be fielding the questions. But if he dodged the reporters, it would just make things worse.

He held his ground, aware that Fiona was watching him from a spot not far from the cemetery wall. He wasn't going to escape the reporters, and he definitely wasn't going to escape her.

"Detective DeFarge?" Andy Larkin had apparently assigned herself to be the spokeswoman for the media crew. "We've heard a young woman has been found—drained of blood. Who was she? Do you think we have some kind of cultists at work in the area? Was it a ritual sacrifice?"

He lifted a hand as a clamoring of questions arose, one voice indistinguishable from the next.

"Ladies, gentlemen, please! We've just begun our investigation into this case. Yes, we *have* discovered the body of a young woman in a mausoleum, but that's all that I can really tell you at the moment. We'll have the preliminary autopsy reports in a day or so, which will answer any questions about the state of the body. We don't have an identity for the victim, and it's far too early for me to speculate in any way on whether this is a singular incident or not. However, at this time I have no reason to suspect that we have a cult at work in the city. As soon as I have information, you'll have information. That's absolutely all that I am at liberty to say at the moment."

"But—" Andy Larkin began.

"At any time that I *can*, without jeopardizing our investigation, I will be happy to see to it that the news media is advised."

"Wait!" A man from one of the rags spoke up; he was probably in his early twenties, taking the best job available to a young journalism graduate. His hair was long and shaggy, and he was wearing jeans and a T-shirt, and carrying a notepad rather than an electronic device of any kind. "Shouldn't you be warning the citizens of New Orleans to be careful? Shouldn't you be giving them a profile of the killer?"

Jagger hoped his sunglasses fully covered his eyes as he inadvertently stared over at Fiona MacDonald.

She had a profile of the killer, he was certain.

"We don't know anything yet. I repeat—we've just begun our investigation. I'm going to give young women in this city the same warning I give all the time: be smart, and be careful. Don't go walking the streets alone in the dark. Let someone know where you're going at all times, and if you go out to party, don't go alone. People, use common sense. That's my warning."

"But aren't serial killers usually young white men between the ages of twenty-five and thirty-five?" shouted a tiny woman from the rear. She was Livy Drew, from a small local cable station.

He reminded himself that he had to stay calm—and

courteous. The public affairs department was much better at that, though, and he fervently wished they would hurry up and get there.

"Livy, there's nothing to indicate that we have a serial killer on our hands."

"You're denying that this is the work of a serial killer?"

"I'm not denying or confirming anything," he said, fighting for patience. "One more time—our investigation is just beginning. Yes, young women should take special care, because yes, a young woman has been killed. Now, if you'll let me get to work, I'll be able to answer more questions for you in the future. Though we have no ID on her yet, we may make a hit with fingerprints or dental impressions, and we'll have a picture available for you soon. And, as always, the department will be grateful for any information that can help us identify the victim—and find her killer. But no heroics from anyone, please. Just call the station with any information you may have."

Someone called from the back of the crowd. "Detective, what—"

"That's all!" Jagger said firmly, then turned to head for his car, parked almost directly in front of the gates. He looked for Fiona MacDonald, but she was gone.

He knew where he would find her.

He got into his car and pulled away from the curb, glancing expectantly in the rearview mirror. She was just sitting up. Her expression was grim as she stared at him.

"What the hell is going on, DeFarge?" she asked.

He nearly smiled. If things hadn't been quite so serious, he would have.

"I don't know."

"Well, *I* do. You have a rogue vampire on your hands. And you have to put a stop to this immediately."

He pulled up the ramp to a public parking area by the river. He found a quiet place to park along the far edge of the lot and turned to look at her.

Fiona was young, somewhere around twenty-nine or thirty, he thought. Young in any world, very young in *their* world.

They knew each other, of course; they saw each other now and then at the rare council meetings in which several underworld groups met to discuss events, make suggestions, keep tabs on one another and keep the status quo going.

He suddenly wished fervently that her parents were still alive. The savage war that had nearly ripped through the city had been stopped only by the tremendous sacrifice the couple had made, leaving their daughters to watch over the evenly divided main powers existing in the underbelly of New Orleans, a world few even knew existed.

Naturally the war had been fought because of a vampire.

No, not true. A vampire and a shapeshifter.

Vampire Cato Leone had fallen deeply and madly in love with shapeshifter Susan Chaisse, who had fallen in love with him in return. The two had been unable to understand why they weren't allowed to fall in love. Frankly Jagger didn't understand it, either. Old World prejudice had done them in. It had been a *Romeo and Juliet* scenario, a Southern *West Side Story*, a tale as old as time. Young love seldom cared about proper boundaries. Man and every subspecies of man seemed prone to prejudice, and it was usually born of fear and or economics. Either way, the outcome was almost always the same. In this case, just as in Shakespeare's tale, it had been cousins of the young lovers who had caused the problems. Susan's first cousin Julian had taken on the form of a monster being, half vampire, half werewolf, and attacked Cato. Shapeshifters were truly gifted; they could take on whatever shape they chose, and mimic not only another's appearance but take on their powers, as well. Cato hadn't even known who he was battling, and in the thick of the fight his own cousin jumped to his aid and was killed by the shapeshifter. That raised an uncontrollable rage in Cato, who in turn killed his attacker, and because the shapeshifter had taken on a guise that was partly werewolf, Cato's family had attacked the werewolves, and the violence had threatened to spill over into the streets. The power that Fiona MacDonald's parents had summoned to defeat the warring parties had cost them their lives. No Keeper, no matter how strong, could exert that much power and survive.

They had known what they were doing. But they had known as well that if the battle had erupted into the human world, it would have brought about the destruction of them all. Humans far outnumbered the various paranormal subspecies, not just here, but across the world, though the largest concentration of any such creatures was right here, in New Orleans, Louisiana, commonly referred to locally as NOLA. History had decreed that they all learn how to coexist. Werewolves learned to harness their power at each full moon, and vampires learned how to exist on the occasional foray into a blood bank, along with a steady diet of cow's blood. The shapeshifters had it the easiest, subsisting in their human form on human diets. Hell, half of them were vegetarians these days.

"Fiona," he said quietly, "I can only repeat what I've said to the media. I don't know anything yet. I have to investigate. God knows there are enough idiots living here, and more coming all the time, who want to *think* they're vampires. You can't deny that this city does attract more than its share of would-be mystics, cultists, wiccans, psychics and plain old nuts."

"I heard that she was entirely drained of blood," Fiona said flatly.

He wished that he were dealing with her mother. Jen MacDonald had lived a long life; she had been a fine Keeper, along with her husband, Ewan. The two—both born with the marks of each of the three major subspecies—had been fair and judicious. And wise. They had never jumped to conclusions; they had always done their own questioning, conducted their own investigations. They had loved those they had been born to watch, never interjecting themselves into the governing councils of their charges but being there in case of disputes or problems—or to point out potential problems before they became major bones of contention.

Jagger took a deep breath. He had become a police officer himself because he didn't want history to keep repeating itself. Most of the underworld—Keepers included—had come to NOLA after years of seeking a real home. The church's battle against "witchcraft" had begun as long ago as the 900s, and in 1022, even monks—pious, but outspoken against some of the doctrines of the church—had been burned. Witchcraft had become synonymous with devil worship, and the monks were said to cavort with demons and devils, indulge in mass orgies, and sacrifice and even eat small children. In 1488 the Papal Bull issued by Pope Innocent III set off hundreds of years of torture and death for any innocent accused of witchcraft. Jagger found it absolutely astounding that any intelligent man had ever believed that the thousands persecuted through the years could possibly have been the devil worshipping witches they were condemned for being. If they'd had half the powers they were purported to possess, they would have called upon the devil and flown far away from the stake, where they were tied and allowed to choose between the garrote or burning alive.

Sadly thousands of innocents had perished after cruel torture. The Inquisition had thrived in Germany and France, and many of those who truly weren't human left to escape possible discovery. Many of the main subspecies, as well as the smaller groups, came to the New World from the British Isles. Pixies, fairies, leprechauns, banshees and more fled during the reign of James VI of Scotland, also known as James I of England. Before 1590, the Scots hadn't been particularly interested in witchcraft. But in that year James—as a self-professed expert—began to enforce the laws with a vengeance and impose real punishment. He was terrified of a violent death, and certain that witches had been responsible for a storm that had nearly killed him and his new wife at sea. His orders sent the witch-finder general into a frenzy, torturing and killing for the most ridiculous of reasons, using the most hideous of methods.

When the Puritans headed for the New World in the early 1600s—intent, oddly enough, on banishing anyone from their colonies who was not of their faith, despite the fact that they had traveled across the ocean in pursuit of religious freedom—the various not-quite-human species began to make their way across the sea to a new life, as well.

There were other witchcraft trials in the New World before Salem, but it was the frenzy of the Salem witchcraft trials that caused another mass migration. The French in America had little interest in witchcraft, and French law allowed for a great deal more freedom of belief.

By the time of the Louisiana Purchase, most Keepers and their charges alike had made it down to New Orleans. And there, though not particularly trusting of one another, they had still found a safe home.

Until the elder MacDonalds had been killed. Their deaths, their sacrifice, had been noted by all clans and families. And not only had peace been restored, there had been a sea change in the way the different species felt about each other. There had been a number of intermarriages since that time. Of course, there were still those who were totally against any intermingling of the bloodlines, those who thought themselves superior.

But overall, there had been peace. America was a free country. They were free to hold their own opinions about sex, religion, politics—and one another. They obeyed the laws, the countries and their own. And their most important law said that no one was to commit crimes against humanity—and bring human persecution down upon them.

"Yes," he said quietly, "she was drained of blood."

"And a vampire did it?" Fiona demanded.

"Fiona, I'm trying to tell you—I've only just begun to investigate," he said.

"Oh, please. I'm not with the media."

He looked at her in the rearview mirror. "And you haven't the patience, knowledge or wisdom of your parents, Fiona."

Maybe that hadn't been a good thing to say. She stiffened like a ramrod. But, somehow, she managed to speak evenly.

"My parents died to keep you all from killing one another and preying upon the citizenry of the city in your lust for power and desire to rip each other to pieces. My parents were unique—both of them born with all three of the major signs. But that was then, and this is now. My sisters and I were born without the full power of my parents, but you know that I was born with the sign of the winged being, Caitlin with the mercurial sign of the shapeshifter and Shauna with the sign of the fang. But here's where we do have an edge—I have all the strengths of the vampire, and the vampires are my dedicated concern, just as Caitlin must watch over the shapeshifters and Shauna is responsible for the werewolves. Don't you think I wish my mother was here, too? But she's not. And I will not let the vampire community start something up again, something that promises discovery, death and destruction for hundreds of our own who are innocent. Do you understand? Whoever did this must be destroyed. If you don't handle it, I will."

He swung around to face her. "Back off! Give me time. Or do you want to start your own witch hunt?"

"You need to discover the truth—and quickly," she

said. "And trust me—I will be watching you every step of the way."

"Of course you will be," he said, regaining his temper. He couldn't let her unnerve him. "Damn it! Don't you think I realize just how dangerous this situation is? But these *are* different times. Hell, I'm a cop. I see violence every day. I see man's inhumanity to man constantly. But I also see the decency in the world. So let me do what I do."

She was silent for a minute.

"Just do it quickly, Jagger."

"With pleasure. Now would you be so kind as to get out of my car so I can begin? Or should I drop you off at the shop?" he asked icily.

"I'll get out of your car," she said softly.

Oh, yes, she would get out. She wouldn't want to be seen around her shop in a police car—even an unmarked car. Especially *his* car.

The rear door slammed as she exited. She paused for a moment by his window, staring at him through the dark lenses of her glasses.

So fierce.

And so afraid.

Yes, whether she wanted to admit it or not, she was afraid. Well, she had a right to her fear, as well as that chip on her shoulder. She'd been nineteen when her parents died, and she had fought to prove that she could care for herself and her sisters, who'd been only seventeen and fifteen at the time. She had taken on the mantle of responsibility in two worlds, and thus far she had carried it well.

The wind lifted her hair. Despite himself, he felt something stir inside him.

She was so beautiful.

She was such a bitch!

"Good day, Fiona. I'll be seeing you."

"Good day, Detective. You can bet on it," she said, and turned to walk away, the sunlight turning her hair into a burst of sheer gold.

Chapter 2

New Orleans was her city, and Fiona MacDonald loved it with a passion.

She tried to remember that as she walked away from Jagger DeFarge's car.

The parking area was new and paved, and sat on an embankment right at the edge of the river.

She paused to look down at the Mississippi. It really was a mighty river. The currents could be vicious; storms could make it toss and churn, and yet it could also be beautiful and glorious, the vein of life for so many people who had settled along its banks.

The great river had allowed for the magnificent plantations whose owners had built an amazing society of grace and custom—and slavery. But even in the antebellum days before the Civil War, New Orleans had offered a home for "free men of color." Ironically, black men had owned black men, and quadroons had been *the*

mistresses of choice. In Fiona's mind, the city was home
to some of the most beautiful people in the world even
now, people who came in all shades. God, yes, she loved
her city. It was far from perfect. The economy was still
suffering, and, as ever, the South still struggled to gain
educational parity with the North.

But everyone lived in this city: black, white, yellow,
red, brown, and every shade in between. Young and old,
men and women.

And the denizens of the underworld, of course.

She took a deep breath as she stared at the river. She
was furious, yes. She was afraid, yes. And what might
have been bothering her most was the fact that she didn't
think Jagger DeFarge had actually intended to wound
her with his words.

God, yes! Her parents would have handled this much
better. But they were dead. They had known what they
were doing would cost them their last strength, their
last breaths. But they had believed in a beautiful world,
where peace could exist, where everyone could accept
everyone else.

She walked down to Decatur Street and paused.
St. Louis Cathedral stood behind Jackson Square, its
steeple towering over the scene before it, including the
garden with its magnificent equestrian statue of Andrew
Jackson. Café du Monde was to her right—filled with
tourists, naturally. It was a "must see" for visitors,
perhaps something like the Eiffel Tower in Paris, even
if it wasn't nearly so grand. It was a true part of New
Orleans, and she decided to brave the crowd of the
tourists and pick up a nice café au lait for the three
block walk back to the shop on Royal Street.

Though an actual drink might be better at this

moment. A Hand Grenade or a Hurricane, or any one of the other alcoholic libations so enjoyed on Bourbon Street.

But she couldn't have a drink. She couldn't drink away what had happened—or everything she feared might be about to happen next.

She made her way through the open air patio to the take-away window, ordered a large café au lait to go, then headed on up toward Chartres Street and then Royal. Her love for the city returned to her like a massive wave as she walked. She returned a greeting to a friend who gave tours in one of the mule-drawn carriages, and headed on past the red brick Pontalba Building. She passed shops selling T-shirts, masks, the ever-present Mardi Gras beads, postcards and sometimes, true relics, along with hand-crafted art and apparel.

Some of the buildings along her path were in good repair, while others still needed a great deal of help. Construction was constant in a city that was hundreds of years old, where the charming balconies often sagged, and where, even before Hurricane Katrina, many had struggled through economic difficulties to do what was needed piecemeal.

But there was something she loved even about the buildings that were still in dire need of tender care.

The French Quarter's buildings were an architectural wonderland. The area had passed through many hands—French, Spanish, British and American—but it had been during the Spanish period in 1788 that the Great Fire of New Orleans had swept away more than eight hundred of the original buildings. And then, in 1794, a second fire had taken another two hundred plus. The current St. Louis Cathedral had been built in 1789, so it, like much of the "French Quarter," had actually been built in the Spanish style.

She reached her destination, a corner on Royal, and paused, looking at the facade of their shop and their livelihood.

A Little Bit of Magic was on the ground floor of a truly charming building that dated back to 1823. She ran the shop with Caitlin and Shauna, her sisters, and she supposed, in their way, they were as much a part of the tourist scene as any other business. When you got right down to it, they sold fantasy, fun, belief and, she supposed, to some, religion. She remembered that, although they attended St. Louis Cathedral regularly, her mother had once told her, "All paths lead to God, and it doesn't matter if you call him Jehovah, Allah, Buddha, or even if you believe that he is a she."

She knew that her parents had always believed in two basic tenets: that there was a supreme being, and that all creatures, including human beings, came in varying shades of good and evil. The world was not black and white. Like New Orleans, it was all shades in between.

And so, in A Little Bit of Magic, they sold just about everything. They had expansive shelves on Wiccan beliefs, voodoo history and rights, myths and legends, spiritualism, Native American cultures, Buddhism, Hinduism, Christianity and Judaism and more. She ordered the books for the shop, and she loved reading about different beliefs and cultures.

Caitlin, however, was their reigning mystic. She was brilliant with a tarot deck. Shauna was the palm reader, while she herself specialized in tea leaves—easily accessible, since they had a little coffee and tea bar of their own.

They also sold beautiful hand-crafted capes, apparel, masks—this was New Orleans, after all—jewelry, wands, statues, dolls, voodoo paraphernalia and, sometimes, relics and antiques. The shop had always done a good business, and despite occasional disagreements, the sisters got along extremely well.

She sipped her café au lait, hoping it would give her what she needed: patience, wisdom and strength.

In a way, at the beginning, it had been easier. She'd been nineteen, an adult. Caitlin had been right behind her at seventeen, but Shauna had been only fifteen. It had been quite a fight to get the family courts to allow her to "raise" her sisters, but she had managed. She'd had help from a dear old friend, August Gaudin—a werewolf, of all things—but he had a fine reputation in the city, and he'd been her strength. At first, her sisters had been young, lost, so what she said was the law. But she had never wanted to hold them down, and now they were women in their own right, with valid thoughts and opinions.

And they were both going to be in a state of extreme anxiety now!

Squaring her shoulders both physically and mentally, Fiona entered the store. Caitlin was behind the counter, chatting with a woman who was selecting tea. She eyed Fiona sharply as she entered, but continued her explanation of the different leaves.

Fiona saw that Shauna was helping a young couple pick out masks.

She nodded to both her sisters and walked through

the store to the office in the rear, where she pulled up the chair behind her desk.

First things first. Then, tonight, a trip to the morgue.

A minute later, Caitlin burst in on her.

"Is it true? A dead woman in the cemetery, *drained of blood?*"

Fiona nodded. "I saw Jagger DeFarge. He's lead detective on the case. Naturally I told him that he has to find the killer right away, and obviously we don't care if it's one of his own, the murderer must be destroyed."

Caitlin sank into the chair on the other side of the desk. Fiona knew that the three of them resembled one another, and yet there were also noticeable differences. Her sister had the most beautiful silver eyes she had ever seen, while Shauna's had a touch of green and hers were blue. Her own hair was very light, Caitlin's a shade darker and Shauna's had a touch of red. Their heights were just a shade different, too. She was shortest at five-seven, while Caitlin had a half an inch on her, and Shauna was five-eight.

Right now, Caitlin's eyes were darkening like clouds on a stormy day.

"He admits the killer has to be a vampire?"

"No, of course not. He didn't admit anything."

"But we all know it has to have been a vampire."

Fiona hesitated. The last thing she wanted to do was defend Jagger DeFarge.

She had kept her distance from him, for the most part. Keepers were not supposed to interfere with everyday life. They did have their councils—kind of like a paranormal Elks Club, she thought with a smile—but as long as the status quo stayed the status quo, each society dealt with their own.

She knew, however, that Jagger did well in life passing as a normal citizen of the city. He was a highly respected police detective and had been decorated by the department.

She'd seen him a few times on television when he'd been interviewed after solving a high profile case. She remembered one interview in particular, when Jagger and his squad had brought in a killer who had scratched out a brutal path of murder from Oregon to Louisiana.

"Frankly, most of the time, what appears on the surface is what a perpetrator *wants* us to see. Any good officer has to look below the surface. In our city, sadly, we have a high crime rate much of it due to greed, passion or envy, not to mention drugs and domestic violence. But in searching for those who murder because of mental derangement or more devious desires, we can never accept anything at face value," he had said.

Before she could reply to Caitlin's question, Shauna came rushing into the office breathlessly. "Well?"

Her youngest sister's hair was practically flying. She was wearing a soft silk halter dress that swirled around her as she ran, and even when she stopped in front of the desk, she still seemed to be in motion.

"Jagger won't admit that it was a vampire. Maybe I'm phrasing that wrong. He said that he has to investigate. He reminded me that this is New Orleans—that we attract human wackos just the same as we attract those of us who just want to live normal lives. He didn't insist that it wasn't a vampire, he just said that he needs to investigate."

"Vampires!" Caitlin said, her tone aggravated, as if

vampires were the cause of everything that ever went wrong.

"What are you going to do?" Shauna asked.

Fiona frowned. "I don't know. But look, we can't all be back here. We can't leave the shop unattended."

"I put the Out for Lunch sign up in the window," Shauna said.

"Out for lunch? It's ten-thirty in the morning!" Fiona protested.

"Okay, so we're having an early lunch," Shauna said with a shrug.

"What do you intend to do?" Caitlin asked. "And don't say you don't know, because I know that's not true."

"Investigate myself," Fiona said with a shrug. "Vampires. It's my duty. I *will* find out the truth, and I *will* fix the situation." She sighed. "Obviously I'll be out most of the day. Oh, and even if we have to have 'lunch' several times in one day, never leave the shop unattended with the door open. We need to be especially careful now, all right?"

Her sisters nodded gravely.

Fiona rose. She had to get started. The situation demanded immediate action.

"Where are you going first?" Caitlin asked her.

"To see August Gaudin," Fiona said grimly.

Usually werewolves were not her favorite beings, though she tried very hard not to be prejudiced and stereotype them. It was the whole transformation thing that seemed so strange to her—so painful. And the baying at the moon.

Vampires were capable of certain transformations, as

well, it was far more a matter of astral projection and hypnotism. A vampire could take on a few legendary forms, such as a wolf and a bat, but they were weakened in such states, and since no vampire wanted to go up against an angry werewolf, for example, in the creature's own shape, the legendary transformation seldom happened.

Like vampires and shapeshifters, werewolves lived among the human population of the city, controlling themselves—with Shauna as their Keeper. But August Gaudin had fought alongside her parents, and in his human shape he was a dignified older man with silver hair, a broad chest and broad shoulders, and benign and gentle powder-blue eyes. He was an attorney by trade, and he had been elected to the city commission, and also worked with the tourism board. He had been genuinely wonderful to Fiona and her sisters, helping them when they truly needed a friend.

His offices were on Canal Street, and she walked there as quickly as she could, not wanting to call ahead, because trying to explain on the phone or, worse, leave a message would be too difficult.

August would see her. He always did.

The office manager stopped her when she would have absently burst right through to see him, but they had met before, and the woman knew that August wouldn't turn Fiona down. Still, the woman pursed her lips and said, "Please, sit, and I will let Mr. Gaudin know that you're here."

"I'll stand, thank you," Fiona said. Silly. The woman was just wielding her power.

August Gaudin came out to greet her, reaching out to

take her hands. "Fiona! Dear child, come on in, come on in. Margaret, hold my calls, please."

Gaudin's office was a comfortable place. He had a large mahogany desk, and leather chairs that were both comfortable and somehow strong. The office conveyed the personality of the man.

He sat behind his desk as Fiona fell into a chair before it.

"I was expecting you," he told her.

"I suppose the entire city has heard by now," she said. She leaned forward. "August, the girl was murdered by a vampire. I'm sure of it. She was drained of blood. Completely. The wretched creatures are at it again!"

"Now, Fiona, that's not necessarily true," August told her. "First, we all know that—"

"Yes, yes, there are ridiculous human beings out there who think they're vampires, who even cut each other and drink each other's blood."

"It *is* possible that such a lunatic killed the woman," August said.

"Possible, but not likely."

"I take it that Jagger DeFarge is the investigating officer?"

"Yes. Imagine," she said dryly.

"That's good, *cher*. He'll know how to investigate properly, and he won't get himself killed in the process," he told her.

"August, this is my fault," she whispered.

"Now, stop. It's not your fault. It's your duty to see that the perpetrator is caught and punished. But it's not your fault any more than it's your fault when some crackhead falls on top of his own infant and kills him, or when drug slayings occur on the street. Crime exists.

And it's unreasonable to expect that crime will never exist in—our world just as it does in the human world," he said softly.

She stood and began pacing the room. "Yes, but…if the vampires respected me as their Keeper, they wouldn't have dared attempt such a thing."

"Not true. There will always be rogues in any society."

"August, you've always helped me. What should I do?" she asked.

He leaned back. "You tell me."

"All right. Tonight, I make sure that the victim isn't coming back, that…that she rests in peace. I'll go as soon as the morgue is closed, and hopefully before…well, before. Then I'll go to see David Du Lac at the club and make sure he's ready to deal with what's happened."

"The perfect plan. Here's another," August told her.

"What?"

"Trust in Jagger DeFarge. He's a good cop. He became a cop to make sure he regulated things that happened among our kind. He's thorough in every investigation. He'll be especially vigilant on this one."

"He's a vampire."

"He's proven that he has integrity and honor."

"He won't want to destroy another vampire."

"He'll do what is right. You have to trust in that."

"I'd like to," she said.

"But?"

"He's a vampire," she repeated.

Jagger headed straight to Underworld, the club owned by David Du Lac, the head of the vampire population of the City of New Orleans. His rule stretched farther, but the city was his domain. He was essentially considered the vampire mayor.

And he did a better job than some of the human beings who had been entrusted with the city's human citizens, Jagger thought.

Naturally Underworld was frequented by vampires. But David Du Lac prided himself on running an establishment where everyone was welcome. He brought in the best bands and kept the place eclectic, and the human clientele never had any idea just who they were rubbing shoulders with.

Underworld was located just off Esplanade, on Frenchman Street. The edifice was a deconsecrated church. Beautiful stained-glass windows remained, along with a cavernous main section, balconies and private rooms. The old rectory, David's home as well as a venue for jazz bands and private parties, was right behind the old church. There was a patio, too, open during the day, and a jazz trio played there from 11:00 a.m. to 3:00 p.m. every day, while the clientele enjoyed muffalettas, crawfish étouffée, gumbo and other Louisiana specialties—along with the customary colorful drinks served in New Orleans and a few designer specials, dryly named the Bloodsucker, Bite Me, the Transformer and the Fang.

Jagger paused for a minute after he parked just down the street from the club. David took good care of the place. The white paint sparkled in the sunlight. The umbrellas in the courtyard were decorated with pretty fleur-de-lis patterns—naturally boasting the black and gold colors of the home football team, the Saints.

He got out of his car and walked through the wrought-iron gate to the courtyard, where a crowd had already gathered, and where the jazz trio was playing softly pleasant tunes.

"Detective Jagger!"

He was greeted by Valentina DeVante, David's hostess. She worked all hours, although she was almost always at the club at night. She was a voluptuous woman, with a way of walking that was pure sensuality. She had the kind of eyes that devoured a man.

He didn't actually like being devoured, so he'd always kept his distance.

"Valentina, is David up and about?"

"Actually, he's over there in the courtyard, toward the back. Tommy, the sax player, is sick, so the guys brought in a substitute. You know how David loves his jazz. He's making sure he likes the new guy so he can fill in again if he's needed. Come on. I'll take you to him."

She turned. She walked. She swished and swayed. Half the men in town, especially the inebriated ones, would trip over their tongues watching this woman. He was surprised to find himself analyzing his feelings toward her. Too overt. He liked subtlety. Sensuality over in-your-face sexuality. He liked a woman's smile, a flash in her eyes when she was touched, amused, or when she flirted. He liked honesty, an addiction to decency…

Fiona MacDonald.

God, no.

Yes. She was sleek and smooth, and she never teased or taunted; she was simply beautiful, and even when she was angry, there was something in the sound of her voice that seemed to slip beneath his skin. Her hair was like the sunlight, and her eyes…

"David, Jagger is here," Valentina said, leading him to David's table and pulling out one of the plastic-cushioned patio chairs. As he took the seat and thanked her, she leaned low. Her black dress was cut nearly to her navel, displaying her ample cleavage right in front of his face.

But then, since Valentina was a shapeshifter, she could shift a little more of her to any part of her body she desired.

"Hey, Jagger, I was expecting to see you," David said. He had half risen to greet Jagger, but Jagger lifted a hand, silently acknowledging the courtesy and assuring him that he was welcome to keep his seat.

"David..." Jagger said in greeting.

Since they were both wearing dark glasses, there was nothing to be gleaned by seeking out honesty in David's eyes, though Jagger knew from past encounters that they were fascinating eyes, almost gold in color. David was Creole, mainly, with additional ancestors who had been French and Italian, so his skin was almost as golden as his eyes, complemented by dark lashes and dark hair. He was a striking man and had always been a friend.

He couldn't tell what his friend was thinking right now but...

David tended to be a straight shooter.

"Obviously, yes, I've heard about the body," David said quietly.

"Any suspects?"

"You think it was one of us?" David asked. He didn't have to keep his voice low; the music was just right, and the courtyard was alive with the low drone of conversation. They wouldn't be heard beyond the table, even if Jagger did note that customers—most of them women—did glance in their direction now and then.

"David, the body was bone-dry. Not a drop of blood."

David nodded, looking toward the band. "They're good, don't you think?"

"Yes, very good. Your taste in music is legendary. Listen, right now the investigation is wide-open. Obviously no one but me suspects anything…out of the ordinary. But we've got a serious problem, because it certainly looks to be the work of a vampire. And pretty soon it's not going to be just me hanging around here and questioning people."

David groaned.

"The Keeper?" he said quietly. "Oh, Lordy."

"She found me right after I made it to the crime scene."

"That one has some attitude, too," David said with a sigh, then shrugged. "Oh well, comes with the territory, I guess. She had a hell of a lot to contend with at a very young age, and so far, we've all kept the peace. She hasn't had the time—or the need—to acquire the wisdom of her parents. And she's got that strict code of ethics thing going on, too. Guess it comes with being the oldest." David grinned suddenly. "Beautiful little thing, though, huh? If we were back in the old days… yum. And I wouldn't have let anyone interfere with her birth into a new existence, either. Hell, she's the kind who might have made me monogamous. For a century or so, anyway."

Jagger wasn't at all sure why he immediately felt protective. Fiona MacDonald certainly wouldn't expect or even want him to defend her.

Maybe David's words irritated him because they had touched a little too close to home.

"Well, she is nice eye candy," David continued. "And everyone is welcome at my club. She has to do her job, right, Jagger?"

"No, *I* have to do *my* job. I have to find a murderer. I hope that it doesn't prove to be a vampire, but if it does... well, we have to handle it as a community."

David looked away. "It's against nature," he said softly.

"Our lives are against nature. We drink blood that's inferior to what our ancestors craved, but we've evolved, we've adapted to it. Louisiana has the death penalty. And since we don't have any vampire prisons, we have no choice. Rogues die, and it's a community affair."

"What do you want me to do?"

"Call a meeting."

"All right. And I'll make it known that everyone's presence is required, though I can't guarantee that we'll get everyone."

"I think most of our kind will be extremely concerned, since they know the other races will be breathing down our necks. This is frightening, David. Frightening for everyone. A young woman was killed, drained of blood. The whole city will be up in arms. And you can guarantee our friends in the underworld of New Orleans society will all be staring at us."

"I'll call the meeting," David assured him. "You'll be presiding?"

"You bet."

"I think I can manage it by late—*late*—tomorrow— the following morning, really. Make it 3:00 a.m. Those who are still hanging out here will probably be three sheets to the wind, not likely to interrupt. The rectory, 3:00 a.m."

"That will work. Thanks, David."

"So, will you have some lunch? As my guest, of course."

"I appreciate the offer, but it's going to be a long day."

"Where are you off to now?"

"The morgue," Jagger told him.

Fiona arrived at Underworld while lunch was still being served. She walked up to the hostess stand, and the woman standing there looked up at her with patronizing patience. She looked Fiona up and down, and would have sniffed audibly if it weren't against all sense of Southern courtesy. She was dressed in black, and had long black hair, black eyes and enormous breasts.

"Yes? A table for…one? I'm afraid there's a wait," the woman said.

Shapeshifter, Fiona thought.

And she probably knew damned well who she was, and what she wanted.

"I'm sorry, I'm not here for lunch at all. I need to see Mr. Du Lac," Fiona said.

"Ah," the woman said, just looking at her.

Fiona wasn't in the mood for a staring contest.

"If you would be so kind, I would deeply appreciate it if you would tell Mr. Du Lac that I'm here."

"Do you have an appointment?"

"I'm quite certain that he's expecting me," Fiona said.

"He's a very busy man. Perhaps you could leave your card."

"Perhaps you could inform him that Fiona MacDonald

is here. In fact, I strongly suggest that you do so right now."

The woman lifted her chin. Fiona could tell that she was about to stall again.

Fiona hated *changing*. She seldom had to do so, but she was adept at the art that was her birthright. She could do so in an instant, and change back so quickly that anyone seeing her who didn't *know* would assume it had been a trick of the light. So...

She *changed*. She gave something that was a warning growl, fangs dripping and bared.

And then she changed back instantly.

"You don't need to get huffy," the woman told her. "Right this way."

She led Fiona past the scattered tables in the courtyard. Beneath one of the lovely umbrellas with its fleur-de-lis in black and gold, she saw David Du Lac comfortably seated.

He had been leaning back, eyes shaded by his dark glasses, hands folded, toes tapping to the sounds of the jazz band.

His pose was casual, but he had seen her coming. He rose, extending his hands to her, a broad smile stretching out across his features.

"Fiona, my dear, welcome, welcome to my club."

She accepted his hands, along with the kiss he gave her on each cheek. "Valentina, be a dear and see that Miss MacDonald receives a libation right away. What will it be, my dear? A Bloody Mary is always a lovely concoction for lunchtime."

"I'm fine, really."

"You must accept my hospitality," David insisted.

"Iced tea, please," Fiona said.

She noticed that Valentina, the bitchy shapeshifter, as she would always think of the woman from this moment forth, did sniff audibly then.

"Certainly, David," the woman crooned.

"David, you know why I'm here," Fiona said, watching the bitchy shapeshifter swish away.

"Don't mind her. She's a jealous vixen if ever I've seen one."

"She's a triple D with feet," Fiona said. "Hardly likely to be jealous of me."

"Ah, my sweet child, what you don't know about your own sex!" David said, then grew serious. "But never mind. I do know why you're here."

"David, this wasn't just someone who went insane and attacked a woman, then tried to hide her body. It wasn't someone trying to create his eternal love. This was an act of…war, really. She was left where some city guide with tourists in tow would find her. She was put on display, stretched out…David, this is extremely serious."

"I do know that, my child," he said.

"I'm not a child, David," she reminded him quietly. "I'm the Keeper."

"Fiona, no offense meant. But you're supposed to step in when we can't police our own."

"This was the action of a rogue, David."

"Yes, yes, of course. And I promise you, if we'd known he—or she—was out there, we would never have let it happen. But have some faith, Fiona. Please. Jagger DeFarge is working the case and—"

"He's a vampire, David. He doesn't want to believe that he's hunting down one of his own."

David leaned back, stretching his arms out as if to

encompass not only his club but the entire city. "Fiona, I love my life. Or death. Or afterlife. However one chooses to refer to this existence, I'm a good man."

"David, I wasn't accusing you of anything."

"My point is that I don't want anyone taking this away from me. I enjoy the money, frankly, not to mention the beautiful creatures of all kinds who cross my threshold. I revel in the music. Would I risk losing this? If I knew who had done this, I promise you, I would see to it that Jagger DeFarge knew, and that our own council handled the matter immediately. You must believe me."

A friendly ash blond waiter with a broad smile delivered her ice tea and asked if she wanted anything else.

"The crawfish étouffée is to die for today," David told her.

"Thank you, but—"

"Please," David said.

She *was* hungry, and she had to have lunch somewhere. "Fine, thank you," she said.

David grinned broadly, delighted, as the waiter moved on to place her order.

"David, you know that I will follow this all the way through, that I'll be in everyone's face everywhere," Fiona said.

"It will be charming to have you here," he assured her. "Fiona, I swear, I will do my utmost to help you in any way that I can. But I am asking *you* something, too. Give Jagger DeFarge a chance."

"I have to give him a chance, don't I? He's with the police—he'll be front and center in the investigation," she said dryly. "But here's what I won't get from Jagger, David. I don't believe he'll tell me when he's suspicious

of someone. He'll protect his own until the very end—
and he may cause more deaths by his unwillingness to
believe the killer is a vampire."

"That's not true," David said.

A throat was cleared behind them. "Crawfish
étouffée," the young waiter announced, giving Fiona a
fascinated smile. She thanked him as he refilled her tea
and handed David another Bloody Mary.

"Who do you suspect?" she demanded, when the
waiter had left them at last.

"No one," David said.

"You're a liar. But if you point me in a certain
direction, I will be discreet as I investigate," Fiona
said.

"No one, really...."

"Liar. Who is the most belligerent? Who wants to go
back to the old ways?"

David looked away.

She followed his line of vision toward a tall man
across the courtyard, just on the other side of the small
stage reserved for the jazz band. He was flirting with
a woman seated at his table. She was middle-aged,
slim and elegant, with fingers that dripped jewels. She
was laughing delightedly at something the man was
saying.

"Who is he?" Fiona demanded, staring at David.
"He's a newcomer to the area, but a vampire, I can smell
him a mile away."

David sighed. "Well, of course, you can," he murmured.
"All right, all right. That man is Mateas Grenard, and
yes, he's not been here long. He immediately sought out
the council, though, before anyone had to find him and

'welcome' him to the city. He has openly disagreed with some of our rules, but isn't that the American way?"

"There's not much else I can tell you," Craig Dewey said. They were in autopsy. The corpse of the beautiful blonde still looked as angelic as when it had first been discovered. "I haven't opened her up yet—we'll get to that tomorrow. We've done the death photographs and taken what blood we could for tests—which was hard, since she's been drained almost completely dry. If there's a quarter of a pint left in her body, I'd be surprised. Cause of death—well, I could be wrong, but it looks pretty obvious that she bled out. It's as if it was siphoned from her body. We've tried to find semen stains, and we ran a rape kit…with intriguing results, particularly given what we just found out in the last few minutes. Determining sexual assault has been almost impossible."

"What? Why? Was there evidence of semen? Or condoms?"

"At least seven different brands," Dewey said dryly. "We're taking it step by step. I'm sorry, but it's the only way, even though—I know you want to catch this killer before panic fills the city."

There was something that seemed eternally sad about the snow-white body on the table, though the white gown had been replaced by a morgue sheet.

"You said you found something out in the last few minutes," Jagger said. "You know who she is?"

"Got a match on her prints. The results posted to your office and mine about five minutes ago," Dewey told him, an odd look on his face.

"What is it?"

"Snow White here isn't what she appears to be. Her

name is Tina Lawrence. She worked at Barely, Barely, Barely, which is a pretty lowbrow establishment across Rampart from the Quarter," Dewey said, offering him the report folder.

Jagger scanned it quickly.

The angelic Miss Tina Lawrence had a rap sheet a mile long. Drugs, prostitution and assault and battery.

"Wow," he said.

"Not a nice young lady," Dewey said.

Jagger winced. "She knifed a college student for being four dollars short," he said quietly.

"Keep reading. She tried to cut the balls off another john. Get this, she *admitted* she wanted to kill him. Amazing she wasn't in jail," Dewey said.

"We can pick people up, but we can't always get them past the legal systems and the pleas and the deals," Jagger said. "Seems she got off that because she had some drug connections and the D.A. offered her a plea in order to pick up a few of her friends who were higher up in the drug chain."

"Not a nice girl. Actually a *deadly* girl—and now a dead one," Dewey commented. "Well, anyway, there you have it. I guess you'll be heading off to the strip club," Dewey said, punching him lightly on the arm. "Have fun."

"Thanks."

Jagger walked out of the autopsy room and left the morgue. He called Tony Miro, and told him where to head to start questioning Tina Lawrence's friends, coworkers and employer, and to pull the credit card receipts and find out who had been in attendance at Tina's last show. He needed to hang around near the morgue.

Waiting for the sun to fall.

As Dewey had said, Tina Lawrence hadn't been a nice girl. She'd been a deadly one.

He could only begin to imagine the horror that would be Tina Lawrence as a vampire.

Chapter 3

The coroner's office never closed. It employed all manner of forensic specialists, along with financial and clerical staff. Under the Napoleonic Code of Law still in effect in Louisiana, the New Orleans coroner's office was responsible not only for the classification of death, but also the evaluation of sex crimes and the overall general health of the citizens of the city, specifically recognizing serious threats from disease. It was a busy place. By day pathologists, forensic psychiatrists, patient liaisons, nurses in charge of sexual assault exams, forensic anthropologists, forensic odontologists and more clogged the corridors.

Death didn't stop at any particular time of day, so naturally a morgue couldn't close.

But by nightfall the accountants, assistants and usually even the experts in such fields as toxicology, entomology and more had called it quits for the day, and only a skeleton crew—if the pun could be forgiven—were on duty. The dead, after all, were dead.

Usually.

Fiona headed down Martin Luther King Boulevard and arrived outside the building's entrance while it was still early; she watched as people came and went, and then kept on watching as they mainly went.

There was no choice then but to go through the change, to concentrate and enter as a vampire would, in a shroud of mist.

The guards never suspected a thing as she went by; the outer offices, where a few doctors were still working, were easily breeched; and she breezed by the night attendant sitting outside the morgue without being noticed. Because several people had died in recent days, she took a chance and searched through the records to find the right body.

Then she headed into the dim, chilly room.

To her surprise, the body of Tina Lawrence had not been slid away neatly into a refrigerated slot but she was stretched out on an autopsy table.

The room smelled heavily of antiseptics and chemical compounds, not so much of death itself, yet the very antiseptics made it seem that the scent of death was prevalent in the air.

She slipped in and concentrated hard on regaining her customary form, aware that during the good times she should have been practicing her transformations techniques. But all the while she couldn't help wondering why they had left Tina Lawrence as she was.

Fiona knew that the tenor of the investigation had changed; the news media had released the woman's identification and touted her past record. Reporters had a knack for finding out what the investigators had barely discovered themselves.

While the media had no doubt thought that releasing the victim's background was a good thing—a reassurance to most citizens that they were safe—Fiona was certain that Jagger considered the knowledge to be dangerous. It was hard to catch a killer when everyone knew too many details about the victim and the crime. Cranks, crackheads and anyone else looking for a little notoriety might decide to confess to the crime. But New Orleans was still raw, still learning painful lessons after Katrina's devastation, and Fiona was certain that most of the media believed they had done a good thing by releasing the information that the victim had led something much less than a blameless life. A majority of the city's women would be able to think, *I'm safe. I'm not a stripper or a prostitute, and I've certainly never been arrested.*

On the other hand, the news about the victim's past had made Fiona incredibly nervous. Tina Lawrence must *not* be allowed to go through the change. Fiona had known what she had to do from the beginning; the information about Tina's past had only made it all the more urgent.

And so, as she retook her human form there in the autopsy room, she worried that the medical examiner assigned to the body might come back any minute to begin working on it still, that the assistant she'd passed in the hall might step in at any time, or that she might be caught by someone else entirely unanticipated who could enter any second.

A sheet covered the body, and all she had to do was

pull it back and use the stiletto sharp stake she had brought, making sure that she pierced the heart.

She wasn't surprised that Tina Lawrence wasn't yet marked by the Y shaped incision of autopsy. Given the circumstances, Fiona was certain that it had taken some time to transfer the body to the morgue, and then the victim would have been fingerprinted, photographed and…

She wasn't sure what else.

She actually didn't want to know what else.

All she had to do was make sure that Tina Lawrence did not wake up.

But as she approached the corpse, she heard a noise in the hallway and the door started to open, so she dived behind a stainless table holding an array of instruments, most of them totally unfamiliar.

The night attendant stuck his head in, looked around briefly, then closed the door and left.

She started to breathe a sigh of relief, then realized that she was hearing something in the room. No, some*one*. She glanced quickly up at the table, but the corpse hadn't moved. She held her ground, listening, her heart pounding.

Nothing. She looked around in the dim light and waited. Still nothing. She started to rise and saw a flurry of motion behind her.

Instantly alarmed, she started to change, but she wasn't quick enough.

Someone tackled her hard and forced her down to the ground.

She instantly went into combat mode, lashing out with her arms and legs, delivering one solid punch that brought out a startled "Oomph," from her attacker before he caught and secured her arms, straddling her.

She found herself looking up into the eyes of Jagger DeFarge.

"Fiona!"

"DeFarge!" she lashed back angrily. "Get off me."

He didn't comply, though he released her arms as he remained straddled over her, staring down at her angrily.

"What the hell are you doing here?" he demanded.

"It's obvious what I'm doing here—cleaning up the mess," she replied.

"It's my concern," he told her.

"No, it's *mine*. I'm responsible in circumstances like these, and I have no guarantee that you'll do the right thing," she replied.

"Well, I'm here, and I'm handling the situation," he said, crossing his arms over his chest and staring down at her.

"Will you please get off me?" she inquired.

Before he could respond, the door opened. The young night attendant walked in, flicking on the bright overhead lights.

Jagger and Fiona stared at one another as the attendant let out a startled cry.

Jagger rose instantly to his feet, shushing the man with authority. "It's all right. I'm Detective DeFarge, just looking for Dr. Dewey and the results of this autopsy."

"I'm about to put her on ice for the night," the attendant said. "Dr. Dewey will be in first thing in the morning to start the autopsy."

As he spoke, the corpse on the gurney jackknifed into

a sitting position, the sheet falling to reveal her naked torso.

The young man opened his mouth to let out a scream, but Jagger leaped over the table in an instant, slipping behind him and silencing him with a hand over the mouth, pulling the door shut with his other hand.

Tina Lawrence glared around, a hissing growl coming from her lips.

Then she parted those lips to reveal dripping fangs.

Despite her calling in life and the way she'd died, Tina Lawrence was still beautiful. Her blond hair cascaded over the white flesh of her shoulders, and despite the terrifying distraction of her fangs, she had lovely wide blue eyes, which settled on the attendant with hunger.

He spoke from beneath Jagger's hold, his words muffled but audible. "She's alive. She's alive!"

Jagger stared at Fiona. "Take him—quickly. Silence him."

She hurried over to where Jagger was struggling with the attendant—both to hold him still *and* to keep from hurting him. She grasped the young man's arms, staring into his eyes. "Quiet now, quiet. It's all right. You're dreaming this. You're asleep at your desk, and you know that you have to wake up, that you have a job to do…."

She kept speaking softly. Jagger apparently assured himself that everything was fine and turned toward the corpse of Tina Lawrence, but as he did, the corpse leaped naked from the table, ready to pounce on Fiona and the young attendant.

Jagger slipped between them just in time.

As she continued trying to calm the attendant, Fiona saw that Jagger had taken a weapon from his jacket.

It was far superior to her own, a long stake, honed

to a sharp point, even narrower than hers. He took Tina Lawrence into his arms, and, just before her newly grown fangs could tear into his throat, he struck hard, delivering the lethal blow directly through the wall of her chest and straight into her heart.

The corpse collapsed against him.

Despite her prowess with hypnotic mind control, Fiona began to lose the young morgue attendant.

He began to emit a low moaning sound and started to slip lower in her arms.

She had a feeling then that he must be a football player—a blocker or a tackle—with Tulane or Loyola, because she simply didn't have the strength to stop him from falling. Though she tried to hold him upright, she began to slip to the floor.

She heard Jagger swearing softly as he shoved the corpse of Tina Lawrence quickly back onto the table and came to help her.

But by then the attendant had passed out cold.

"We've got to get him back to his desk," Jagger told her.

"What if someone else is in the hallway? There are still people in the building," she warned.

"Get out there and make sure no one is coming," he told her. "Quickly."

"Why me?"

"Well, you obviously can't lift him."

"All right, all right, I'm going," Fiona said, and pointed an angry finger at him. "But you don't give me orders. I am the Keeper!"

"And you're going to have a hell of a lot to keep if you don't get moving," he told her.

She wanted to reply; she wanted the last word. But they needed to hurry. She rushed out into the hallway.

It was clear.

"Now," she told Jagger, sticking her head back into the autopsy room.

Luckily the attendant's desk was just down the hall. She rushed toward it, ready to fend off anyone who might come by.

Jagger had lifted the attendant as if he were no more than a ten-pound lapdog and was hurrying toward the desk. Just beyond the desk, Fiona saw a door opening. She rushed toward it just in time to see an older man in a lab jacket about to come through.

"Oh!" she said, staring at him, trying to lock her eyes on his and demand his attention.

Apparently she succeeded, because he stared curiously back at her.

"Hello," he said weakly.

She smiled. "You're so tired—you've been working very hard. Go and get your things, then go on home and have a nap. You're hallucinating, you're so tired."

"I'm so tired," he echoed. "You're a lovely hallucination."

"Thank you."

He was of average height and weight, with close-cropped white hair. He was usually very dignified looking, she was certain, but right now he was staring at her with wide-eyed wonder.

"You're daydreaming, sir. You have to go home. You need some rest."

"Yes, yes, but…why don't you come, too, and make this a really good daydream? An erotic daydream, maybe. Please?"

Fiona groaned inwardly.

"That wouldn't be a very good idea. You probably have a wife, and I think *she's* your daydream."

"All right."

He stepped back the way he had come, closing the door.

As she turned, she almost screamed herself. Jagger had come up quietly behind her.

"He's at his desk. He'll wake up confused. Poor boy may never be the same. He'll have some memory…but he'll just think that he imagined everything," Jagger told her. He was staring at her with amusement, and she could tell that he must have heard her conversation with the middle-aged man in the lab coat.

She pushed against his chest. Like a rock, but he moved back. "This is a disaster," she said, her voice a low and angry whisper. "You need to let me handle things."

"With what? A sledgehammer? So you could let the whole world know something was going on in here?"

Fiona ignored that. It was true that he had definitely… taken care of things.

But he was a vampire. And a vampire was normally loath to kill another vampire.

"The corpse?" she asked briskly.

"The corpse will have nothing but a tiny hole through the heart. If you had done this, it would have been obvious that someone had been here. Do you understand?"

"Your weapon is the right one. I'll see that I improve on my arsenal," she snapped.

"We need to finish up quickly," he said.

He hurried back to the autopsy room, checking the

hallway after she followed him in, then closing the door.

"The sheet," he said, which irritated Fiona, since she was already returning Tina Lawrence to her original position on the table and covering her with the sheet.

Jagger just had to straighten it.

"Now let's get the hell out of here," he said.

He changed in a split second, appearing to be no more than mist, and heading out. Cursing silently, she did her best to make the change as quickly and efficiently.

Still, he looked impatient when she met him back on the street, though she couldn't have been more than a few seconds behind him.

"You could have caused a real problem in there tonight," he told her.

They had met on the street corner, beneath the shadow of a giant oak that dripped moss. He was tall, dark, lean, strikingly handsome—and deadly—in the glow of the flickering electric streetlight. Powerful in a way that was frightening, that stole her breath.

She wasn't afraid of him, she told herself.

She was the Keeper.

"I was there to see that the right thing was done," she said with dignity. "And I would have managed just fine—if you hadn't come in and messed everything up."

"I'm a cop, and I know how to manage any situation—especially one that has to do with vampires."

"I repeat. I am responsible. I am the Keeper. *Your* Keeper."

He bristled at that, and took a step closer to her. He used a body wash or aftershave that was subtle and masculine, and despite herself, she took a step backward, not sure if it was because she was intimidated—or because she found herself too attracted, too tempted to lay her hands on the broad expanse of his chest.

She forced herself to stay still as he took a step closer to her, pointing a finger and touching her just above her cleavage.

"You *are* the Keeper. But you're overstepping your bounds. You're supposed to step in when we can't handle a situation ourselves. In this case, I was handling the situation just fine."

She shook her head. "I can't trust you to kill a vampire," she said, her words soft.

"You *have* to trust me."

"A vampire has committed murder," she reminded him.

"That's not proven," he insisted. "Look—we're on it. Give us a chance, Fiona. Good God, learn from your parents. They were amazing, because they understood delegation."

"My parents are dead," she reminded him angrily.

She was surprised when he seemed to soften, when something in his eyes became gentle, almost tender.

"I'm sorry. Please, give me a chance...as a cop—and as a vampire. I *will* get to the bottom of this, but none of us will be in good shape if we get the city abuzz with rumors, and all the underworld starts getting edgy and worried. Please."

She nodded. "I don't want a panic erupting, either, but that's the point. I have to keep watching—that's what Keepers do," she reminded him. She was overwhelmed by the sense that she needed to get away from him. She didn't want to be this close, didn't want to be noticing his physique or realizing that his scent was extremely evocative. She wanted to be irritated from a distance; she wanted to solve the problem herself, because she was the Keeper.

"I have to get home," she heard herself say a little nervously.

"I'll drive you."

"I have my own car," she told him quickly.

"I'll walk you to it," he told her.

"I'm all right. This is my city."

"And like every city, it has crack houses, drug addicts and plain old thugs. I'm a cop—I do my job even when the denizens of the underworld *aren't* out causing trouble. I'll walk you to your car."

"Honestly, Jagger, I'm a Keeper."

"And a Keeper—just like a vampire, werewolf, shapeshifter, pixie, pooka, leprechaun or even a lamia— can be taken by surprise. Why the hell do you think our kind had to escape the old world, then flee places like Salem, to find a place where we could blend in? We're all vulnerable, Fiona, despite whatever strengths we have. We're all vulnerable—in so many ways."

He took her arm as they walked down the street. She wanted to wrench from his touch, but…

The lady doth protest too much, methinks, she thought.

But she was so acutely aware of him!

They reached her car.

"Good night, Fiona," he said, as he opened her door for her.

"You'll keep me apprised—of everything going on? From a cop's standpoint *and* a vampire's?" she inquired.

He nodded.

"I have to follow up and investigate. You know that."

"Have some faith in me, please," he said.

"I'm having faith. But I'm using what I've got, too, that's all."

"I'll report in daily," he said.

"Yes, you will."

He smiled suddenly.

She frowned, looking at him. "I don't see anything to smile about in any of this, Jagger."

"Oh, certainly not. Not in the situation."

"Then?"

"You just have to have the last word, don't you?" he asked.

She didn't reply, just slid into the seat, and he closed the door. She stared at him and turned the key in the ignition. He stepped away quickly as she gunned the engine, then started to ease out onto the street.

A good exit, she told herself.

Except that she could hear his husky laughter even as she drove away.

Chapter 4

Fiona had just slipped into the long, soft cotton T-shirt she loved to wear to bed and crawled under the covers when she heard the tap on her door that announced Caitlin's arrival. Her sister knocked, but didn't wait for an invitation.

"Well?" Caitlin demanded.

The room was dark, but with the hall lights on, Fiona could see her sister's anxious face.

"It's done," she said.

"Thank God," Caitlin breathed. "For some reason the media have been trying to hide the details of Tina Lawrence's life, but finally—one of the anchors started reading her police sheet, and...I literally shivered. Can you even imagine? The best vampire is a bloodthirsty beast and—"

"Caitlin, please. We know plenty of vampires who are fine citizens. And let's get serious. There's no more violent beast out there than man, when he chooses to be," Fiona argued.

Caitlin sighed softly. "Look, I know that they're your charges, but…well, I just don't believe there's ever been a truly good vampire."

Jagger DeFarge.

The name came unbidden to Fiona's mind.

She realized that despite her earlier misgivings, she believed that he was a force for good. After all, was anyone really all good or all bad? Everyone, every being, every creature, came with a form of free will, and free will led to behavior that was good, bad and everything in between.

"Jagger DeFarge was there," she told her sister. "He was already attending to the matter, as he should have been."

Caitlin sniffed. "Was he? Or did he decide he had no choice, once he saw you?"

"Caitlin, please. I have to have some faith in his ethics and his commitment to our laws. The vampires, like all creatures, are supposed to police their own, and I believe that they will do so. I also went to see David Du Lac, and I know that the higher-ups among the vampires are deeply concerned. Caitlin, they like their lives. They're not going to risk everything they have, all to protect a rogue."

Caitlin looked at her gravely, the softly glowing hall light making her appear angelic.

"I'm just worried," she said. "Worried…for you."

Fiona rose and walked over to the door, where she took her sister into a warm hug. "I understand."

They stayed close for a minute, sisters who had seen the worst. Then they broke apart, and Fiona smiled.

"I'm fine, honestly. Have some faith in me, if not the vampires. The truth is, I need your help."

"My help? We're talking vampires. Not my thing, remember?" Caitlin said.

Fiona nodded. She had been born with the sign of the bat, a tiny birthmark at the base of her spine. Caitlin had been born with the sign of the mist, shape-shifting. She loved her sister's birthmark, which was magical, changing continuously, though most who saw it thought it a trick of the eye.

Shauna bore the mark of the werewolf Keeper, the wolf, howling at the moon. No tattoo artist had ever created a work of such perfection.

Their friends had marveled at the marks on those rare occasions when they'd been revealed by a low-cut bathing suit. They hadn't tried to hide them, had merely shrugged them off, leaving their friends to wonder how and when they'd come by them.

Before Fiona could reply, Shauna popped up behind Caitlin.

"So? What's going on? Do you know who did it?" she demanded.

Fiona gave up and turned on her light. "Come in. Actually I don't know—yet—but I do have a plan for finding out."

The three of them sat cross-legged on the bed as Fiona went on.

"I want to attend the luncheon at the Monteleone tomorrow."

"The lunch to honor Jennie Mahoney?" Caitlin asked, frowning.

Jennie Mahoney was the untitled queen among the shapeshifters. She was a beautiful woman, a socialite and a member of the local literati. If it was happening in New Orleans, Jennie was in on it.

She was going to be honored for the work she had done in soliciting funds to redo a coffeehouse just outside the Quarter. The place offered open mike nights to poets at least once a week, along with hosting up-and-coming musicians and decorating its walls with works by local artists. Since Jennie and several of her friends considered themselves poets, Fiona wasn't sure that all the effort Jennie had put in wasn't a little self-serving, but the coffee house had been a local landmark that was completely ruined by Katrina, and the fact that it was now open again was a big boost for a city in need of every boost it could get.

"Are you going?" Fiona asked Caitlin.

"Of course. It would be incredibly rude of me not to attend," her sister said.

"Can we all go?"

"If I'd known you wanted to go, I should have gotten tickets ages ago," Caitlin said.

"Do *I* want to go?" Shauna asked, frowning as she looked at Fiona.

"I think all three of us should be there. I'd like to talk to Jennie," Fiona said.

Caitlin was frowning. "If you talk to Jennie, she's going to think you're suspicious of her—and her kind."

Fiona shook her head. "Not at all. I'm hoping *she* can tell *me* about anything suspicious going on."

Caitlin nodded slowly, staring at Fiona. "But you know this was the work of a vampire," she said.

"Certainly not a werewolf," Shauna said. "A werewolf…well, a werewolf kill is never subtle or pretty, you know?"

That was true, beyond a doubt.

"Caitlin, I really need your help," Fiona said.

Caitlin nodded slowly. "All right. I'll text a few people right now. The lunch was sold out weeks ago, but… there's always someone who has to cancel."

"Thank you."

"It's late. We should get some sleep," Shauna said, as she rose and yawned. "Boy, what a relief."

"What's a relief?" Caitlin asked.

"That it wasn't a werewolf."

Fiona glared at her.

"Sorry…" Shauna apologized. "I'm not saying…I mean, I'm not accusing anyone. For all we know, it might have been some drugged out weirdo who *wants* to be a vampire."

"No," Fiona said.

They both looked at her.

"Tina Lawrence…she started to rise from the dead."

"But you said Jagger DeFarge was there to handle the matter," Caitlin pointed out.

"Yes," Fiona said, meeting her sister's eyes. "I'm afraid it's in our jurisdiction. She was definitely killed by one of ours."

Caitlin stared at her steadily. "Good night," she said finally, then turned and left.

"What's wrong with her?" Shauna asked softly.

"She thinks I'm accusing a shapeshifter. I'm not. I just have to keep my mind open, and if it wasn't a vampire, then it had to be a shapeshifter. No other creature could take on—or pass on—the abilities of a vampire."

"It probably *is* the work of a vampire," Shauna said softly.

"I know," Fiona assured her, then smiled with what she hoped was reassurance. "It's our first real challenge. We will meet it."

Jagger spent his time checking out the city's streets.

Bourbon was crawling with tourists, as usual. He heard excited conversations, visitors talking about the "vampire murder," girls teasing boys about taking care of themselves in strip clubs—and boys teasing girls about the same.

A stripper-slash-prostitute had been killed. It was worthy of gossip, not of great concern.

Walking along, he came upon mounted officers, Reginald Oaks and Vickie Gomez. He slowly patted Gomez's horse, Enrique, and questioned his fellow officers about what was going on.

"Seems like a regular night in Boozeville," Vickie told him.

"Frat boys are singing karaoke, dancing in the streets, throwing beads around…it's not Mardi Gras, but it's busy. Nothing to suggest anything going on," Reginald told him. "Have you been up past Rampart?"

Jagger nodded. "I've been everywhere tonight. Uptown, Garden District, Frenchman Street…you name it. I even cruised the Central Business District. But that's the way it's going to have to be until this is settled. Anything, anything at all unusual, you have me on speed dial."

"Yes, sir," Vickie assured him , flashing a quick smile. "Sir, there's a weaving group behind you looking for a picture with the mounted cops and the horses."

He turned away just as a group of inebriated tourists came weaving over, looking to take a picture with the horses. He started to step away.

"Oh, please. Stay," one girl told him.

"Sorry—official business," he said, flashed his badge and quickly moved away. His partner, Tony Miro, was supposed to be meeting him at Barely, Barely, Barely, the strip club up past Rampart where Tina Lawrence had worked. He hurried down the cross street to where his car was parked by the station on Chartres.

Tony Miro was waiting for him in front of the club when he pulled up a few minutes later.

It was odd to think that the club was really only a degree below plenty of the other clubs in town. Even on Bourbon Street, you could find some truly sleazy down and dirty places, but…Barely, Barely, Barely seemed even more worn around the edges, and he knew the girls working the poles in the place were going to be a little harder, a little more beat-up by life, physically and mentally.

He had met strippers who only worked the clubs to get through college—it was good money, and sad but true, good money that seemed like easy money often twisted people, and led to worse ways of making more money, and plenty of bad things to spend it on. Not that all strippers were prostitutes. But in his time on the force, he'd seen far too many girls who started out stripping on the weekend, only to discover they enjoyed the drugs they often started taking to give them the courage to strip in the first place. Drugs cost money, and prostitution paid better than stripping.

He left the car on the street, his police insignia evident. Tony approached him with a long-legged stride. He was wearing a work suit, and when he eased a finger around his collar, Jagger realized he was uncomfortable.

"Everything all right?" Jagger asked.

"I questioned everyone in the place, and I got a list of their charge customers," Tony told him. "Some of the girls weren't working last night, so I've listed them at the end. I highlighted a few names—" he pointed to the list he was offering to Jagger "—because those two were bartenders, and those two were the girls who went up right before and after Tina Lawrence, and that name—Trish Bean—belongs to the cocktail waitress who was working the floor while Tina Lawrence was working the pole."

"Thanks. Did you see anything, hear anything, among the workforce? Do we have a reason to compel a search warrant and start looking for blood?" Jagger asked.

"No. And I don't think she was killed here," Tony said. "But then again, I don't seem to have your nose for blood."

Jagger nodded dryly and said, "It's acquired. Let's go on in."

Tony opened the door, wincing. "Back into Dante's Inferno."

It wasn't really Dante's Inferno. It was a strip club where very little was spent on a cleaning crew and every effort was spared when it came to the decor. Animal-print upholstery that looked to be from the sixties or seventies covered the ratty sofas and chairs. There was a main stage, along with a number of small circular tables cum stages with their own dance poles, surrounded by C-shaped couches covered in the same retro animal prints.

The place was dark, filled with smoke, and what

seemed like a miasma of pain and loneliness that stretched back through decades of human existence. Two girls were dancing on the main stage, while the small stages Tony said were for "private screenings" were all empty.

"The bar?" Tony asked.

"No, let's check this one here, in the back," Jagger said, heading toward one of the tables with its own stripper pole.

Tony, wide-eyed, looking torn between fascination and repulsion, joined him, groaning softly as he sat down.

"What?"

"Something sticky—I just sat in it," Tony said.

"Is it blood?"

"Some kind of fruity drink," Tony said.

"Then ya just gotta live with it a bit," Jagger told him, grinning. "Who's on stage now?"

"The one girl over on the left is called Rosy Red. Her real name is Martha Hamm. And the other one, the blonde, is Jamaka-me, real name Tammy Curtis. Jamaka-me was on stage just before Tina Lawrence— who was known as Ange-demonica when she was working. They all have stage names," Tony explained. "Hers was pretty grotesque, if you ask me."

Jagger grinned at his partner. Tony was twenty-eight. Both his parents had been born to Italian immigrants in an area of Boston where Italian was still the most commonly heard language. Tony had gone to Loyola here in town and fallen in love with New Orleans.

He was still a good Catholic Italian boy, though. He had grown up quickly working New Orleans' rough streets, but he had a pure heart that seemed to be something of a birthright.

A tired, skinny cocktail waitress wearing some kind of a costume—Jagger wasn't sure what, but both the tail and the ears were drooping—came up and asked them what they'd like. She noted Tony's badge hanging from his breast pocket and said, "Oh. Cops. You want some coffee...?"

"Are you Trisha Bean?" Jagger asked her.

She nodded glumly.

He was sure she'd never worked the stage. Trisha Bean, who worked with coffee beans, he thought dryly, and she even looked a bit like a string bean, she was so thin.

"Yeah, Bean's even my real name. Go figure, huh?" she said. She was clearly long past seeing any humor in the situation. "Coffee? Speak up. Believe it or not, I'm busy, and I need the money. I've got a kid to feed."

"We're actually off duty, so I'll have a beer," Jagger said. "Something in a bottle, please," he added, as Tony held up two fingers to tell her to double the order.

Trisha Bean laughed. "Good call. Don't think the beer taps in here have been cleaned since year one. Be right back."

"Don't you want to question her?" Tony asked.

"I will. Let her get the drinks first." Jagger loosened his tie and set a foot on the coffee table. "Chill. Keep your eyes open. Watch everyone in here. I would bet money that the killer came in here to find Tina Lawrence. I'm not sure where he'll go next, but I think it was a conscious decision to go with a stripper."

Tony looked at him with surprise, then gave serious attention to the room.

Jagger laughed. "Tony, casually, or these guys will make us for cops and be out of here in two seconds flat. Ease it back."

Tony flushed and relaxed as Trisha Bean returned with their bottled beers. "Here you go," she said.

Jagger set a large bill on her tray, telling her to keep the change.

"They're paying cops well these days," she commented, but he saw the smile of appreciation in her eyes.

"I have to confess, family money," he told her.

"'Family money?'" she said. "I'd be living the life of luxury. A little pad dead center in the Quarter, no crack whores banging around the building at all hours of the night. Anyway, what can I do for you? I wasn't holding out on you before," she told Tony. "I just didn't see anyone being any more of an ass than usual in here the night Tina was taken and killed. You think she went with the murderer willingly?"

"I think she met him here, yes," Jagger fudged.

Trisha was thoughtful. "Oh!" she said suddenly. "There *was* one guy I noticed…." Clutching her tray to her, she spun around and pointed to a private-screening table that was a few rows closer to the stage. "He wasn't being a jerk, though. He was in here alone, sitting right there. He was drinking, but he wasn't smashed, and he tipped me and the girls pretty good. I remember now, because Tina…went to that table. Here's the thing I noticed most, though. He was young, and really good-looking."

"Young. How young?"

"Twenty-five, thirty…maybe thirty-five. And he was almost…pretty. Beautiful skin. Thin, tall…pretty."

"Dark? Light?" Jagger asked.

"Dark hair, nice cut, lean face."

"What color eyes, do you remember?" Jagger asked.

"You know, I don't remember his eyes at all," she said. "Kinda dark in here."

"How about I get you to see a sketch artist?" Jagger asked her.

"Can I do it in the morning?"

He nodded. "Give me your address, and I'll pick you up and get you home after. Thank you," he said.

She nodded. "I just gotta get my kid to school first, you know?"

"Of course. I really appreciate all help," Jagger assured her.

She walked away, and Tony turned to stare at Jagger. "I talked to her at least twice today. She didn't remember the guy then."

Jagger shrugged. "You were being a cop then, looking for someone who'd made a stink. She was nervous. Now you're being human. You're having a beer. People think better when they don't feel threatened."

As Jagger spoke, Jamaka-me did a flying leap onto the main stage, spun around the pole athletically and leaped down to the floor.

Her action was greeted by whoops and catcalls and applause.

She moved through the audience, accepting tips stuck in the string that passed for a thong but managed to hide nothing at all.

Finally she leaped on their table and stared at Jagger before doing a slow, sultry spin around the pole.

Jagger met her eyes.

Werewolf, he thought.

* * *

At 3:00 a.m., Fiona was still wide-awake. She gave up tossing and turning, threw her covers off and walked to the windows that led to her balcony.

She loved this house, as did her sisters. It was huge and old, filled with memories of their family. Its long hallways were hung with photos of the three of them and their parents. Skiing in Aspen—and meeting up with other Keepers. A holiday to Jamaica—and a meeting with another Keeper family from New York City. The father was in charge of Leprechauns, which weren't nearly as plentiful in New Orleans as they were in Boston and New York. But then, no one had the workload her parents had always managed, except those working in places like Transylvania, Edinburgh or the true home of all the magical creatures of the earth: Ireland.

Out on the balcony, she looked across to her sisters' rooms. Shauna had the middle bedroom, and Caitlin's windows were just beyond.

Shauna's room was dark, but Caitlin was pacing. Her light was still on, and Fiona could see her walking back and forth, back and forth, behind the curtains.

Caitlin despised vampires. She believed that they were the eternal troublemakers, and she blamed the deaths of their parents on vampires.

Fiona wished that she could ease some of the hatred in her sister's heart. It wasn't that she didn't know that her own reason for existence was to keep the vampires' bloodlust in check or that she thought her job was easy. In truth, all the beings of the underworld were so much stronger and, often, craftier than humans, or at least they came with talents that allowed them to carry out feats of tremendous deceit.

But Fiona had realized at an early age that evil came in all sizes, shapes and races. Human beings were capable of as much cruelty and torture as any paranormal being, and though she had suspected from the first that they were looking for a vampire, she knew that a human being was perfectly capable of the murder, even if not the method.

She had to stay on top of the situation, had to investigate as if she had been trained at Quantico. This was her responsibility.

And yet...

She was paradoxically glad to be sharing that responsibility.

With Jagger. Jagger DeFarge.

She left the balcony, locking the double doors behind her once she was back inside. This was a time to be careful, and she didn't intend to be taken unaware by anyone.

Or any*thing*.

She had to get some sleep.

She lay back down, closed her eyes and wondered if anyone had ever really managed to fall asleep by counting sheep. She tried. It didn't work.

Instead she kept seeing Jagger DeFarge. The rugged and yet ascetic lines of his face. His eyes, gold and entrancing. The richness of his dark hair. The sense of security she felt when he was near. Surely, she told herself, that was only because he was tall and strong.

At last she began to drift to sleep.

But even then, she kept seeing his face, hearing his voice. She saw his smile of gentle amusement when he looked at her, the hardness that locked his jaw when she annoyed him. She felt his hand, touching her.

When she drifted to sleep at last, she was imagining his voice, husky in her ear, and his fingertips, stroking her. His lips were coming closer to hers as he whispered words she couldn't quite comprehend.

He was a vampire. She knew vampires. He was probably getting ready to sink his fangs into her throat and drink her blood.

No…

She was imagining what it would be like if his lips touched on hers and he drew her close to him. He wouldn't be cold to the touch—that was a myth. He would be warm, maybe hot as fire. He would draw her into an embrace that was secure with vibrant warmth, hot and edgy and erotic. His kiss would be filled with passion, searing and wet, and crushed against his body, she would feel the electricity of his being….

The alarm suddenly rang, persistent and irritating. Fiona bolted awake, jerked from the arms that had seemed so real.

She was drenched in sweat. Swearing, she leaped from her bed and headed for the shower.

The ballroom where the luncheon was being held had seating for approximately a hundred and fifty people. The room was beautifully decorated with flowers everywhere, and a large banner stretched across the top of the small stage area boasted, In Honor Of Jennie Mahoney, Philanthropist Extraordinaire.

A jazz trio had played while they were seated and served their salads, followed by a main course of jambalaya, which was delicious. The hotel had always boasted top-notch food, even when serving hundreds of meals for a formal function.

After the entrée, there had been several speakers. Some talked about Jennie's humanitarian work. Others spoke about her talent for poetry. Then Jennie herself spoke, reminding them all that New Orleans was unique, a breeding ground for art in all its guises. The coffeehouse they had managed to get back on its feet recognized new talent, from poets to visual artists, violinists to drummers to jazz musicians, as well as those who hoped to one day climb the pop and rock charts.

Her speech drew thunderous applause.

"Son of a bitch," Caitlin, seated to Fiona's right, suddenly muttered.

Fiona looked up to see Jennie Mahoney welcoming Jagger DeFarge to the stage.

She hadn't even seen him here.

Admittedly, the attendees were mainly women, but she had noticed a number of men there, as well. A few of the city commissioners were there, including their old friend August Gaudin. He was at their table, in fact, along with Jill Derby, Sue Preston and Sean Ahearn, who were a couple, and Mya Yates, shapeshifters like Jennie, and supporters of her philanthropic efforts.

The only vampire she'd noticed was Lilly Wayne, an octogenarian and philanthropist in her own right, well-loved by everyone, human and supernatural alike.

Fiona realized now that Jagger had been seated at Lilly's table near the stage, but her view of him had been blocked before he rose to take the microphone.

"How very odd," Shauna, at Fiona's left, said softly. She didn't sound suspicious or angry, just curious.

"What in God's name is *he* doing here?" Caitlin asked.

"Well, since hc's about to speak, I'm assuming he was invited," Fiona told her dryly.

Caitlin's lips were pursed; she didn't answer, only looked on with disapproval.

"He's so cute," Sue, a pretty redhead, whispered to Mya.

"Dreamy," Mya agreed.

Dreamy? Who used that word these days? Fiona wondered, annoyed.

Like it or not, Jagger DeFarge was a presence. His height gave him an immediate advantage, and he had such dark hair. His shoulders were broad, making him stand out in any room. He moved with impressive agility for such a large man, and his smile could only be called compelling.

Because he was a vampire. A vampire with the innate ability to seduce his victims.

But to the best of her knowledge, Jagger DeFarge lived his life like a man. A human being. He worked for the city, a city he truly seemed to love.

They had that in common.

Caitlin made a sound of distaste. Fiona glared at her sister, who looked away, but her cheeks were touched with color.

Just then Jagger began to speak.

"Jennie, I'm here as an officer of law, one who speaks for us all, all of us who love this city and work for all the good things that make up the Crescent City, the Big Easy—our New Orleans. We honor you for the beauty and the creativity you tirelessly work to promote, and we thank you from the bottom of our hearts. We've been through bad times in this city, but bad times teach us how we must cherish all that is fine in life, and for that we thank you. Now, I believe I'm the last speaker, and I think I'll stop here, so we can hear the Mountjoy trio spin their magic again—and enjoy the bourbon-pecan pie."

His words were met by thunderous applause, and Jennie went over to give him a big hug.

"Detective!" someone cried as he started to leave the stage.

He paused, then returned to the mike.

"Yes? Miss Chase, is it? Julie? What is it?"

"Do you have any leads on that bizarre murder?"

"Unfortunately, no, we don't have the answers yet. But we're pursuing the case twenty-four hours a day."

"Do you think there's a killer going after the…fallen women of this city? Are the rest of us safe?"

"Julie, I don't know yet, but we're pursuing any and all leads, and I promise you, we won't stop until this killer is caught."

Another woman stood up.

"Detective—is it true she was drained of blood?"

He didn't hesitate. "Yes. And before everyone starts running for cover, my advice to all of you is the same advice I always give. This is a big city, full of very fine people, along with some very unusual ones and, yes, an admitted criminal element. Ladies, be smart. Go out at night in groups. Lock your doors. Don't let strangers in. If you're at work late, make sure you don't walk to your car alone. Think. Always think. And be smart at all times. And now I'm leaving this luncheon to go back to work on the case—rejoining my partner, along with a team of top-notch officers and forensic investigators. As for you, go about your lives, just be smart, including street smart."

His words were met by another round of applause. Jennie Mahoney took his arm, waving a hand to indicate that there would be no more questions as she walked with him off the stage.

"Oh," Mya sighed, watching him flash a smile at Jennie as he seated her back at her table, then drew out the chair next to hers.

He'd not only been invited, he'd also been given a place of honor.

"I'd feel safe if *he* was sleeping with me at night," Sue said, grinning.

Caitlin made a sniffing noise. Fiona kicked her beneath the table.

Sean Ahearn laughed, having noticed the exchange, and reached across the table to cover Sue's hand with his. "Honey, please. I *am* right here, you know."

They all laughed then. "And you know I love you," Sue told him.

"I'm not in a relationship," Mya pointed out.

August Gaudin spoke up then. "Ah, my dear, I hear that a handsome young football player has his eye on you."

Mya flushed. "Randy Soames. Yes."

"And he's your kind," August said softly, as aware as Fiona and her sisters were that their table was filled with shapeshifters.

Sue flicked her hair back. "That, Monsieur Gaudin, sounds both prejudice and archaic, though I'm sure you didn't mean it to."

"He's right," Caitlin said, her tone hard. "Certain... aspects of society should simply remain separate."

"Oh, look! The pie is coming," Fiona said, wanting to hush them all. Her tablemates might be denizens of the underworld, but there were well over a hundred other people in the room, emphasis on "people."

Fiona rose as the pie was brought to the table, acutely aware that Jagger DeFarge was rising, too—ready to go back to work, if what he had said on stage was true.

"Excuse me," she murmured.

"I'll be right back."

She hurried out to the hallway, managing to get there just as Jagger did—with Jennie Mahoney right behind him.

"I'm so sorry, but I should have expected the question to come up," Jennie was saying. She stopped short when she spotted Fiona.

"Hello, dear. I'm so pleased you were able to come today." She was a very attractive woman, somewhere in her mid to late thirties, with flashing green eyes, deep auburn hair and a slim, shapely build.

Of course, she could have any build she wanted, but changing required effort, and most shapeshifters were consistent in the appearance they donned in their day-to-day lives.

"It was my pleasure, Jennie," Fiona said.

"I knew your sister was coming," Jennie said. "But—"

"I'm afraid I have to get going," Jagger said, interrupting. "I'm praying we can catch the killer before the city falls into a state of panic."

"How intriguing that you're in such a hurry to be off," Jennie said, "Since, quite honestly, I'm assuming that Fiona is here today not as a friend, but because she is willing to entertain the idea that a shapeshifter is the guilty party rather than a vampire."

"Actually, Jennie," Fiona said, "I'm here because I want to ask you for your help."

"My help?" Jennie said, her ruffled feathers smoothing over almost visibly.

"Yes. Jennie, you know everyone…I'm hoping that you'll be on the lookout and let us know if you see anything that might be a clue, or anyone behaving oddly in any way."

Jennie arched her brows. "But Jagger is on the case." She lowered her voice, looking around to be sure she wouldn't be overheard. "And he's a *vampire*."

"A vampire who has to be on his way, Jennie.…" He gave her a kiss on the cheek, and then his eyes met Fiona's. She was sure she saw a sizzle of amusement. "Miss MacDonald."

He didn't touch her.

She hated that she wished he had.

He walked away down the hall, his strides long and sure.

"Jennie, I'm really sorry if I gave you the wrong impression by being here," Fiona said. "I really do think we need all the help we can get."

Jennie sighed. "Well, I can assure you, this isn't the work of a shapeshifter." She looped arms with Fiona, leading her back into the ballroom. "Why don't I join you at your table for a few minutes?" she suggested.

As they approached the table, Sean quickly went to find an extra chair for Jennie. There was gushing all around as she sat, her fellow shapeshifters congratulating her, Caitlin mentioning her pride in her, and August Gaudin announcing she was a wonderful example for everyone in the city.

Jennie thanked them, then glanced around quickly, making sure no one was nearby.

"Listen, we all have to focus on solving this murder. It looks like we have a rogue vampire among us, though I do have to acknowledge that Fiona may be concerned because the only other entity who could have pulled this off is a shapeshifter."

"It was obviously a vampire, it's just that I'm afraid neither my sister nor DeFarge wants to admit that," Caitlin said.

Fiona controlled her anger; Caitlin should never betray a breech between the three of them.

"We know it wasn't a werewolf," Shauna said happily.

"And I'm quite certain it wasn't a shapeshifter," Jennie said. "You have to understand our kind, Fiona. We're pranksters, not violent at all."

"It's true," Sue said. "I love to shapeshift into some hot movie star and tease the paparazzi."

"Or a rock star," Mya said, giggling. "I've met the most interesting people that way."

"You two are wicked," Sean said.

"Hey, you like to impersonate politicians," Mya reminded him.

"My favorite, ever, was being Tom Cruise," Jill Derby announced in a whisper, grinning.

"You didn't!" Mya said.

"I did," Jill said.

Fiona forced herself to laugh along with the rest of the group. "I'm just asking all of you—help us out, please."

"None of us want another war," August Gaudin said quietly.

"No," Fiona said, rising. "We don't want a panic, and we don't want a war. And we have to live by the law, just like everyone else. The difference being, of course, that we have to handle our own criminals. If a vampire *is* guilty, I guarantee you he will be brought to justice."

She looked at her sisters.

"Whoever is guilty, he will be brought to justice. I swear it."

Chapter 5

David Du Lac groaned audibly.

Jagger, standing at the head of the table, looked up and saw that Fiona MacDonald had arrived.

Of course, she had.

He wanted to stride over to her, take her by the shoulders and shake her.

She had to give them some space. She had to give them a chance to police their own.

"Gentlemen, ladies, please proceed, I'm not here to interrupt," she assured the assembled group.

There were about fifty people there, including several vampires who held positions in the highest echelon of city politics. There were also two football players, a local DJ, a TV anchorwoman, a singer, a float designer, a costumer, a woman who worked at the city's most successful wig shop, several restaurateurs and others who weren't well-known but were still important in their own right.

"Fiona!" Gina Lorre, the anchorwoman said, smiling. "How lovely to see you."

"Thank you," Fiona said, as gracious as if she'd just been welcomed by the queen—or at least the voodoo queen. This *was* New Orleans, after all. One of the football players rose, insisting she take his chair. She thanked him, giving him a patented Fiona-smile.

He smiled back, smitten. Their Keeper *was* a stunning young woman, Jagger admitted to himself. She was also capable of radiating confidence. Not arrogance—just confidence. Along with her beauty, her manner, her silken voice and her undeniable grace meant she was not just accepted but, he saw, truly welcomed.

Was he the only one who didn't want her there?

"I didn't mean to interrupt. I'm so sorry," Fiona said. "Please, Detective DeFarge, go ahead. I'm just here to keep abreast of what's going on. I have complete confidence that you'll quickly and efficiently solve this problem by yourselves."

Like hell! he thought, not believing her for a moment.

But he smiled. "Of course. And naturally we're all pleased that you're *keeping abreast*, and that you have *complete confidence* in our ability to handle this situation."

He looked from her to the assembly and made a point with his next words. "As of yet, there's no proof positive that this is the work of a vampire rather than a shapeshifter. However, since the evidence does point in our direction, I want to make sure that we're all aware of just how deeply this may affect our lives. We've worked extremely hard around the world—and especially here in New Orleans—to be a part of society. We work, we play, we fall in love. Right here in this city, we enjoy our jazz, our homes, our world—and when that world needs protecting, we come out and fight natural disaster alongside everyone else. We have proven that we are among the city's finest citizens."

"Jagger, that's just it," Billy Harrington, a college student, said. "I don't understand why any of us would have done this and put everything at risk. It just doesn't make sense."

"Billy, in a way it does," Jagger said. "Take human beings. Everyone's born with a capability for good and evil, and with natural instincts that drive them toward one rather than the other. People can be almost unbelievably evil toward each other, practicing torture and murder—sometimes for love, sometimes for hatred, sometimes in passion and often for greed. We have the same instincts as humans do, but we try harder to control our baser impulses—we have to, because our natural craving is for blood. Why couldn't there be one among us whose instincts are baser than most, who is weary of the restraints we put on ourselves so we can live something approaching normal lives? We have to bring that person to justice. Each of us has power and strength, but together we are less than half a percent of the population, and we can be brought to extinction, even though each of us would take down dozens of 'them' if it came to a fight. That's the reality—even beyond the fact that most of us *like* our lives and enjoy our neighbors, human and other, making it imperative that we police our own."

"We do police our own," David Du Lac said firmly.

"I know that. And we're not alone in this," Jagger said. "Jennie Mahoney intends to keep watch among the shapeshifters, and August Gaudin has always been a friend, and a supporter of peaceful coexistence among all the races. We've had a decade of ease, with any disagreements being solved quietly among our own, but now we must be vigilant. Rumor and suspicion can lead to hurt and bitterness, and I don't want us all to start looking at our neighbors and suspecting them of being responsible. But I do ask that if anyone among you find something suspicious, you bring it to me. It's easy to cause a world of hurt by casting accusations without solid evidence, so we all need to stay calm and be discreet at all times. First, because we don't want to sow suspicion among ourselves, and second, we don't want to cast blame where it doesn't belong and drive our fellow races to see us as monsters."

"I'm sure they already do," Billy said dryly.

"Why not? We *are* monsters."

The comment came from a relative newcomer at the end of the table, Mateas Grenard.

"Mateas, would you care to speak?" Jagger asked. If the man wanted the floor, it was better to give it to him now than listen to subtle barbs that would get beneath everyone's skin.

Grenard stood. He was a hair shorter than Jagger, a little stockier, but he bore himself with confidence and a certain charm.

A man who could easily influence others, Jagger thought. A vampire to be noted.

"We are monsters—that's why we have a Keeper," Grenard said, smiling and nodding toward Fiona.

She watched him without expression, waiting for his words.

"When I arrived, I was amazed at the self-control you—*we*—exercise here in New Orleans. I love being here, but I've often wondered why we don't do as they do in other places and feast on occasion upon the dregs of society. How often does the murder of a prostitute really get noticed? And this state has a death penalty—why waste the blood? There are drug lords and gangs out there. I keep thinking that an organized kill now and then—especially one supervised by an officer of the law—would not be out of order."

"I don't know about that," Gina Lorre said. "Someone would be bound to notice that even a hooker or a criminal was drained of blood. I don't know exactly what happened, but when we were looking into this murder, our reporter found out that the young man working the graveyard shift at the morgue quit the day after the body of Tina Lawrence was brought in." She looked worried for a minute. "Jagger, she's not out there, is she?"

"No, she's not out there," Jagger said quietly.

"Even if she were, this is a forgiving city, and we all know that dozens of human beings in the area *think* they're vampires," Mateas Grenard pointed out.

Fiona stood. "That may be true, sir, but no human being is capable of taking blood as a vampire takes blood. As Detective DeFarge has pointed out, we don't know for a fact that a vampire is guilty—but suspicion falls that way. And to address your other point, if the vampires justified the taking of a human life, no matter how seemingly worthless, then the shapeshifters would want to kill, and the werewolves would be hungry, and those three groups are just the largest and strongest of the underworld. What if every race decided it had a right to take a life now and then?"

"Excellent point," David Du Lac commented.

One of the city commissioners stood. "More than an excellent point. I can tell you that the city government is already up in arms, arguments have started with the tourist board, and there's trouble brewing, despite the fact that the victim was hardly an innocent and there are plenty who claim she only got what she deserved. Luckily for us, because of the way she was displayed, so far the majority opinion is that some nut case psycho committed the murder. But I know for a fact, the department brass are breathing down Jagger's back, wanting to know where she was killed, and how, not to mention how all her blood was drained.…We need to work to keep the status quo. Everyone has to help by doing exactly as Jagger has asked and bringing anything odd, any suspicion, to his attention and only his attention, so we can retain the peace among ourselves."

A murmur of approval rose from the group.

"Ah, well, then I fear I am in the minority," Mateas Grenard said.

"That's fine," Jagger told him. "Discussion is always welcome."

"Open discussion, yes," David Du Lac said. "Mateas, we thank you for speaking candidly."

"Yes, and I thank you for understanding our position here in New Orleans," Fiona told him.

"I bow to wiser heads," Grenard said.

"All right, ladies, gentlemen, I thank you all for coming," Jagger said. "David will call for another meeting, if need be. For the time being, please be on the alert, and come to me with anything you feel might be relevant."

Murmurs of consent went all around, and the group began to break up. David Du Lac, always the perfect host, had arranged for refreshments and a table at the rear of the room was set with food and wine.

Jagger greeted friends, nodded to acquaintances and made his way to the table, procuring two glasses of wine.

Fiona was still at the rear of the room, talking to David and Gina, when he walked up and offered her one glass. "Thank you for coming, Fiona."

She flashed him a quick glare. He knew what it meant: thanks for inviting me.

"David told me about the meeting. I thought it was important for me to be here," she said.

"Well, of course it is, sweetheart," Gina said, walking up and giving her a hug.

Jagger met Fiona's eyes and raised his own glass in a toast. "To all involved doing their best to find a speedy solution to our problem," he said softly.

Fiona stared at her wine suspiciously.

David laughed softly. "It's nothing but merlot, and an excellent vintage, I swear."

Fiona blushed and drank.

"I promise you, I will be totally vigilant," Gina said. "I have to go, my darlings, David, Fiona…Jagger, you handsome hunk of…well, whatever." She looked at her watch. "Goodness, I have to be at the studio in a little over an hour. See you all soon."

"Take care, Gina," Jagger told her.

She laughed softly. "Just hope the killer, who and

whatever he is, doesn't come after me, or he'll be sorry."

Others were filing out. There were pleasant goodbyes all around.

It might have been a late night buffet thrown by the tourist board.

Jagger offered David his hand, and the two men shook. "Thank you," Jagger told him.

"I am always ready to serve," David said graciously.

Billy came by. "Fiona, thank you," he said. "I think it's cool that you're our Keeper."

He was so young and cute and sincere that even Fiona could ignore his blatant admiration.

"Thank you, Billy. Will you be okay this late? Aren't you living in a frat house?"

He grinned. "I am, but don't worry. I'm great at sneaking back in. Oh—and guess who's the new late-night morgue attendant?"

"You?" David asked him.

He grinned. "Seemed perfect for me. I start tomorrow night."

"I just hope you get nothing but the elderly dying of natural causes," Jagger told him. "I don't want to have to come in and see you anytime soon."

Mateas Grenard left right behind Billy. He, too, stopped to thank David for his hospitality.

Then the man looked at Fiona with a twinkle in his eye and took her hand, planting a kiss lightly on it. "Miss MacDonald, a sincere pleasure. And, DeFarge," he said, turning to Jagger while still holding Fiona's hand. "I speak my mind, but I didn't make the kill. I swear it."

"Did you think that I was suspicious of you?" Jagger

asked. He wanted to wrench Fiona's hand away from Grenard's hold.

Grenard chuckled softly. "I'm a newcomer and not shy about expressing my views—and I'm not stupid. Of course I would fall under suspicion. But I didn't do it. Don't waste your time on me."

"I never waste time, and I always discover the truth," Jagger told him, then turned to Fiona. "Miss MacDonald, are you ready for me to see you home?"

"If you've business to attend to, DeFarge, I can see our Keeper home," Grenard offered.

"That won't be necessary, thank you. I have a few matters to discuss with Fiona," Jagger said, but he didn't look at her, afraid she might say that she preferred to go with Grenard.

But she didn't.

"I'm ready whenever you are," she said.

"Alas, well, then, good night, my friends," Grenard said, and departed.

Jagger doubted that she was going to let him see her home for the pleasure of his company. Maybe she distrusted Grenard. Or maybe she was hoping that he had something to say.

"Good night, David, and thank you," Fiona said, kissing him on the cheek. "Thank you very much."

"Don't be a stranger, sweetie," David told her.

She shook her head. "I won't be. Just, please, tell Dragon-lady to let me in when I come."

He laughed. "Consider it done."

"Dragon-lady?" Jagger echoed, and was surprised to see Fiona flash a smile.

"Bitchy shapeshifter," she said.

"Valentina," David explained. "She seems to have

claws when she sees our dear Keeper." He smiled. "I shall inform my hostess that you are always welcome here, Fiona. Come back some night, when the music is sweet and the 'joint is a hoppin' and a poppin'.'"

Fiona promised him that she would. Then Jagger nodded to David and led Fiona toward the door, steering between the tables in the courtyard to reach the street.

It was the rare hour of "tween" in New Orleans. The clubs often stayed open until five, and a few of the late night pizza, chicken or burger joints boasted twenty-four-hour service. But, for the most part, the last partiers had finally called it quits, and it was too early for the workaday world to have begun stirring.

The streets were quiet.

And beautiful.

"You walked?" Jagger asked.

"Yes."

"Alone?"

"Yes."

He sighed deeply. "Don't you ever listen to intelligent advice?" he asked her.

She lifted her hands. "I'm a Keeper," she told him.

"And you're vulnerable. Any vampire could take you by surprise, and a werewolf could be on you before you blinked. Not to mention that a shapeshifter can be and do pretty much anything. And let's not forget our normal run-of-the-mill crackheads, heroin addicts, thieves, rapists and murderers."

She had the grace to flush.

"I can change pretty quickly myself, you know. And anyone can be taken by surprise."

"Right. So don't let that anyone be you," he said.

She glanced up at him with her beautiful, opalescent

eyes, a dry grin curving her lips. "I'm glad to hear that you genuinely seem to want me to survive."

"Protect and serve, that's my motto," he said.

"And you resent my intrusion," she said.

He shook his head. "No, I don't resent you. I just don't understand why you won't believe that I'm not shirking my responsibility, that I *am* policing my own, that I *will* act when necessary—even against my own breed. My...people are committed to the 'lives' we lead here, Fiona. For the most part, we're extremely good citizens. If someone is guilty, they will be brought to justice. And I won't be acting alone. The entire vampire community will be behind me."

"Get real," she murmured.

"Pardon?" he asked.

She squared her shoulders. "What have you discovered?" she asked. "Anything?"

He looked ahead as they walked, weighing his answer. They were into the Quarter, and the moonlight and soft glow of the street lamps hid anything that might mar the perfection of the buildings, with their balconies and decoration. He thought there was little in the world as picture perfect as the architecture in the French Quarters. People loved their balconies, and ferns grew profusely in pots and planters, along with flowers in an array of colors, and insignia plaques that held the city's symbol, the fleur-de-lis, adorned more than one building. Banners still proclaimed the city's pride in the New Orleans Saints, and beautifully fashioned signs advertised various shops and restaurants.

"Jagger?" she asked.

"I spent part of last night at Barely, Barely, Barely— the club where Tina Lawrence worked. I met a woman there, a waitress, who came in this morning and worked with a police artist to create a sketch of a man she thought was suspicious. I met a werewolf who worked with her, and verified that Tina carried on a conversation with the man and intended to meet him after work. I don't know if he's the one who killed her, but I didn't recognize him."

"Do you have a copy of the sketch on you?" Fiona asked.

"Of course," he said. "I didn't want to show it tonight, because I didn't want anyone to go off half-cocked, but it will run in tomorrow's paper, and they'll show it on the local newscasts. No one at the club had ever seen the man before, so we're not putting it out that he's under suspicion, just that we're hoping he may have some information regarding Tina Lawrence. Thing is, if he's a married man, he'll probably be afraid to come forward, won't want to admit where he was. But, one way or another, someone out there must have seen him. And if we find him, with luck he will lead us somewhere."

He paused beneath a streetlight on St. Ann's and took out his phone, then brought up the picture.

Fiona stared at it for a long minute.

"Anything?" he asked her.

She shook her head. "No, I've never seen him before."

He slid the phone back in his jacket pocket as they started walking again. "Before the meeting, I went back to the club, and the girls who'd seen him all agreed that it's a good likeness of him."

"I hope it leads us in the right direction," Fiona said.

A moment later they had reached her house, which

was surrounded by a ten-foot brick wall, with a wrought-iron gate that led to the front walk.

She hovered before opening it. "Do you want to come in? Can I get you anything? Although after that wine, we should probably get some sleep."

Mixed signals. Did she want him to come in? Or was she just being polite?

He shrugged. "It will probably be another hour or so before I wind down."

"Do you only sleep when it's light?" she asked him.

He laughed. "I long ago learned to sleep whenever I get the chance. And, yes, I wear sunglasses, and slather on the sunblock, but in general my 'life' is as normal as anyone else's."

She smiled. "I'm sorry, I wasn't implying anything, just pointing out that we all must be tired."

"Are *you* tired?"

She looked away from him. "I'm…keyed up, I guess." She grinned suddenly. "Want to watch a movie? Pay-per-view has everything—adventure, horror, thriller, you name it."

He laughed. "I can actually sit through a chick flick, you know."

She grinned again, pulled out her key and opened the gate. "Please, come in, then."

"Thank you, Miss MacDonald, I believe I will."

He had never been in the MacDonald house, though he had heard it was spectacular.

He'd heard right.

The front path took them through a small garden to the door, which led up one step to a tile entry. There was a small mudroom before the grand foyer, which offered two hallways, one to the left and one to the right. Straight ahead, a grand stairway led to the second floor.

Fiona walked down the hallway to the right.

"We've basically divided the house," she explained. "I'm in this wing, Shauna is in the center upstairs, and Caitlin has the left wing. There's a huge dining room-slash-ballroom at the back of the first floor, and the kitchen is back there, too, though we all have little kitchenettes of our own. There's a third floor, a little garret, above Shauna's rooms, so the division of space is about even. We live and work together, so we have to give one another a little privacy where we can."

"Nice," he murmured.

They had reached what was clearly Fiona's living room. He quickly saw that she liked antiques and eclectic art. There was a huge fireplace against the wall, all done in red brick, with a pink marble mantel. Books were everywhere, and pictures of her family and New Orleans adorned several of the tables and the mantel, along with small sculptures of cats, dogs and other animals, gargoyles, ornate wands and more. She was clearly fond of Rodrigue, judging by the many prints of his Blue Dog pictures.

"The TV's upstairs, sorry," she said, her words a little awkward. "Does that make you uncomfortable?"

"Does it make *you* uncomfortable?" he asked.

She hesitated. "I don't think so."

They were caught there together in the soft glow of the few night-lights she'd left burning when she went out, and everything was quiet around them, as if they were alone in the world.

He suddenly found himself speaking the truth. "Any

man in creation would want to be with you anywhere," he said softly.

Soft color suffused to her cheeks, but she didn't blink, and she didn't turn away.

"Isn't it forbidden?" she asked.

"Only if we forbid it," he told her.

"But…before…what happened…the war when the races mixed…"

"We would never allow that to happen again," he said.

She continued to stare at him. He wanted to move closer, but he wouldn't allow himself to. He drew upon his every reserve of strength to keep his distance from her. He imagined holding her, really holding her, inhaling the scent of her hair, feeling the warmth of her, feeling her heart beating, the rise and fall of her breath, her skin, so silky, crushed against his…

He had to go or he would be screaming in frustration in a matter of seconds.

Then, to his astonishment, *she* moved toward him.

In a second—no, less than a second—she had crossed the few feet that separated them. She was in his arms, against him, and instinct demanded that his arms tighten around her, that he bury his face against her sun-colored hair to inhale the sweet feminine scent of her . He didn't know if he was dreaming at first, if his imagination hadn't been taunting him so completely that he was hallucinating the wonder of the moment. But it was real.

She was real.

And more than his imagination could ever have predicted. She trembled slightly in his arms, and he felt her warmth, her vitality, the heartbeat that had so fascinated him. Her skin was as soft and smooth as silk, and even more tempting than he'd imagined. For seconds that felt like an eternity, he just held her. Then he drew away far enough to lift her chin, to look into her eyes and whisper to her, "Fiona...I don't...I'd never..."

"You'd never hurt me," she said softly.

"Never," he swore.

She smiled. "I believe you."

"But...I am what I am."

"I know what you are."

"Others may...talk."

"Let them."

"Are you sure?"

She nodded, staring up at him with a beautiful honesty, heart and soul bared, something he'd never imagined he would receive from her. "Truthfully I didn't want to feel this way. I didn't even want to like you," she told him.

He had to laugh softly. "Sorry about that."

"I am the Keeper, after all," she whispered.

"What better way to keep me?" he teased.

"I dreamed about you," she told him.

"I hope I can live up to the dream."

Then he touched her lips gently with his own. Hers were soft and welcoming, parting beneath his tender touch. And then he was locked with her in the soft light, his tongue reveling in a wealth of sensation, heat that led to slow burning fire, something that wasn't just beautiful and angelic, but deeply passionate, as well. Stepping backward, her lips still locked with his, she drew him toward the staircase. Step by step they went up, never breaking the kiss. The stairs led to a large room where he glimpsed the promised TV, and on the back wall, a door. They made their way to that door.

He closed it behind him when they entered her bedroom. Gentle, pale light streamed in through the soft white curtains that covered the doors to the balcony without blocking the moonbeams or the artificial light from the street. As they broke apart at last, he saw a room that felt instantly welcoming. Her bed was large and covered with a homemade quilt, her shelves were filled with more bric-a-brac, and there was local art on the walls, a rocking chair by the fireplace…everything warm and individual, and uniquely the woman who had demanded his attention, and seduced his senses and his heart.

Fiona never hesitated. She kept backing up until they reached the bed, and there she studied his eyes, as if she could see into his soul. Perhaps she could. If so, she would know he was trembling inside.

His existence had gone on for more years than she could probably imagine, and he had known battle and peace, family, friends…and enemies. But he had seldom, if ever, felt so in awe, so touched, and all from a woman's eyes upon him. Eyes that promised honesty and an exploration of the heart, eyes that he could never, not even in the full span of his near-eternal lifetime, betray.

He kissed her again—hard and passionately—feeling as if he were drowning in nothing but a kiss. His lips traveled to her collarbone and, impatiently, he began to undo the tiny buttons of her blouse. At the same time, he felt her hands on him. Her fingers were like pure magic, moving down his spine, slipping beneath his waistband.

She shrugged impatiently, letting the blouse slip from her shoulders, then slipping her hands beneath his jacket. He stood up, shedding the jacket, along with his holster and gun. And then she was against him again. A dream. Silk in his arms. He pressed his lips to her breast, felt the intake of her breath, the press of her body against his. He eased her skirt down, found the tiny line of her string panties, let them fall. A second later he'd shed the rest of his clothes and was with her at last. Naked flesh to naked flesh. Feeling the play of muscle beneath her smooth skin, as she arched against him.

It hadn't been that long since he'd had sex.

But it felt like forever since he'd made love.

His desires seemed to burst instantly and almost savagely to the front the instant they came into contact, but he brutally willed them under control. Being with her in this moment, this seemingly impossible moment, was something to cherish and savor. And he did. He stroked her flesh in wonder. Kissed her with reverence and wanton need. He explored the length of her body with his touch, with his lips. She was not to be outdone. Her hands moved along his back, teasing his spine, his buttocks. Her lips found his chest, his abdomen, below. Soft groans escaped him, and he took the lead again, bearing her beneath him to the mattress, finding her breasts with the pressure of his mouth, the teasing touch of his tongue, then moving lower, down to her ankles, her knees, the luxurious length of her thighs…and between.

She cried out, dragging him to her. Their lips met again as he entered her, drawing her long legs around him, sinking together so completely that he felt as if they were sharing their very beings. All that had been slow became desperately fast, subtle became bold, and they seemed to both give way before something so urgent it was almost cruel, and yet there was still time for kisses of liquid fire, caresses and whispers as tender as the softest breeze.

He held himself in check as he held her, felt her shudder and jerk and climax, and at long last he allowed himself to release the shattering volatility that he had held in check, the entire world darkening and then exploding along with him. She fell against him, drenched and liquid, spent and limp, and he held her, feeling as if he actually had a heart himself, one that hammered along with hers as they both eased down from the pure carnal ecstasy of incredible sex.

Together, they lay entwined on the bed, with the soft white light slowing bringing the world into focus again. He didn't want to leave—ever.

She stirred against him. He slipped an arm around her, drawing her head down to his chest, gently threading his fingers through the tangled mass of her hair, marveling at the color in the light. Where she went, he thought, there was sun. A sun that didn't burn or hurt, just brightened the world.

She could be the most infuriating individual in the world. Stubborn. Pig-headed, actually. But being with her was amazing. Making love with her was even more amazing. Lying beside her, just being near her…

He must be insane. Being with her was the most wonderful experience in his memory, in his life, in his death…in his entire existence. But he needed to be careful. His emotions were running rampant.

He didn't care. He didn't think all the powers in

heaven or hell could have stopped him from making love to her tonight.

And then he stopped, amazed at the tenor of his own thoughts. He was a *vampire*.

And he was falling in love.

She moved slightly, getting more comfortable against him.

He wondered if she realized just what they might have to face as he continued to stroke her hair in silence. Then, he couldn't stop himself.

"Are you sorry?" he asked softly.

She shook her head. "No...actually, I haven't felt this...I don't know...so..."

"So...what?" he asked, setting a finger on her chin to lift her face so that she had to look at him.

She was smiling. "I was about to say 'at peace.' I haven't felt so at peace in years. But I didn't want you to think that your lovemaking was peaceful. I mean, I'm not sure that would be a compliment, and I wouldn't want to insult you. At all." She was suddenly flushing, but he laughed, not in the least bit offended.

"I won't take it as an offense against my masculinity, I promise," he assured her.

Her smile suddenly faded. "I want you to know...I mean, I have no expectations. I...don't think I meant to do this when I let you walk me home tonight. I...I don't mean to intrude on your life. I mean...I *do*, as far as discovering what happened goes. So far..."

"So far," he said firmly, wrapping his arms around her, "so far, there's nothing we can do until morning. Tonight...tonight, I'm in awe, and I don't want to give up a minute of the time that's left."

"I think it's already starting to get light."

"Then hush, and let me love you."

Fiona awoke with his words echoing in her mind.

Of course, he hadn't meant it as "love." He'd meant it as "make love." But still, she believed with her whole heart that there was something between them more than sex. She really hadn't wanted to want him.

But she had. And she did.

She'd dreamed about him.

She'd felt a pang when others had talked about him. She had admired him.

But he was a vampire, and she shouldn't have been with him.

Why not? It wasn't forbidden. Just because her parents had died to stop a war because beings from two different societies had fallen in love…

Hadn't they learned from that war? People were people, even when they were creatures of the night or the underworld. Surely they had learned that society's dictates could never control the heart.

After all, look at her. She was lost in a whirlwind over him. Falling deeply. She didn't have affairs; she had never been the type. Sex was the most intimate act possible between a man and a woman, and she had never taken it lightly.

But…

She didn't even know how old Jagger DeFarge really was, or how long he had existed, or…

If he knew how to feel emotion.

She started to roll over, certain that he would still be there, when she was stunned as her door flew open.

She pulled up her covers, suddenly self-conscious.

Jagger was gone.

But Caitlin, wearing a look of pure fury was standing in her doorway.

Chapter 6

"Oh, my God!" Caitlin said. And then again, "Oh, my God!"

"Excuse me, what happened to knocking?" Fiona demanded.

"When did we ever knock?" Caitlin said, then gave her anger free rein again. "I would think, if there was a need to knock, *you would have told me!*"

"Would you excuse me?" Fiona said, ignoring her and wanting only to get away to think—about Caitlin's words, Jagger's absence. "I'd like to grab a shower."

"A shower? You need to be decontaminated," Caitlin snapped.

"*What?*"

"You were with—you were with Jagger DeFarge!" Caitlin said.

How did she know? Fiona was certain that her sister hadn't seen Jagger. She was positive. He never would have put her into that position. He could be far faster than any speeding bullet. Even if he had been sound asleep, with his acute hearing, he would have known when Caitlin twisted the knob, and he would have been gone, rather than let her sister catch him there.

"Caitlin, this isn't really any of your business," Fiona said.

Caitlin stared at her, her jaw clenched. Finally she spoke icily. "I'm afraid that, because of who we are, it is very much my business."

Then she slammed the door and was gone.

Ruing the situation—but never the deed—Fiona hurried into the shower. Afterward she brushed her teeth, dressed quickly in a soft knit halter dress, grabbed her sandals and sped down the stairs. A glance at her watch assured her that she hadn't missed opening time at the store—again—and that her sisters would be at the breakfast table.

Caitlin might have been angry, but Shauna was just amused.

"Ah, there she is at last. The fallen woman. Thank God! I've thought for a very long time that you needed to get in bed with somebody," Shauna said.

"But a vampire!" Caitlin said, almost spitting out the word.

"Does somebody want to run up to the roof and announce it to the city?" Fiona asked.

"Honestly, Fiona. I can't believe that in the middle of everything going on, you brought a vampire into our home," Caitlin said.

Fiona sighed and walked over to the coffeepot on the buffet. Antonia—a shapeshifter—came and helped them out three days a week. She was a natural housekeeper and a warm mother figure. She'd been with them for over five years, after coming into the shop one day and overhearing them admitting that even between the three of them, they were having trouble keeping up with the house and the store.

Antonio made the best coffee in the world. It was strong and bracing, with a slight touch of pecan.

Fiona got her coffee, then turned to face Caitlin. She loved her sister so much, and she knew that Caitlin loved her, too. She hated it when they were at odds.

"August Gaudin has been coming here forever. Antonia is a shapeshifter and she might as well live here. They're good…beings. So is Jagger DeFarge."

"How can you say that? You hardly know him," Caitlin said.

"One way or another, we've known him forever, actually," Shauna said in Fiona's defense. "Caitlin, come on. The city trusts him. We might as well, too."

"None of us should become involved," Caitlin said quietly.

"Perhaps we shouldn't," Fiona said, walking over to where her sister was sitting at the dining room table. "I'm sorry. Maybe I should have…maybe I should have told you both how I was feeling, but I didn't really know myself until. . . Look, that's not the point. We have to worry about the real problem here, not whether or not I choose to have sex, or with whom."

Caitlin inhaled a deep breath. "I'm trying not to overreact. Honestly." She took another deep breath and stood, her hands on her hips. "But the vampires started the war, the war that killed our parents, Fiona."

"They—they didn't start it alone," Fiona said.

"They started it over an affair—a love affair—between

a vampire and a werewolf," Caitlin reminded them grimly.

"Well, there you go," Fiona said quietly. "I'm not a werewolf. And no one's going to war."

"Everyone will start to think that mixed affairs are all right," Caitlin said accusingly.

"Would that really be such a bad thing?" Fiona asked.

"Let me tell you why it's a bad thing," Caitlin said. "It's not you or me or Shauna—it's not Jagger. It's the rest of the underworld. It's people. It's the world around us. I'm sorry, but the world is filled with prejudice, and that's simply the truth."

"Then shouldn't we work to change things?" Fiona asked.

Caitlin looked at her and sighed. "I don't want you to feel the hurt the world can dish out," she told her sister.

Fiona hugged her, suddenly at a loss for words.

"Get serious. Half the shapeshifters were drooling over him at that luncheon," Shauna said. "I think things are going to be fine. When is the wedding?"

"Wedding?" Caitlin gasped.

"Shauna! Stop, I beg you. There *is* no wedding," Fiona said. "Seriously, there's a killer out there, and catching him is my only focus at the moment."

"Except for having sex with a vampire," Caitlin noted sourly.

"Yes, I'm sorry, forgot to throw that in. I'll probably have a few meals and sleep for a few hours in the midst of all this, too. Caitlin, please…"

Caitlin bit her lower lip, looking away. "I'm sorry. I do

love you, and you know it. I don't mean to be difficult. It's just that Jagger is…"

"Jagger is a vampire. Yes, I am aware of that. And I'm the oldest of the three of us, and I need to act responsibly. And I will. I swear, I would never do anything to risk the two of you or myself—or anyone else, for that matter," Fiona said.

"Responsible, intelligent and aware—and sleeping with a vampire," Caitlin said, then lifted a hand when Fiona would have spoken. "And vulnerable. We're all vulnerable. That's life. Just don't let it be your death."

The artist's sketch of the man from Barely, Barely, Barely who had probably met up with Tina Lawrence after her last night at work was everywhere.

It was shown on every local news channel. It was in the newspapers.

In some neighborhoods the residents printed up fliers and plastered them all over trees and poles and shop windows.

But not a soul called in to say that they had seen the man.

Jagger had returned to the scene where the body had been found, though with very little hope that he would find anything, but he had to start somewhere.

Of course, it was still early days, he told himself. The sketch had just started making the rounds. They could still hear something.

Meanwhile, he was standing in the tomb in the old cemetery just on the edge of the Quarter when the call came that a body had been discovered in a cemetery in the Garden District.

In ten minutes time he was standing in the Alden

family vault, last interment 1921. He noted everything about the vault as he went in, the architecture and the inhabitants. The first interment had been in 1840, soon after the cemetery was established in 1833. The gated door was guarded by two angels, now minus their heads. That detail fit in well with the asymmetrical rows of little stone houses in this particular city of the dead. As for the Alden mausoleum itself, there was an altar at the far end, a small table in the center of the room, and rows of divided shelving for bodies, most of them sealed in. A few of the oldest had broken—or been broken—open, but not even bones remained. The heat in New Orleans provided for burial of another family member or loved one in the same space in "a year and a day." In that time, the corpse was basically cremated by the intense heat alone, and what was left of the remains could be raked to a "holding cell" at the end of each tomb so that someone else could be interred in the first body's spot.

This tomb itself was slightly different from the one where Tina's body had been left, so this time the killer had left his victim on the altar that stretched across the back wall.

She was beautiful—blonde and beautiful. Her face was perfect, like porcelain. Her hair was almost platinum, and curled over the edges of the stone. She was laid out in a white halter-necked gown, as if she had just been to a dance. Maybe a prom. This one was young.

There didn't appear to be a mark on her.

"Oh, God," Tony breathed.

Jagger turned to him. "Apparently she was also found by a tour guide. Can you head out and talk to him? I don't think he found her until eleven, and the first tours go through around nine, so maybe we'll get lucky and someone saw our killer. Can you find out just how he stumbled on her?"

Tony nodded, looking almost as ashen as the corpse.

When he was gone, Jagger slipped on his gloves and began his intense search of the corpse.

As before, the marks he was looking for were there.

He sighed softly. This time the killer had gone for the major artery in her left thigh.

"Now we're in serious trouble," a voice said from the entryway.

He turned around.

Craig Dewey had arrived. He was standing in the doorway, caught in the dust motes that played against the rays of sunlight seeping into the tomb.

Dewey laughed dryly. "Hey, buddy. You look like a character out of a movie, standing there all 'Son of Dracula,' bending over his last meal."

Jagger didn't laugh. He knew Dewey wasn't trying to be funny.

The other man strode on in, stared down and shook his head.

"They have an ID on her yet?"

"Nothing certain, but she matches up with a missing co-ed call that came in this morning. Abigail Langdon, last seen at a frat party last night. One of the uniforms is getting me her college ID picture. If it's her, we'll have to bring someone in to make a positive ID. One of her friends, maybe," Jagger said.

Dewey slipped on gloves and stepped closer to the body. "Skin as white as snow. The killer seems to like blondes. And he's bold. Wants his victims found, and found by ordinary citizens. This is considered one of the safest cemeteries in the city to visit."

"I'm not sure any cemetery is safe at night," Jagger said. "There are too many places for someone to hide. We call them the cities of the dead, and the dead don't call the cops when you run in to escape observation."

Dewey looked at the victim's eyes, turned her, touched her and took her body temp, then turned to Jagger. "Well, we're looking at exactly the same kind of killing—late last night, very late. Can't say much about lividity, because there was no blood left to pool beneath the skin. Again, I can't help but think she was killed elsewhere, since I'm not seeing a drop of blood around the body anywhere. What a shame. This one looks like a kid."

"Rape?" Jagger asked.

"I'll need a kit, but no obvious signs of violence or trauma…." He looked at Jagger. "I'm not a vegetarian, and I don't avoid leather, but I'd never buy fox fur. They electrocute the poor little things with a rod up the rectum. Quite gruesome."

"She wasn't electrocuted," Jagger pointed out.

"Just don't ever buy fox fur," Dewey said, stabbing a finger at him. "The point is that she looks as pure as the day she was born. The killer didn't leave a mark on the body that I can see so far. I'm not even sure she suffered. It's almost as if she were hypnotized and told to go to sleep or something. Poor child, so beautiful."

"Well, we've got to let the crime scene unit in, and then you can take her to the morgue," Jagger said. "How soon can she be scheduled for autopsy?"

"Not right away, I'm afraid. First thing tomorrow.

I'll have her photographed, bathed…set for first thing tomorrow morning."

"I thought she'd be a priority."

"You would think so, right? But a city bigwig—potential candidate for mayor—died in his home last night, and his children are making waves against the stepmother."

Jagger groaned inwardly. Another night he'd have to head for the morgue. Slip in. Maybe traumatize a few employees.

Then he remembered that Billy Harrington had taken the job of night attendant. He could just call Billy and ask him to handle the matter.

No, he couldn't. This was his responsibility.

He stepped outside and saw that Officer Gus Parissi was standing at the gate, patiently waiting, presumably for him.

He saw, too, that the media were already there, being held on the far side of the gates. Tour groups were being sent away.

"Parissi, you waiting for me?" Jagger asked.

The other cop nodded. "The brass are keeping the same group of uniforms working both murders," he said, then winced. "This that missing college kid?"

"Looks to be," Jagger said.

"I brought a yearbook," Gus told him.

Jagger took Parissi's elbow and led him behind one of the tombs. A winged cherub set to guard an ironwork-covered window stared at them balefully.

"Let me see the missing girl," Jagger said.

Parissi silently opened the book to a marked page.

She was a junior, a nursing major. She was in the chess club.

She was the latest victim.

"Family?" he asked Gus Parissi.

"The sisters at the convent," Gus said. "She was orphaned at seven and never adopted. They say only babies stand a chance to—"

"Gus?"

"Sorry. She doesn't have a family. Just the sisters."

"All right. I'll let them know. Parissi?"

"Yessir?"

"Keep the mob out. Let the M.E. and the crime scene unit take their time in here. The Catholic Church still has control of the cemeteries just outside the Quarter, but this place is managed by a historical foundation. See that it isn't reopened until tomorrow. Understood?"

"Understood."

Jagger turned away. Celia Larson, her bag in hand, was headed toward the tomb. She glowered at him. "How can you think that we'll turn anything up when the crime scene has been trampled by hordes of tourists?" she demanded.

"Celia, if I knew where a crime would be discovered, I'd be there before the damned thing happened," he said, trying to maintain his temper. "Come on, surely you've been briefed. She was discovered at eleven. The first tours are at nine. What do you think I could have done?"

She sniffed and walked on past him. Dewey was standing at the door to the tomb. He rolled his eyes toward Jagger as she approached, and Jagger shrugged.

He had to go see the nuns.

"Oh, God, there's been another one!"

So far the three of them had been doing well, considering the way the day had started.

But Fiona knew the minute her sister spoke that there was real trouble ahead.

Caitlin was behind the desk, focused in on the news on the store's computer. So far, the identity of the victim hadn't been released to the public, but from what the news media had been able to gather, the method of murder and the disposal of the body matched the first, just a different cemetery.

Fiona felt as if her stomach pitched down to her feet.

She moved to stand behind her sister. Jagger was on the news, caught by the media as he exited the Garden District cemetery.

"The police will not lie, nor will we hedge," he said. "Yes, we have discovered a second body. We have formed a task force, and every officer will be on overtime, following every possible lead. We will not stop. We ask the citizens of the city to help us, and we ask the women of New Orleans to be especially vigilant. We will be working tirelessly to find this killer. Please, don't panic, but be smart. That's all that I can say right now. We have to let our crime scene unit and our coroner's office do their work."

Gina was at the head of the crowd.

"Detective DeFarge, we've heard that the dead woman was a blonde, and that she was drained of blood. Should the blonde women of New Orleans be dyeing their hair?"

"The women of New Orleans need to be vigilant and not go out alone after dark. Don't walk through parking lots alone, don't leave a party alone, stay with friends and family. We've released a sketch of a possible witness to the disappearance of Tina Lawrence, so please, if anyone has seen the man, notify the police. If anyone sees anything out of the ordinary, notify the police. We need your help. Thank you. Now, please, I have work to do."

Despite the barrage of questions that followed him, Jagger made his way out of camera range.

Caitlin glared at Fiona. "There's a rogue vampire out there, Fiona. You have to stop him. This will turn into a panic and create a mess in more ways than most people in this city can possibly expect."

"She's right," Shauna said. "I'm going to a meeting tonight of the were clans. I'll do my best to keep them from flying into a fury, but…two murders, Fiona. This is bad."

"We need to call a general assembly," Fiona said, forcing herself to remain calm. "All the races need to be invited—and the voodoo priests and priestesses, as well. And Father Moran."

Father Moran was a priest, and a human being. But like the city's most powerful voodoo priest, Antoine Geneset, who would also be invited, he had an instinct for all creatures and often attended the general assemblies, which were usually held no more than twice a year.

This was an emergency, however.

"I'll stop by and see David Du Lac. He'll make the arrangements," Fiona said.

It was a terribly duty, informing people someone that someone they loved was dead.

Jagger felt out of his league, even though he'd had to perform the same sad duty before.

The sisters who had raised Abigail Langdon had loved their charge dearly, and caught in the midst of their grief, he felt as if he had been overwhelmed by a flock of penguins.

But the sisters had a powerful faith, and eventually their tears gave way to prayers. Listening to those prayers, Jagger felt his resolve doubled. He *would* see to it that their beloved Abigail was allowed to rest in peace, to return to the tender hands of her Maker.

Sadly, the sisters were unable to help him in his quest for the killer. Abigail had been living in a dorm. She had a roommate, and they had talked to the roommate just before the girl had called the police, which was how they had found out that she was missing to begin with. The roommate, Linda McCormick, had called them to tell them that she had last seen Abigail at a frat party. When Linda was ready to head home, Abigail was nowhere to be seen. Linda assumed her roommate had headed out without her, but when she reached the dorm and found no sign of Abigail, she had begun to worry. But she had known that Abigail was an orphan, and where she had been raised, and she had called the sisters.

Jagger's next stop was the dorm, where he met up with Tony Miro and went to speak with a teary-eyed Linda McCormick.

"It was a party, just like any other party," she told him. "Yeah, there was beer. There's always beer…we *are* in college, and this *is* New Orleans," she said, sounding a bit defensive.

"What about drugs?" he asked.

"Sure, some kids do drugs. But I don't, and Abigail didn't."

"What about the kids at the party? Was there anyone there you didn't know?"

"No, I don't think so."

"Can you give me a list of names?" Jagger asked.

She started crying again, and he took her gently by the shoulders. "Linda, we need your help. I know you cared about your roommate. I need you to be strong, though. I need a list with the name of every person who was at that party. No one is going to get in trouble for underage drinking, I swear. Okay? I need every name."

Linda stopped crying long enough to shudder and nod. Tony provided a paper and pencil, and she went to work.

They headed out of dorm as soon as she was done. Jagger called in the ten officers he'd been given as his "task force," so that they could all begin questioning the frat boys at the house where the party had been held, before starting to track down the other attendees. Before long Celia Larson and her team showed up to search for trace evidence.

Jagger wasn't sure what they thought they were going to find. Even if the entire fraternity and all their guests had been full-on inebriated, he was sure they would have noticed if a murder had taken place right in front of them.

The sketch of their possible suspect from the strip club was passed around, but no one had seen anyone who resembled the "pretty" man who had waited for the first victim, Tina Lawrence.

Something big—and bad—was going on.

It was while he was talking to a frat boy who claimed to have been in love with Abigail that he found a possible—and troubling—suspect.

"Hey, have you talked to Billy Harrington?" the boy asked. "He and Abigail were friends."

Jagger frowned and looked at his list. Billy's name wasn't on it.

"Billy was here?"

The young man wiped his wet cheeks and frowned as well. "Come to think of it, Billy wasn't going to come. Said he had to be somewhere else."

That rang true; Billy had been at the meeting at David's last night.

The murder could have taken place in the hour right before the meeting.

"All right, he wasn't supposed to be here. But you saw him?"

The boy suddenly seemed confused. "Did I see him? I don't remember him coming in, and I was by the door. But...I thought I saw him. No, maybe I didn't. But...oh, I don't know!" Fresh tears streamed down his face. "I had a lot of beer."

The kid went on.

It didn't matter.

Jagger knew that he would be seeing Billy that night.

Valentina—apparently chastised by David—was icily cordial when Fiona stopped by the club. She led Fiona right to David, who was in his private quarters, thoughtfully sipping a cup of something when she arrived.

Once they were alone, he lifted a hand before she could speak. "I heard, of course," he said softly.

"We have to call a general assembly, David," she said. "I'm afraid that things will start getting ugly. Everyone—every being—is going to be up in arms."

He nodded. "Let's try for 3:00 a.m. again. Tomorrow

night-slash-morning," he said. He looked at her sadly. "Who would do this? Who would risk everything?"

"I don't know. We have to find out," Fiona said. "And we have to keep the peace while we find the killer, and I think an assembly is going to be the best way. The others have to believe you when you say you want the killer as badly as they do. You have to be beyond convincing."

"You got it, kid," he said softly. "Tomorrow night."

She thanked him, said goodbye and left.

She hoped the next night was going to be soon enough, but there was no way to meet any sooner. It wasn't as if they could broadcast this particular meeting on the airwaves.

Back out on the street, she saw that the sun was setting. She got in her car and headed for Martin Luther King Boulevard.

Darkness was falling, but it seemed as if the entire morgue staff was working late.

Jagger waited, watching the entry, watching the sky.

Finally he could wait no longer.

He turned to mist and entered, aware that some people felt *something* as he passed by. A chill. "Footsteps walking over their grave." Bad expression for New Orleans—there weren't many graves to actually walk over.

He headed to the autopsy rooms, certain that Abigail would be in the same situation as Tina Lawrence. With the autopsy scheduled for first thing in the morning, a tech would have prepared the body. He wondered what thoughts had accompanied the process. Anyone in their right mind would have felt sad at the sight of one so young, with so much hope for a future, lying dead on a cold gurney at the morgue.

He passed the desk where Billy Harrington should have been working, stopping anyone who came to that part of the morgue and requiring them to sign in, but Billy wasn't there.

As Jagger stood there for a moment, he realized that the place had gone very quiet. Most of the day workers had left at last.

He strode down the hall, quietly opening the door to the room where he'd so recently seen Tina.

And there she was: the beautiful young victim.

He entered silently, and there he found Billy.

The boy was standing in front of the gurney, holding a stake. It wasn't nearly as efficient as Jagger's own weapon, but it was apparent that Billy had intended to carry out what he saw as his duty.

Or his necessity?

Was Billy the killer?

Jagger glared at him. "You were seen," he said. "One of the frat boys saw you, Billy."

The look Billy gave him as he turned in surprise was one of sheer astonishment. "What?"

"You were seen at the party. The frat party. The last place Abigail was seen."

"I wasn't there!" Billy protested. "You know where I was. I was at the meeting."

"She could have been killed as much as an hour before the meeting."

Billy shook his head, astounded. "Jagger, I'm telling you, I wasn't there. I swear it. I swear it on my soul and any hope of heaven! I've never killed anything, except for a rat here and there. And they're awful! I get my blood the same places you do. I wasn't even born into *human* life before the peace was made, much less reborn as a vampire. And I remember the war. Good God, Jagger, I don't want anything like happening again. It wasn't me, I swear it!"

"You'll have to appear before the council, Billy," Jagger said. "For now, you need to step aside. I'll take care of this matter."

Billy didn't move.

"No," he said softly.

"Billy—"

"No. Jagger. I knew her. Abigail was a sweetheart. She'd never hurt anyone, alive or…dead. She might not even need to be—"

"Billy, the girl was murdered. The entire city knows she was murdered. The medical examiner has seen her. She's been photographed and bathed. Her time of death has been listed."

"She hasn't been cut yet," Billy said. "There are medical miracles."

"Stop this!" a woman's voice said, one Jagger had come to know well.

He turned as Fiona MacDonald stepped into the room.

Billy stared at her and groaned softly. "I…I love her. I'll fight you both. I'll die for her if I have to, and they'll find me here, because—I'm not old enough to turn to dust. I mean it—I *will* die for her."

"Billy, you're already dead, technically," Fiona pointed out gently.

Before he could reply, a sound drew their attention, and the body on the gurney suddenly jackknifed into a sitting position. The sheet fell away.

Abigail, in all her glory, stared at them with huge blue eyes.

"Where am I?" she asked, and looked around. Her mouth fell open; she was going to scream.

Fiona started forward as Billy clamped a hand over the girl's mouth. "Please," he whispered, meeting Fiona's eyes beseechingly.

Fiona stared at Jagger. *You have to do something,* her eyes told him.

"Billy, you have to step away," he said gently.

"Why? She didn't wake up screaming and hungry," Billy demanded.

"I *am* hungry," Abigail said, still so confused. Then she gasped. "I'm naked! I'm naked and I'm—I'm in a morgue!" She opened her mouth to scream again.

Billy put his hand over her mouth again as both Fiona and Jagger moved forward.

"Look," Billy whispered urgently. "She's a nice kid, a good kid—raised by nuns, for God's sake. She'll follow our laws, she'll…she'll be a good citizen. Please, give her a chance."

"Billy, she doesn't even understand what happened," Fiona said.

Billy's hand slipped from Abigail's mouth. "Please, be quiet, okay?" he begged her.

She let out a little whimpering sound and leaned against him. "Billy, I really *am* hungry. Starving. For a rare steak. Or for…"

She stared at Fiona.

At the pulse in Fiona's throat.

Abigail lowered her head and started to cry. "I'm hungry for blood."

Jagger stepped close to her, showing her that he had his stake at his side, not ready to strike.

"Abigail. My name is Jagger DeFarge. I'm a cop. I need to know what happened to you. You went to a party, and then…?"

She stared at him, confused, humiliated. She suddenly realized that she had a sheet and pulled it over her breasts.

"There was a lot of beer," she whispered.

"Think, Abigail. Please."

Billy moved between Jagger and Abigail, and shook his head angrily. "No! You can't try to use her and then… You can't. For the love of God, Jagger!"

"Someone is going to hear us soon," Fiona pointed out.

"They'll hear us when I fight you!" Billy promised. "I don't want to hurt anyone, but don't you see? I love Abigail."

"Oh, Billy, really? I've been in love with you for ages, too," Abigail cried softly. "I was just too afraid to say anything."

Jagger stared at Fiona. She was not untouched.

"Look," Billy said quickly. "We'll just say she wasn't really dead. There have been mistakes before, medical miracles."

"Dead?" Abigail's voice shook with horror.

"Shh," Billy pleaded.

"Billy, this is the real world," Fiona pointed out gently. "A team of doctors will start performing tests. At best, she'll become a freak, and there won't be anyone who can tend to her, who can make sure she gets the nourishment she needs." She touched his shoulder gently, looking like a caring angel. "Billy, a lot of people would wind up dead."

Billy whipped out the stake he had brought, intending to kill the love of his life.

He aimed it toward Fiona. "No, please," he pleaded.

Jagger grabbed Fiona, drawing her behind his back.

"Billy, don't you dare threaten her," he whispered fervently.

Billy paused for a moment, staring at him, and understanding entered his eyes.

"So that's the way it is," he said softly. "The powerful old vampire is in love with the Keeper."

"Billy, don't be ridiculous. And step away from the girl. I can make the change in a split second, and when I do, I'm powerful," Fiona said. "So don't threaten Jagger, and don't threaten me."

"Please," Billy entreated. "You have to understand. I'm not threatening you. I'm *begging* you. I'll do anything, anything at all. And how can you?" he demanded. "You're the Keeper—can't you see that she would be an asset to our community?" When Fiona didn't say anything, his shoulders sagged and he lowered his stake. "Fine. Kill us both," he said in resignation.

"Billy..." Abigail protested, putting a hand on his arm.

If the situation weren't so dire, Jagger thought, it might have been amusing. There was the lovely Abigail, hiding in back of Billy, clutching the broad young shoulders of the one she loved.

And facing Billy—him. With a rock hard determination that he would die for the woman *he* loved as willingly as Billy had vowed to do. Was she in love with him, as Abigail was in love with Billy? He didn't know.

He did know that there was something between them. He did know that he felt as if he had waited several lifetimes to feel for someone the way he did about her.

"There is no easy solution," Fiona said softly, sadly.

Jagger was electrically aware of her standing behind him. Felt the length of her body against his own. Felt her whisper against his skin and trembled inside at the sound of her voice.

Love.

Was it real? Something growing, something more precious than life, that went far beyond death?

Fiona groaned softly. "What do we do?" she whispered. "In the name of God, what do we do?"

Jagger sighed, hanging his head for a moment.

"I guess we steal a corpse," he said at last.

Chapter 7

During the following hours, Fiona decided that she was insane.

She kept wondering what her parents would have done.

Handled it. They would have handled it. Gotten there earlier, they would have made sure Abigail was dispatched before...

Maybe. Or maybe not.

Billy had probably hovered over the corpse from the moment he had reached the morgue, maybe even proclaimed his love.

Would her parents have been so uncertain? So hesitant to act?

Maybe. They had certainly believed in love. They had known all about evil, along with good, and they had coped—because they'd always had each other....

As she—maybe?—had Jagger now.

She stood guard at the door as Jagger and Billy started explaining the situation to Abigail. The girl was still in shock, still whining that her stomach hurt, as if rats were gnawing at it.

Billy tried to explain that the faster she paid attention, the faster they could appease that hunger. Jagger was a stronger personality, and he dispensed with the preliminaries and demanded that she listen to him, which she finally did. He explained the process changing into mist, and how it was imperative that she listen, so they could get her out of there. Quickly.

Finally she tried it herself. At first, she was so bad at it that Fiona began to regret their decision to let the girl "live."

But finally Abigail got it.

"Billy, you can't come with us. Fiona will have to knock you out," Jagger told him.

"But…"

"Billy, do you want me arresting you in a matter of hours for stealing Abigail's corpse—and maybe for having killed her in the first place?" Jagger demanded.

Billy understood. He clutched Fiona's arm. "You're the Keeper," he whispered to her. "You'll—you'll take care of her, right? Keepers don't lie, not to anyone they're responsible for."

"I promise I'll watch over her," Fiona said.

"I'll get her out of here," Jagger told Fiona. "Follow as soon as you can."

She nodded, knowing he was far more prepared than she was to handle the situation if Abigail panicked or something went wrong.

"Meet at my place," he said softly.

She nodded, wincing inwardly, certain that her sisters would be expecting her to come straight home from the morgue. They might not like it, but they might even be expecting her to come home with Jagger.

But she couldn't bring a freshly turned and completely ignorant vampire home.

Once Jagger and Abigail had turned into mist, Fiona followed Billy out to the desk. She'd put on surgical gloves before she entered the building, not wanting to leave fingerprints, and now she looked around for a weapon. Finally she picked up the computer keyboard from the desk and creamed him with the flat side.

Mist herself, she left the morgue, and she didn't regain her shape until she reached her car. She drove away, praying that no one saw her, and headed for the French Quarter.

Though she had never been inside Jagger's home, she knew where it was, two blocks in from Rampart, halfway between Canal and Esplanade.

It was one of the few houses that had survived the great fires in the early 1800s, standing on a manmade rise, the better to display its charming facade. He lived behind a wall and gate almost as tall as hers, but his courtyard was in front of the house, rather than behind, and his property stretched from street to street.

The gate opened as she arrived; obviously he'd been looking for her car. She drove up to the front of the house as the gate closed and locked behind her.

When she got out of her car, Jagger was already there.

"Come, quickly, I'm afraid to leave her alone for long," he said softly.

She nodded.

Though he'd said he wanted her to move quickly, for a moment he paused and stared down into her eyes. Then his lips touched hers with a kiss that was tender and yearning...and brief.

Then he caught her hand and hurried her into the house. The entry was large and impressive, leading into a tiled foyer, with a curving stairway to one side.

They hurried past the stairway toward the dining room and kitchen, moving through both rooms so quickly that she had no time to note a single detail. At the rear of the kitchen there was a door, and when he opened it she saw a stairway heading down, and she realized that the lot had been built up to allow for a small basement in an area of the country that was prone to serious flooding, because most land was—barely at sea level.

As he led her quickly downward, she expected dank earth—with a coffin in the middle of the room.

But what she saw was nothing like her expectations. There was a canopied bed instead of a coffin, the floor was red brick with a Persian carpet, and there were attractive paintings on the walls, along with a massive entertainment center.

There was also a small kitchenette, complete with refrigerator.

Abigail, still wrapped in her sheet, was greedily drinking from a large pitcher.

Of blood.

Fiona could feel her eyes widening

"Don't look at me like that," Jagger said to her. "It's pig's blood. You eat bacon, right?"

"I wasn't staring at you," she said. "I'm used to blood. I'm the Keeper, remember?"

He nodded and touched her cheek. He didn't say

anything, but the look in his eyes seemed to wrap around her heart.

What the hell had they done? she wondered. There were going to be terrible repercussions from tonight. She was sure of it.

"I have to ask you to stay here, to…teach Abigail," he said.

"No! You…have to teach her," Fiona said.

"I've already been called about her corpse being stolen," Jagger said. "I'm the detective on the case, remember?"

She opened her mouth, desperately wanting to protest, but then Abigail made a slurping sound, and she knew someone had to do something.

"But I'm not a vampire."

"Make the change. It will help you," he advised. "Please, Fiona."

She nodded jerkily. "All right. And, Jagger, an assembly has been called for tomorrow night."

"Good. It will definitely be necessary."

"My sisters will be calling me soon."

"I'll be back as soon as I can," he swore.

With that, he pulled her to him and kissed her, hard.

And again, quickly.

Then he was gone, and she was left with a naked young woman slurping blood in the center of the room.

Billy was good. If Jagger remembered correctly, his major was engineering, but he might as well be majoring in theater arts, he was playing his part so well.

Tony was already there at the morgue, along with two

beat cops, a few night-shift employees and a city security officer. Tony had started questioning Billy Harrington, but he took a break and pulled Jagger aside the minute he arrived.

"He was hit on the head with a computer keyboard. He doesn't know how or why someone took the body. Why the hell steal a corpse?" Tony asked.

Jagger jerked his head in a manner that suggested he couldn't fathom the question himself. Then he pulled up a chair across the desk where Billy Harrington was sitting, an ice bag pressed against his temple.

"What happened, son?" he asked.

Billy looked at him and shook his head gravely. "I was doing paperwork. The next thing I knew, I woke up on the floor with a cop standing over me."

Jagger stood up and turned to the remaining morgue personnel. "No one saw anything?" he asked.

"Nothing," said a buxom middle-aged clerk. "Nothing at all. And the door was still locked."

"There must be other doors," Jagger said.

Looking embarrassed, people ran to check other possible means of entry.

To his astonishment and vast relief, someone had actually forgotten to lock one of the doors where the bodies were wheeled in from the ambulances that brought them to the morgue. As accusations began to fly among the workers, guilt bit into Jagger.

He lifted a hand, stopping the flow of conversation, and sighed. "The crime scene unit will be here shortly. We'll do our best to settle this as quickly as possible, but meanwhile, be prepared. The press are going to have a field day."

Several people urged Billy to go to a hospital, but he

adamantly refused. Jagger offered to take him home, and Billy agreed.

"You're going to take the kid home?" Tony asked him, incredulous.

"Maybe I can get him to remember something," Jagger suggested. "My guess is that something might come to him after a while, and I'll be right there to find out what it is. Go home, Tony, and let the night guys handle the scene. Get some sleep tonight. Tomorrow is going to be hell."

A few minutes later Jagger led Billy out to his car.

As soon as they were inside, Billy let out a sigh of relief. "Sweet Jesus, bless you," he whispered, his eyes closed.

Jagger marveled at the fact that so many vampires were religious; in fact, they were often some of a church's best attendees. They were always praying that they really did have souls.

"You're one hell of an actor," he told the boy.

"So are you." Billy frowned, then, and shook his head. "Look, you can't still believe I'm the one who did this, can you?"

"Billy, if my thoughts were running in that direction, you'd be dead, along with Abigail. Dead—as in stone dead. Staked through the heart. But I do want to talk to you about that night. That frat boy really thinks he saw you, though he admitted he was drunk. But he also said you didn't originally intend to go to the party because you had something else to do."

"Yeah, I went to the meeting," Billy said, and he sounded genuinely lost. He twisted in the passenger's seat to stare at Jagger. "She's all right, isn't she? Abigail.

You didn't whisk her away and—and stake her, did you?"

"No, we didn't stake her. I left her with Fiona."

"She's going to be so confused," Billy said.

"Fiona is the Keeper," Jagger said. "She'll manage just fine."

"Dead?" Abigail said, staring at Fiona. "What are you talking about? Vampires don't exist. They're just a myth. They're not real."

"Abigail, you woke up in a morgue, remember? You escaped by turning into mist," Fiona pointed out.

The girl strenuously shook her head. "No. No, no, no. They made a mistake. They thought I was dead, but I wasn't. I'm alive. You can see that."

"Abigail, you're a vampire now. You just drank a gallon of blood, and you'll have to keep drinking blood to stay…alive."

"I will not run around killing people!" Abigail exclaimed, horrified.

"No, you definitely will not. If you make a single kill, I'll consider it my responsibility to stake you through the heart and end your existence."

The girl stared at her, then leaped to her feet in horror, letting the pitcher she'd been holding slip to the floor. "You…you want to kill me." She gasped, pointing a finger at Fiona. "I know you—you're…you're some kind of a witch or a voodoo priestess or something. You own that shop that sells potions and things. You do tarot card readings—"

"That's my sister, I read tea leaves," Fiona said wearily. "And I'm not a witch."

"You are! You want to hurt me. Where—where's Billy?"

"Billy will be here soon. Abigail, I know this is really hard to comprehend, but please, think. You woke up in the morgue. Billy, Jagger and I were there, and we got you out. But you are not alive. You have become a vampire."

Abigail shook her head, looking as if she were about to burst into tears. "No! It can't be true. They just made a mistake."

She rushed forward, clutching her sheet to hold it in place as she fell to her knees at Fiona's feet. "I'm alive. They made a mistake. I'm a college student, for the love of God. Let me go home to the sisters! They raised me. They know me. They'll tell you I'm alive."

"No! Of all places you can't go now, number one is home," Fiona told her. "Come on, let's get you something to wear." She looked around and spotted a folding door. "That must be Jagger's closet. At least we can get you a T-shirt or something." She opened the closet door, and just for a second, she closed her eyes and inhaled deeply. She must be falling in love with the man. Just the clean scent of his aftershave, lingering lightly in the air, seemed to seep right into her. To remind her that she wanted to be with him. That she could be with him. That he wanted to be with her...

She pulled herself back, reminding her that she had a dead girl on her hands.

"All right, here's a shirt," she said and turned around.

Abigail was gone.

Jagger drove into the French Quarter and down his street. As he neared his gate, he hit the electronic opener on the dash. The gate slowly opened inward, allowing the car access.

He drove in, parked and got out of the car. Billy did the same.

As Jagger looked toward the house, he was astounded to see Fiona, who'd made the change, perched atop the wall toward the rear of the house. As he watched, she made a leap down to the street.

"Oh, hell," Jagger muttered.

"What?" Billy demanded.

"They're out!" Jagger said.

Moving faster than the human eye could follow, with Billy on his heels, he made a flying leap up to the wall himself. He was just in time to see Fiona adeptly landing on the sidewalk, and for a moment he paused to thank God that he didn't live on Bourbon Street, where a hundred tourists would have been there to see.

He jumped lightly to the street himself, searching the road, the houses, the darkness.

Then he saw her.

Abigail, stark naked, a block away and just walking down the street, looking lost.

He swore softly.

Fiona reached her before he could, catching her by the shoulders and quickly wrapping her in one of his long-sleeved tailored shirts.

A woman walked by, leading a yappy Papillon.

"Well, I never!" she declared. She was about sixty, dignified, plump, with graying hair.

The dog wouldn't shut up.

Jagger quickly walked over to her. "Good evening, ma'am."

"That's indecent exposure," she declared.

The dog kept yapping.

Ten feet away, Fiona and Billy were urging Abigail off the street.

Jagger stared at the dog first, and the animal went silent.

"Do something, or I'll call the police myself," the woman began.

"It's fine, ma'am. It's all fine. That young lady is supposed to be in the hospital. We're here to take her back."

"Oh?"

Jagger smiled and stared hard into her eyes. "You won't remember this in the morning," he said quietly.

She blinked. The commotion behind him had quieted; they had gotten Abigail off the street and, hopefully, back into his house without further notice.

"That's all right then," the woman said, smiling. The dog wagged its tail.

"Good evening," he said pleasantly.

"Just getting off work, Detective?" she asked.

"Yes, ma'am." If he knew the woman, he didn't remember her.

"You shouldn't be out this late, you know," he added. "Not walking your dog alone."

"Mrs. Beasley needs her constitutional, Detective."

"Then walk her in your yard. Please, don't wander in the dark alone. There's a killer out there."

She laughed. "I'm old, plump and gray. Not his type at all."

"Please, for me, will you stay inside once it's dark?"

The woman flushed. "When such a handsome young

man asks a favor, I do my best to oblige," she said, and winked at him.

"Where's your house?" Jagger asked.

She pointed.

"I'm walking you back," he said, and offered her his arm.

She gave him a bountiful smile and turned to walk with him.

When they reached her house, she thanked him, gushing, and gave him a kiss on the cheek.

The dog yapped.

He bade her good-night and hurried back to his own place, wondering why on earth human beings couldn't have the common sense to lock their doors when there was a murderer on the loose.

Chapter 8

"How on earth did you let her get away?" Jagger demanded, still unnerved by everything that had been happening that evening.

"I didn't *let* her get away. Did you notice that she was *naked?*" Fiona protested. "I was getting some clothing for her!"

Thankfully, Abigail was at long last clothed—still blonde and beautiful, and now cute, as well, in one of Jagger's shirts.

"I'm so sorry," Abigail said. "Oh, my God. What would the nuns say? I was running around naked." She looked at Billy with her huge blue eyes.

"What would the *nuns* say?" Fiona asked impatiently. "You're a *vampire*." Fiona turned to confront Jagger. "You'll have to excuse me. I have to get back home or my sisters will be calling a city wide meeting, wondering if I'm alive or dead. You chose this course of action, so you—"

"Wait just a minute," he said. "*We* chose this course of action, and you're just upset because you let her escape."

Fiona stiffened. "Then I'm sure you'll find it a relief to manage the rest of the evening on your own, Detective DeFarge. I leave everything in your capable hands." She spun on Billy and Abigail. "You two! Get it right or I will have no choice but to handle the situation—and you know what that means."

She had started for the stairs when Abigail suddenly tore after her. For a moment Fiona felt a rush of fear, sure she was about to be attacked.

But Abigail only touched her arm, and she turned to look into the young woman's anguished eyes.

"I'm so sorry. I understand that you've shown me incredible mercy. It's just that I was so terrified, so confused…and it's still so hard to believe. I went to a party, and now…Please forgive me. I swear, I'll stay here and do anything and everything Detective DeFarge tells me to do."

Lovely. You'll listen to him—now that you've made a fool of me, Fiona thought.

She told herself not to let her own hurt and humiliation affect her handling of the situation.

Before she could speak, Billy Harrington strode over to stand behind Abigail.

"We'll never be able to express our gratitude. We'll both do anything Detective DeFarge says, I promise," Billy told her.

"If you really mean that, then Abigail has to disappear.

The world thinks she's dead, remember? So no one can see her. *No one.* Perhaps David Du Lac will be able to discover that she has a long lost identical twin, but setting that up will take time. And, Billy, you have to go to your classes. You can't spend your days hanging out here with Abigail. If you want this to work, you *have* to do these things, or else leave the city. And this isn't a good time for you to leave the city, Billy. Not unless you want to look guilty of murder. Do you understand what I'm saying?" she demanded.

The two of them nodded in fervent agreement.

She looked back at Jagger. His golden eyes had a glitter in them that told her he was angry with her, but he didn't say anything. Apparently he had chosen not to argue any further, at least not then.

She hurried up the stairs, trying to make a dignified exit.

Then she realized she couldn't get through the gate without Jagger's help, so she waited at the door, arms crossed over her chest, trying not to admire the warmth of the large fireplace in the living room, the masculine and inviting…decor that was earthy, warm and secure, and spoke volumes of the man. She didn't want to fight with him. She just wanted to touch him and be touched by him.

Tonight, however, they had taken a dive into a serious situation that could bring nothing but hardship to either one of them.

Jagger arrived and hit a button on the console by the door. Then he held the door open for her as she watched the massive gate swing open. She started toward her car without a word.

His eyes met hers when she turned back for a moment. "Don't worry. I'll see that everything gets done—just as you demanded."

She didn't answer him, just slid into the driver's seat, wondering how they had managed to agree on a course of action, only to arrive at such a cold impasse.

All in the name of love, she thought dryly. And hadn't some of the greatest tragedies and travesties in history taken place in the name of love?

She drove the few short blocks home, then breathed a sigh of relief as she entered her quiet house.

She walked directly up to her bedroom and opened the door.

And found both her sisters, Shauna curled up on the bed reading a magazine, Caitlin pacing.

They both stopped what they were doing and stared at her.

"A stolen corpse?" Caitlin demanded, practically hissing. "Did you think we wouldn't hear the news?"

Fiona tossed her shoulder bag onto the chair by her dressing table, pressed her fingers to her temple and, ignoring Shauna, flopped backward on her bed. It was a big bed, and there was room.

"She was just a college kid, huh?" Shauna said sympathetically.

"Where is the body?" Caitlin asked.

"Risen," Fiona said dryly.

"You let her get up? What in the world were you thinking?" Caitlin cried, striding over to the bed, arms crossed over her chest, eyes filled with a tempest of emotion.

"I am so tired. If you came here just to lash into me—"

"We're here to find out what's going on," Caitlin said.

Shauna cleared her throat. "This is a real mess, Fiona. All the races are up in arms. Since you've been…busy, I'm assuming you didn't hear about the altercation in Jackson Square. Mateas Grenard was attacked in the park. He's new, and he's not exactly politic about what he says. He fought back, of course. The attacker was one of mine, a werewolf named Louis Arile, who owns a T-shirt shop over on St. Peter's. Anyway…"

"Anyway, Shauna was there, she calmed Louis down, and the cops ended up giving them both a slap on the wrist. It was only Shauna who kept the whole thing from turning into a real disaster," Caitlin said.

Fiona looked thoughtfully at Shauna. Her little sister was coming into her own.

Shauna shrugged casually. "Louis isn't a bad guy, just scared, like everyone else. He loves his shop, and he really loves Jazz Fest, and he doesn't want to be forced out of New Orleans if these murders end up alerting the humans to the existence of the underworld."

"The police didn't figure out that there was something…different about them? Neither of them… made the change?" Fiona asked, concerned.

"No. Shauna got there in time," Caitlin said. "She convinced the cops that they were fighting over a sports bet."

"Clever," Fiona said.

"Maybe, but something tells me that was just the start of our problems," Caitlin said.

Fiona stood. "There's another general council meeting tomorrow night. We'll nip this in the bud."

"Nip it in the bud?" Caitlin said quietly, almost gently. She touched Fiona's cheek. "You're my older sister. I love you, and I admire you. You've held us together. You've done everything for us. But this has gone way past the 'nip it in the bud' stage. I understand how you might have fallen under Jagger DeFarge's spell. He's sex on legs. But you can't forget who and what you are. You're a keeper. And this is serious. The races will be up in arms—they're not stupid. They'll figure out that you made the choice to let that girl rise, and they'll know she's young, that she's almost certain to make serious mistakes that could ruin things for everyone—like going out in public and being recognized, when she's supposed to be dead. And if one of them, just one, decides to take matters into his own hands…Frankly, Fiona, I'm terrified. We've seen what a war can do."

"There won't be a war, Caitlin." Fiona sat down at the foot of her bed. "There won't be a war," she repeated, trying to sound convincing. "It was easy to see that Tina Lawrence had to be…dispensed with. Even as a human, she was frightening. She'd hurt people. She was dangerous. But this girl…she was eighteen and raised by nuns. She's a college student."

She saw that Caitlin was about to protest and raised a hand. "*Was* a college student. The girl hasn't a whiff of evil in her. She'll be fine."

Shauna shook her head, scooting closer so that she was sitting next to Fiona. "How is she going to be fine?"

Fiona was quiet for a moment, surprised by the tide of emotion that swept over her.

"David Du Lac. He'll make it fine. Mom and Dad went to him a few times over the years. God only knows all the places he's lived during his...existence, but no one loves this city more, and no one's better at creating new identities. We'll bring Abigail to him. He'll take care of everything."

Caitlin laughed. "And when will that be? After the funeral? Don't forget that everyone out there thinks you've stolen a corpse."

"No one thinks I've done anything," Fiona said firmly. "People may know her corpse was stolen, but I wasn't seen."

"What about DeFarge?" Caitlin asked.

"No one saw him until he went to the morgue after the report that the corpse had been stolen and the attendant had been knocked out," Caitlin said. "Look, both of you, I beg—no, I demand—that you both show me some respect and faith here. I fought hard, really hard, to keep us all together—and I managed it. Now we're facing our first real crisis, so please, remember that I came through for you before and just trust me."

Both of them stared at her for a long moment. Then Shauna leaned over and kissed her on the cheek. "Of course. And we're here, ready to do our part," she promised.

"I love you, you know that," Caitlin said.

"Yes, I do, but how about some faith, too?" Fiona asked.

Caitlin nodded. "Right." She turned to leave, then paused at the door. "Vampires. It's just—well, vampires," she said, and walked out.

When she was gone, Shauna looked at Fiona. "I'm sorry. You know Caitlin adores you."

"Yes, I do."

"But—she really doesn't like vampires," Shauna said.

"I've noticed. Hey, kid, good work tonight," Fiona said.

Shauna grinned, but her grin faded quickly. "Thanks. I do think there are some scary times ahead."

"No doubt," Fiona agreed.

"Good night," Shauna said, then kissed her cheek again and left the room, closing the door quietly in her wake.

Fiona was exhausted, but she had been at the morgue. She was afraid she would never sleep with the smell of formaldehyde—real or imagined—in her nose.

She headed into the shower, turned on the spray and reached for the large container of coconut-and-almond shampoo.

The tropical scent rose around her, and she inhaled deeply as she massaged the shampoo through her hair, wishing that the pressure of her fingers could make the whirlwind in her mind come to a halt. Did she know that she had done the right thing?

No.

Would she feel any better now if she had been coldly efficient and dispatched Abigail and Billy both?

No, definitely not.

Admittedly they were stuck working around the disappearance of a corpse, but it could have been worse.

They could be dealing with a dead morgue attendant.

She rinsed her hair and groped blindly for the soap,

then nearly screamed when the container of body wash was placed in her hand.

Her eyes flew open, and she gasped.

Jagger was standing there outside her shower, grinning in admiration.

He had no right.

She wanted to yell at him for scaring her, when she was already feeling like an incompetent fool.

She wanted to yell and scream and beat her fists against his chest.

Because she was afraid.

But more than all that, she wanted him there.

The water beat down. The steam rose.

He looked at her without moving. And then he spoke softly.

"I'm sorry, Fiona. I'm so sorry."

Had he really just apologized?

Suddenly her eyes were stinging.

To hide the rising tears, she turned back into the spray.

"All right, I understand," he said.

He was going to leave, she realized.

She groped blindly again, catching his arm, soaking the sleeve of his immaculate jacket.

"No, no…it's just my eyes," she said.

In a second, a dry washcloth was in her hands.

And then he was in the shower, naked and standing behind her, holding her close to him and whispering against her ear, above the rush of the water,

"I really am so sorry."

She turned in his arms, as if she had been starving for years for a human touch. In a way she *had* starved, of course, because she had always been a Keeper, never allowed to forget her responsibilities.

And *he* wasn't human.

He was more than human. Better.

It was true that neither of them really understood the complete ramifications of the extraordinary lives they led. The secrets of heaven and hell were not in their possession. What they did know was that kindness and cruelty, good and evil, were natural attributes of all living things, represented in greater or lesser degrees in everyone.

But Jagger seemed to contain more of the best than anyone she knew, and his strength was greater because it could bend.

And the way he held her…

She turned into his arms.

"Forgiven," she said softly.

It was deliciously erotic, making love in the water, the slickness of soap lubricating their flesh, the steam hot and luxurious, and his hands…

Touching her. Holding her. Making her feel as if she were completely savored and cherished, as if he worshipped every part of her.

His lips, hot and slick. His tongue, teasing.

His whispers echoed in the close confines of the shower.…

He held her against the tile, oddly cool against the heat, and the complex mix of emotions and sensations seemed to heighten every touch, every movement. When she fell against him in release, she could still feel his lips against her shoulder, his arms around her, his body against hers. She reveled in the security of his support and her immersion in another—a man, no matter that his heart didn't beat.

He fumbled for the faucets, turning the water off at last, and lifted her easily to the bathroom rug, following her out and wrapping a large fluffy towel around her, then reaching for one for himself. She smiled as she met his eyes, longing to tell him how glad she was that he had come, how much it meant to her that they stood together. And more than anything, how it made her tremble to realize that he was willing to ask her forgiveness when he felt he'd been wrong.

He pulled her to him, cradling her against him, and looked into her eyes.

"It's frightening, what we've done," he said.

She nodded, then grinned slowly. "Yes, but I realized we only had one other choice. A dead morgue attendant."

"True."

"Where are the young lovers?"

"Sound asleep."

"What if they wake up?"

He laughed softly, gently stroking her wet hair.

"Billy is back in the frat house. And I took Abigail to David Du Lac, who welcomed the challenge and is ready to forge ahead. He thinks we made the right decision, said we did what was right."

"There will still be hell to pay," she said.

"I know."

"My sister broke up a fight tonight between Mateas Grenard and a werewolf named Louis Arile."

Jagger was quiet. "And unless I catch this killer quickly, we're going to see a lot more of the same."

"My sisters are up in arms."

"I tried to make a hasty exit and not get you in trouble with them."

"Excellent work. But they're not fools."

"Of course not. They're Keepers."

"I'm so worried about this. We can't let it come to another war."

"We won't."

"Then…"

"Then," he said, pulling her closer to him by tugging on the towel, "we learn to make each precious moment that we have alone together count."

She smiled, closing her eyes, savoring the simple feel of being close against him.

"Even the seconds…" she murmured.

"Exactly."

He lifted her, his eyes locked on hers, his every movement both romantic and excruciatingly sensual as he carried her to the bed and laid her on the mattress, then moved the towel as if he were unwrapping something exquisite and fragile. He made her skin burn with the intensity of his gaze before his lips skimmed her body with a slow, liquid touch that burned and yet was still somehow tender, awakening an array of incredible desire. She lay still for a moment, in simple awe of the way he could make her feel, and then she burst to life, desperate to return every caress.

The sun was coming up when at last they lay exhausted and spent, entangled in one another's arms.

Fiona drifted to sleep on a dream more wonderful than any other.

When she awoke, he was gone.

Only mist and memory remained beside her.

But even they were beautiful, and more than she had ever dreamed she would find.

There were certain matters of police procedure that Jagger had to follow—no matter what he knew to be true.

The dorms had to be searched. All the dorms in the city, all the frat houses—even all the sorority houses. With the new morgue attendant being a college kid, the police had immediately theorized that the corpse might have been stolen as some kind of sick college prank.

There was also no way to keep the media from becoming a major presence. And once they got wind of the fact that the missing body looked like the stereotypical victim of a vampire attack, the less responsible papers ran with the story.

Has beauty arisen?

Co-ed, drained of blood, seems to have walked out of morgue!

To make matters worse, a recent cable documentary had focused on vampire cults in the city of New Orleans. One group in Uptown that had been given special attention had taken to walking reporters around their communal home, explaining their rites—and need for blood.

Jagger hoped against hope that the entire city hadn't seen the show. He hadn't, but Tony had, and happily told him all about it.

His first order of business once he became aware of what was happening had been to send a couple of black and white cruisers out to protect the residents of the house. Didn't those idiots realize they were courting an attack?

He was in his office, having just arranged a press conference for early that afternoon, when he received a call from August Gaudin.

"What on earth is going on?"

"August, I can't share privileged information with you, but I can assure you that no one is more concerned than I am about the situation."

"And let *me* assure *you* that I am not a fool. If a new vampire is walking, you and Fiona know something about it."

"There's a meeting tonight, August."

"And you had better be prepared to keep the peace."

Jagger looked around. There were three other vampires, two werewolves and one shapeshifter on the force. Only the shapeshifter, Michael Shrine, was on the day crew, and he'd sent him out to the vampire cult house.

They also had one of the largest leprechauns he'd ever met on the force, also working days, and he, too, was out of the office, leaving only human beings surrounding him now.

But no matter who was around, Jagger was always careful to keep this kind of discussion out of his office.

"Got time for an early lunch, councilman?" he asked now.

"Do you?"

"Gotta eat. I'll make time."

"Sure. How about the Napoleon House?" Gaudin asked.

"It will be busy," Jagger warned.

"Which is fine. I want us to be seen together, but it

will be noisy, so we can talk—and not be overheard. Oh, and they make a po'boy I really like," August said.

A little while later, seated in the historic restaurant, they ordered quickly—they were, after all, working men just grabbing a bite.

"You've seen the papers?" Gaudin asked immediately.

"Of course."

"I know that Gina is trying hard to keep the media from going crazy, but she can't ignore the obvious, and she can't protest too much—that's always a dangerous course. So…I want the truth."

Jagger nodded, meeting Gaudin's eyes. "Okay. You were right. No new vampire would be walking without Fiona and me knowing. The girl was eighteen, August. *Eighteen*, raised by nuns and as pure as the driven snow."

"Doesn't snow much in New Orleans," Gaudin noted, his innuendo obvious.

Jagger ignored him and went on. "She's being given a new identity, of course."

"Are you ready to face an argument from the assembly?" Gaudin asked.

"Of course."

"Would you have made the same decision, do you think, if we had been looking at a werewolf or a shapeshifter?"

"You know me, August. You know that I'm always fair."

"I know it. I'm just trying to warn you that everyone else may not be so understanding."

"Warning gratefully noted," Jagger told him.

"I'm sorry to say, I think it's obvious now that a vampire is guilty."

"The only thing I'll admit is that it's obvious a werewolf isn't," Jagger said dryly.

"We also know that no human being, no matter what occult kick he's on, was the killer."

"Yes." Jagger took a long swallow of sweet tea. "The timing of that documentary was really unfortunate."

"I won't argue with you," Gaudin said, then frowned. "I wonder if they realize how much danger they're in. Have you—"

"Officers are watching the house. And I've called a press conference for this afternoon."

August Gaudin nodded thoughtfully. "This is a very tenuous situation we're in. How close are you to finding the killer? Was the girl able to tell you anything useful?"

Jagger shook his head. "She was drinking at a frat party. That's the last thing she remembers. She's with David Du Lac, and he knows to inform me right away if she remembers anything else."

"All right, then. I'll be there to support you—and the peace. Three in the morning. Damn. These old bones could use more rest than they're getting these days," Gaudin said, shaking his head.

Rest would be nice, Jagger thought. But the time he spent with Fiona was infinitely more precious.

"Well, well, gentlemen," a soft, feminine voice said from right beside them.

Jagger turned and almost groaned aloud.

Jennie Mahoney, stunningly and sophisticatedly dressed—no touristy T-shirts for her—was looking down at him.

He rose, pulling out an extra chair so she could take a seat beside him.

"Jennie. What a pleasure."

"I'm sorry, but I'm not here for pleasure, Jagger."

"It's still always a delight to see you, my dear," August Gaudin assured her.

"And you, August, of course," she said, and gave him a gracious smile. Then she turned on Jagger. "Explain yourself, Detective."

"I intend to, I promise. Tonight."

"You saved her, Jagger," Jennie said, studying him. "Why?"

"Innocence," he said.

"No excuse."

"Actually it was, Jennie."

"The Keeper will see that she doesn't join society."

"The Keeper is in agreement with me."

Jennie frowned severely. "Jagger, this is dangerous."

"Not if we all keep our own counsel."

Jennie shook her head. "I'm perplexed. Why hasn't the girl fingered her murderer? She was at a frat party, according to the news. She must know who she was with."

"No, I'm afraid not. All she remembers is a lot of beer."

"Jagger, you need to get out and grill those boys mercilessly. Isn't one of your kind a student? He was at the meeting…was he at the frat party, too? What was his name? Billy…? That's it! Billy Harrington."

"Billy Harrington wasn't at the party, because he was coming to the meeting at David's," Jagger explained.

Jennie made a sound of distaste. "From what I've

heard, there would have been plenty of time for him to kill that girl first."

"There was just enough time, yes," Jagger agreed. "But trust me, Billy didn't do this. I don't see any vampire doing something like this, frankly. It would be a blatant challenge to the rest of us. He'd have to know we'd come after him, that he couldn't get away with it."

"Well, if it wasn't a vampire, the only other possibility is…Jagger! My God. I didn't expect much from the vampire Keeper, but really! You, too? You're accusing a shapeshifter."

"I'm not accusing anyone, Jennie, I don't have enough evidence yet," Jagger explained.

Jennie straightened regally. "You need to get moving then, Detective. You don't have time to be sitting here enjoying a leisurely lunch."

"Jennie, I asked him here," Gaudin said.

Jagger stood, laying money on the table. "August, we'll talk more later. Jennie, I know what I'm doing."

He leaned down and spoke softly.

"And yes, I'm a vampire as well as a detective, but I take my commitment to keep peace in the city very seriously. I *will* discover the truth. When I have evidence, I'll see that the killer is brought down—whether he's a vampire, a shapeshifter or something none of us has ever seen before. I'll see you both at the meeting."

He heard Jennie's indignant gasp as he left, but he wasn't in the mood to give a damn.

It rankled him that Jennie was right about one thing.

He needed to be out on the streets. He belonged at that frat house, asking questions.

Billy Harrington had indeed had the time to kill the love of his life and put her body on display. As for a motive, he was madly in love. Now he could be madly in love forever.

Billy had sworn that he would never harm Abigail. And the truth was that none of them knew what awaited a vampire once his existence on earth was over. Many of them believed in the power of God and the devil.

Would Billy have risked the possibility of sending the object of his devotion to a fiery hell?

Jagger didn't think so, and he was a good detective—vampire or not—because he had gotten to be very good at reading people and their emotions. It wasn't impossible, and he wasn't ruling anything out, but he would need actual evidence before he was willing to even consider it likely.

Then there was the killing of Tina Lawrence.

Billy had no motive in her death. And they hadn't gotten a single call from anyone who had seen anyone who even remotely resembled the police artist's sketch of the man from the strip club.

And in his mind, that could only mean one thing.

Shapeshifter.

Chapter 9

"Shauna, you still have friends in grad school, right?" Fiona asked her youngest sister, while she brewed herself a cup of her favorite English breakfast tea behind the counter in the shop. She spoke softly, because Caitlin was in the back, giving a tarot card reading.

"Yeah, sure, why?"

"I'd like to talk to some of the kids who were at that frat party," Fiona explained.

"Sure—when? The major emergency assembly is tonight."

"How about early this evening?"

"What about Caitlin?"

"She's welcome to come, too," Fiona said.

Shauna was thoughtful for a moment. She joined Fiona behind the counter and absently began brewing a cup of her favorite tea, white peach.

"Fiona, I'm afraid of what will happen if you receive

information that puts…well, casts *you* in an unflattering light," Shauna said.

"What do you mean?"

"Okay, let's face it, you've been bowled over by a vampire."

"I've been bowled over by a *man*," Fiona protested quietly.

"Yes, and I can definitely see the attraction. I think that Caitlin would, too, if…I don't know. It might be different if she were the Keeper for the vampires, but… she still blames that vampire for the fact that Mom and Dad are dead. She blames the vampires for the war."

"And you don't?"

"I blame everyone. I blame intolerance everywhere," Shauna said. "And another thing—the one who helped us through everything was August Gaudin. A werewolf. There's never been a reason for her to trust a vampire." She lowered her voice. "Now come on. We all know you're not telling us everything about letting Abigail the student survive the change. What really went on?"

Fiona hesitated, but it was probably all going to come out eventually, and she felt she owed it to her sisters to be completely honest.

"Billy Harrington—you remember him from the meeting? The college student? He had just started working the night shift at the morgue. They knew each other. In fact, they were madly in love with each other, though neither one had had the guts to tell the other. Anyway, he was willing to fight for her."

"So? You didn't back down from a fight. I know you," Shauna said.

"No. But he offered to do it for her, and we chose to respect his…feelings. Besides, think about it. She was raised by nuns. She's a good kid, with a good soul and I believe in the existence of the soul."

Shauna looked as if she were about to speak, but just then Caitlin and Mrs. Vickery, her client, came from the back room into the shop proper.

"My dear, you are the most insightful reader I have ever met," Mrs. Vickery was saying. She was one of those people who seemed to have been sent into the world just to make it pleasant. She was about sixty, gray hair always coiffed, plump figure attractively attired. She loved children and animals, and was active in the community, constantly giving to others. She was always smiling, and she always came with her tiny Papillon in a designer bag. The dog was as sweet as her owner. Her hairy little head popped out the top of the bag as they neared the counter.

"Thank you," Caitlin said.

Mrs. Vickery smiled at Fiona and Caitlin. "Your sister is so wise. She sees what others don't." She looked down fondly at her dog.

"I *will* find a mate for my little Mrs. Beasley here," she said, delighted.

Caitlin laughed softly. "You didn't need a tarot reader to tell you that, Mrs. Vickery. "You're going to find a mate for Mrs. Beasley because you're so determined."

Mrs. Vickery flushed happily. "Well, yes, there's that, too. Fiona, dear, one day next week, would you read the tea leaves for me? They tend to show such different possibilities."

"Of course. I'll fit you in wherever you like," Fiona assured her.

"I've just been so worried lately," Mrs. Vickery said.

"And," she added, looking at Shauna, "I'm looking forward to another palm reading, young lady."

"I'll give you a freebie right now," Shauna said, taking the older woman's hand. A look of concern briefly crossed her face, and she seemed to force a smile. "See this little line? It's new. It means that you're going in a new direction with a pet project, that you're going to do well, and others will embrace your ideas."

"Oh, how lovely. And it *is* a 'pet' project," Mrs. Vickery said. "I have a friend who owns one of those old plantations who's agreed to open up the old kennels as a shelter where no animal will ever be put to sleep."

"That's wonderful," Fiona approved.

"And it's so reassuring to know others will embrace the idea," Mrs. Vickery said happily.

"Kindness begets kindness," Fiona said.

Mrs. Vickery flushed. "Well, I inherited a fortune. In all honesty, with so much money at my disposal, I owe it to others to help them, at least in my own mind."

"It's a beautiful mind," Fiona assured her.

"I do worry these days," Mrs. Vickery said. "All this horrible business with women being killed, their bodies drained. And now that second girl's body was stolen. What on earth have we come to? I bet it's those cultists in the old Brewer mansion."

"What?" Fiona asked sharply.

"There's a group of so-called vampires living in Uptown, in the Brewer mansion. Can you believe it? They were in a documentary that aired just the other night! If the police don't deal with them, I'm sure someone will," she said knowingly.

Fiona groaned inwardly. Great. Just what they needed at a time like this.

"They're probably just a group of confused kids," Caitlin said reassuringly, glancing over at Fiona.

Mrs. Vickery sighed softly. "All I know is that too many frightening things are happening. And I'm having dreams. I saw a girl turning into a vampire—a real one, like in the movies—and walking down the street naked." She gave an exaggerated shudder. "Well, we'd best get going, my little one and I. Next week, girls."

As soon as the woman had left the store, Shauna turned to Fiona. "A dream, huh?"

Fiona frowned and asked, "What did you really see in her palm?"

"Probably the same thing I read in her cards," Caitlin said.

"What was that?" Fiona asked sharply.

"She's in danger," Caitlin said.

Fiona's heart sank. She hadn't realized that Mrs. Vickery was the woman on the street when she had been trying to corral Abigail back into Jagger's house.

"You…you didn't see her *death*, did you?" she asked.

"A jagged line," Shauna said.

"Danger—that could lead to death," Caitlin told her.

Fiona groaned aloud. "All right, I've got to get going. I need to see what's going on with that cult. Listen for your cell phones. I might need help at any time."

As she grabbed her bag, Shauna went over to the computer and logged onto a local news site.

"Hey!"

Shauna called, and turned up the volume.

Fiona and Caitlin ran to join her.

* * *

Jagger was speaking to the press, and Fiona's heart practically stopped. How was he going to explain things to the public when he didn't know who the killer was but he did know *what*.

And when that "what" wasn't human…

"It's unfortunate for our city that a certain documentary that was shown recently seems to have put some strange ideas in people's heads. Only concrete evidence can lead us to the perpetrator of these heinous crimes, and the police are working diligently to find that evidence," Jagger assured the media.

"But this group claims to drink blood!" one of the newscasters shouted.

"Claiming and doing are two different things," Jagger pointed out. "Listen, please. Protecting these people from a potential lynch mob is costing us police man hours. I'm begging the public to work with us, not against us."

"What about the corpse that was stolen?" another reporter asked, thrusting a microphone closer to Jagger.

"The police are investigating that, as well, I assure you. All I'm asking is that you and everyone in this city stay calm and help us do our work. Don't become an accusing mob, and do inform us if you see anything out of the ordinary, anything that looks dangerous. The police are trying to help the city, and we ask that you all do the same. And now I thank you for your attention, but you'll have to excuse me. I'm needed on the streets."

Jagger walked away, followed by a barrage of questions, but he was firm, politely lifting a hand until he could make it to his car. Fiona saw that his partner was waiting behind the wheel as Jagger slipped into the passenger seat.

The press conference was definitely over.

"I've got to get moving," Fiona said, and hurried out of the store.

"Wait," Caitlin said. "Shauna, cover for us, please. Fiona, I don't want you going alone. I'm coming with you."

Jagger and Tony drew up in front of the cult house. Sean O'Casey—the world's largest leprechaun—was partnercd with shapeshifter Michael Shrine as part of the task force that had been assembled to deal with the murders and the possible rise of violence in the city. They were parked by the entry to the cult house.

Michael Shrine, six feet four of muscle in his human form, was leaning against one side of the car. Sean O'Casey, stretched to his top height of an amazing six even, was just as implacably entrenched on the other side of the car, arms crossed over his chest.

Both men looked grim.

Jagger didn't blame them.

There wasn't a city employee who wasn't worried about the possibility of violence. Of course, most of them were worried that human beings—Baptist, Catholic, nondenominational Christian, Jewish, Hindu, atheist, alien-worshipping or even run-of-the-mill New Orleans voodoo practitioners—would attack other human beings.

Those who haunted the city's underground knew that the situation might be far worse.

"Any trouble?" Jagger asked, approaching the car, with Tony a step behind.

"Well, a truckload of high school kids went by—looked as if they were going to hurl eggs, but they saw us and drove on by," Shrine said.

"Then there was the crazy woman," O'Casey told them. "And her crazy followers."

"What? Who?" Tony asked.

Sean shook his head. "Skinny woman, walked from that way—" he pointed "—to get here, had about ten people behind her. They were all carrying Bibles and saying that disbelievers would burn in hell."

"Scarier than our would-be vampires, if you ask me," Shrine said.

"Fanatics are always scary," Jagger said. "But no one attempted to go to the house, or attack the residents in any way?"

"Not yet. No one in, no one out," Shrine assured him.

"Thanks," Jagger said. He started toward the front door, then turned around so quickly that Tony almost crashed into him.

"Go on, I'll be right along," he told Tony.

Tony headed for the door as Jagger walked back to Sean O'Casey. "How the hell did you get to be so tall?" he asked.

Sean O'Casey shrugged. "Must be the hormones in the milk over here. I've two brothers back home who aren't a full four feet. And my sisters are tiny little things."

Jagger grinned, asked the two of them to be sure to write up full descriptions of everyone who'd come by, then thanked them again and headed back to the door.

Tony had already knocked.

A woman with dyed black hair opened the door.

She was wearing a black dress and looked like a younger Elvira, Mistress of the Dark.

"Hello. I'm Detective Jagger DeFarge, and this is my partner, Detective Tony Miro. We'd like to talk to you and your…group for a few minutes, if we could."

The woman smiled. She had just a touch of bloodred lipstick on her teeth. "Of course. Come in. We're already entertaining guests, so please join us."

"Oh?" Just how long ago had those guests arrived? he wondered, making a mental note to check with the officers who'd been on duty before Shrine and O'Casey.

He stepped in. The house was a basic grand colonial, with a huge entry hall, doors to the left and right and a massive staircase leading up from the middle of the room.

The banisters were adorned with garlands of black roses.

The walls were painted black. Black curtains hung over the windows.

The walls held movie posters celebrating Hollywood's fascination with werewolves, mummies, vampires, witches and every conceivable monster, from a giant lizard that had just crawled out of a swamp to King Kong.

The woman offered him a hand, long fingers, with longer fingernails painted in bloodred, dangling.

"I'm Lucretia. Real name. It goes with Brown. Please, come in. I'm the titular queen of our little group."

She led them to the door on the right and into the next room. For a moment the scent of blood was strong, and Jagger steeled himself against it.

The living room added red to the black of the entry

hall, and instead of movie posters, the paintings that hung on the walls qualified as erotica at least as much as art. A man was seated in a claw-foot chair by a huge fireplace, and side by side on a massive sofa covered in plush red velvet were Fiona and Caitlin MacDonald.

He groaned inwardly. "Fiona, Caitlin, I didn't expect to see you here."

"You all know each other?" Lucretia asked pleasantly.

"I've known these ladies quite a while, yes," Jagger said. "Tony, have you met my friends, Fiona and Caitlin MacDonald?"

Caitlin apparently realized in an instant that Tony was human and decided to be nice to him.

"It's a pleasure," she murmured.

"Fancy finding you here," Jagger said, staring at Fiona. He bent close and said for her ears only, "How the hell did you slip in? The men outside didn't see you. No, wait. Don't tell me. She shape-shifted into a mouse or something, and you went to mist. You just made my officers look like fools."

Fiona flushed, looking away momentarily.

"I thought I should come. I wanted these people to understand that they could be in serious danger. I explained about the shop, and how we know the mood of the city."

Jagger knew his smile looked glued on as he took a seat next to Fiona and said softly, "Great."

"Your officers aren't in trouble. No one knows," she said.

"Tony knows now, doesn't he?" Jagger asked.

"Is everything all right?" Lucretia asked worriedly. "Detectives, can I get you something to drink?"

Yes, a nice cup of the blood I can smell would be great, Jagger thought dryly, wondering why the man in the chair was there. Muscle in case things got out of hand, he supposed.

"We have a full liquor cabinet, soda, tea…coffee?" Lucretia continued.

"No, we're fine, thank you," Jagger said. "We need to talk."

Lucretia's bloodred lips pursed. "As I've been explaining to Fiona and Caitlin, we believe that blood is life. We're not murderers. We drink animal blood. We're no worse than someone who has a nice steak—served rare."

"There's human blood in this room somewhere," Jagger said firmly.

Lucretia looked startled.

"Um…actually, yes, we do keep a few vials—all from our members, and all given quite voluntarily." She sighed, extending her arms. "We've joined together because of our shared beliefs. We…we believe that lovemaking is enhanced by a sip of blood. None of us is on drugs, and in case you've forgotten, the United States offers freedom of religion. I'm a legally ordained minister."

"Did you get your credentials online?" Tony asked.

Lucretia flushed. "Yes," she snapped. "And they're perfectly legal."

"What's the name of your…church?"

"We're the Church of Elizabeth Báthory," Lucretia told him.

Tony stared at Jagger, then turned back to her. "Really?"

"Really and legally," Lucretia said icily.

Jagger lifted his hands. "Look, here's the problem

with your current situation, and it isn't legal, it's human. First, you admit to drinking blood—to using it for religious purposes?" he asked. She nodded, frowning. "The city has two bloodless corpses—"

"One," Lucretia reminded him. "You lost one, remember?"

"The point is that everyone in New Orleans knows that two women were killed and drained of blood. Therefore, I or one of my officers will need to speak with every one of your members. Personally I don't think you're guilty. I *do* think you're going to cost me man hours I can't afford. And frankly, I'm not sure how worshipping Elizabeth Báthory counts as a respectable religion."

"Hey! People worship aliens. And cows—and cats, so I've heard," Lucretia said indignantly.

"Whatever. This isn't a good time to be drinking blood," Jagger said. "And you and your members have to start being careful about what you say and do, all right? This is a…delicate time in the city. All right? Once we catch the killer, knock yourselves out. Go on every news show out there. But until then…"

He noticed that Fiona and her sister had risen. Tony rose, too and he followed suit.

"I think we should leave you to your police business," Fiona said.

"How kind of you," Jagger murmured.

"Thank you so much for coming," Lucretia said, rising as well.

"Tony, you stay here and talk to Lucretia. I'll see the sisters to the door," Jagger said, taking each of them by an elbow and steering them in that direction.

"What are you doing here?" he asked Fiona when they reached the door. "This is police business."

"Jagger, they needed to be warned. And we were doing a better job than you did of explaining that they shouldn't run around right now announcing their devotion to a fifteenth century countess who bathed in blood," Fiona said.

"And," Caitlin added, her glare icy, "when the police can't seem to handle police business, I think we need to lend a helping hand."

Jagger looked at Fiona. "I really don't want to arrest your sister," he said.

"Jagger, don't be ridiculous! I'm the Keeper—"

"And she's not. Not *my* Keeper, anyway," he said. "Get out of here—both of you. Oh, Caitlin, you might want to apologize to the tall fellow at the car—Michael Shrine, shapeshifter. He's going to feel like an ass for letting you walk in right under his nose."

He saw them both out the door and closed it with a bang. Irritated, he headed back to the living room, with its choking red-and-black decor, and wretched paintings.

Hell.

He wanted to be anywhere but here.

He sat on the sofa and pulled out his notebook. Tony did the same.

"We're going to need the names of everyone who is involved in your religion in any way. Now, let's start with you, Lucretia. We'll need to know where you were on the nights of both murders. And I'm going to pray that you aren't all each other's alibis."

This was a total waste of time, he thought. A killer was out there, and he wasn't some deluded wannabe. This killer was the real thing.

* * *

"Oh, man, it was terrible. I haven't had a drink since." Standing on the lawn in front of the frat house, Jude Andre gave a sudden, fierce shiver.

Fiona stared at him, certain it would be a while before he had another drink. His tone had been sincere.

She was with Shauna. Caitlin—who had actually apologized to Michael Shrine, and even to the leprechaun, Sean O'Casey—had gone back to the shop, muttering about Jagger being rude, unappreciative of the role of a Keeper, and an all around…vampire.

Shauna had joined Fiona for their planned visit to the frat house where Abigail had attended her last party, but they'd split up after arrival so they could talk to more people in less time.

The long-haired and lanky young man with the sax case and book bag stared at Fiona and Shauna, shaking his head. "What a party, you know? It was great. The booze was good—no cheap beer. We were jamming, you know? A bunch of music majors, just having fun."

"Sure," Shauna said. "But here's the thing. No one remembers Abigail leaving. I'm trying to get everyone to tell us about the last time they saw or talked to her that night."

He scrunched up his face, thinking. "About twelve. I was in the old parlor, playing my music. I was pretty drunk. She came by and led me to a chair, told me I was about to fall down."

"Okay, you saw her around twelve. Did you see anyone else with her?"

The boy narrowed his eyes in deep thought. "No, she was alone then. I thought it was kind of odd."

"Really? Why?" Fiona asked him.

"Well, hell, everyone knew that Billy Harrington was crazy-mad for her. She was pretty nuts for him, too. They just never figured it out about each other, you know? Went around together all the time like they were just friends. I didn't think I'd see her at a party without him. Hey, wait!" His face wrinkled as if he were a Shar-Pei.

"What is it?" Fiona asked.

Jude looked at her, shaking his head. "He wasn't at the party because he said he had some big shindig in the Quarter he needed to attend. He said he didn't want to come to the party and get started drinking and all, since he had to drive to the Quarter later."

"So you saw him during the day, but not at the party."

"Right. I think," Jude said. "Don't know why, but I have an impression of Billy in the house, but I know I didn't see him at the party." He gasped suddenly. "Oh, God! You think Billy Harrington...that's crazy! You think he murdered Abigail and then stole her body. That he loved her so much he murdered her. You think he's a necrophiliac!"

It sounded as if he thought the latter would be far worse than murder.

"No. No, that's not what I mean at all. I'm just trying to find out what happened, that's all," Fiona said firmly.

"Are you a cop or something?" he asked.

"No, my sister and I are just concerned local businesswomen with an interest in keeping our city safe," Shauna said, walking up to join them.

"Hey, Jude, Shauna!"

The call came from the steps of the frat house, breaking into the awkward conversation. The young man who walked over to join them had long dark hair, neatly kept, and a slender, attractive face. He was tall and lean, and Shauna greeted him with pleasure.

"Jimmy!" she called.

Werewolf. Fiona knew it instantly.

Jimmy smiled and shook hands when Shauna introduced him to Fiona.

"Jimmy, Fiona thinks Billy Harrington is a necrophiliac," Jude said with horror.

"I did not say any such thing," Fiona said firmly.

"Come on, I'll show you two the house," Jimmy offered, drawing them away from Jude.

"Thanks," Fiona murmured in gratitude, grateful for the chance to get away from Jude Andre, as well as the chance to see the house.

"Wrong dude to be talking to if you want useful answers," Jimmy explained to the two of them once they were out of earshot. "Jude is an all right guy, but he loves two things—his sax and his weed. He's not exactly living in the real world, if you know what I mean."

Jimmy had a nice grin—it dimpled his cheeks.

"Were you at the party?" Fiona asked him.

He nodded gravely, pushing open the door. The frat house was painted white, and the door had a beautiful cut-glass oval that sparkled in the light of the setting sun.

Fiona noticed a strange dark substance coating the door.

Jimmy shrugged. "The crime-scene people kind of got carried away…dusting for prints."

"They had to. They're looking for the prints that don't belong," Fiona said.

"Well, they have their work cut out for them. There were a lot of people at that party. And did you know we all had to go down to the station for an interview today? We're all missing classes, and we didn't even do anything."

"Jimmy Douglas, you know it's imperative that the police find the killer," Shauna said.

Jimmy lowered his head and spoke quietly. "We all know the killer's a vampire, so Jagger needs to be interviewing vampires, and that's that. And I intend to say so at the meeting tonight. Anyway, come on upstairs—I see Nathan, Billy's roommate. I'm sure you'll want to talk to him."

Fiona glanced at Shauna, and then they hurried up the stairs in Jimmy's wake. Nathan was sitting on the floor, his back against the wall, a book in his hands. As they approached, he looked up, saw the two women and smiled.

"Hey, I know you two. You run that supernatural shop in the Quarter. I was there with about ten guys a couple of weeks ago. They sure don't have anything like that in Indiana, where I come from."

"Nathan, these are my friends, Shauna and Fiona MacDonald," Jimmy said.

Nathan struggled to his feet. He looked like he was from Indiana. Corn-fed and strapping, with wheat colored hair and bright blue eyes. "Nice to meet you formally."

"They're here about Abigail," Jimmy said.

"Oh." He looked at them gravely. "What happened to her was…horrible."

"Did you see anyone with her? Was she flirting with anyone, or was anyone trying to flirt with her? Did she leave with someone, and do you remember when she left?" Fiona asked.

"The cops asked me that, too. I saw her and all, but I don't think she was flirting. She wasn't the type."

"Did you see Billy Harrington that night?" Fiona asked.

A strange expression crossed his face. "The cops asked *that*, too. He said he wasn't going to be here, but somehow…I have the impression that he was, only I don't actually remember seeing him or talking to him. Bizarre, huh? He's in our room. Poor guy—he's all ripped up over this."

"I'll go see him," Fiona said, and turned to Shauna. "Can you talk to Nathan? Thanks." Then she walked over to Billy's door and tapped gently.

"Yeah?" She heard Billy's muffled voice.

"It's Fiona."

The door opened, and he practically dragged her into the room.

Billy was clean and neatly dressed, the complete antithesis of a man in deep mourning. "Fiona, oh my God, they think I'm in mourning. I'm crawling the walls. I have to see her. I'm terrified. I don't know what she and David are doing, what the police are doing.… I'm going insane here."

"I'm sorry," she said. "But you'll just have to pull yourself together and keep going. Listen, this is serious.

A lot of people *think* you were at that party—even though you said you had to go into the Quarter and wouldn't make it."

He was indignant. "I told you—I wasn't at the party!"

She sighed. He sounded so sincere.

"Even your roommate, who certainly doesn't seem to be out to get you, has the impression you were there."

"And I just told you, I wasn't there," he insisted. "Damn it, Fiona! You know how I feel about Abigail."

"Do you love her enough to want to keep her by your side for all time?" It was the only motive for murder she'd been able to come up with for him, but she had to admit, it made a certain amount of sense.

He drew himself up stiffly. "I would never have turned her. Ever. I swear it. And you know why? Because I would never damn someone I love to the uncertainty every vampire faces every day."

He sounded so sincere.

Then again, she'd seen him act.

An impression. The other kids had an *impression*.

No one knew for a fact that they had seen him.

"I'm innocent. I swear it."

"All right, Billy. Just stay in here as long as you can—alone," Fiona said. "I'll see you at the meeting tonight."

He nodded, and she slipped back out.

She and Shauna spent another hour talking to the kids from the party, but except for a few more who had the vague sense that they'd seen Billy, they didn't come up with anything useful. Finally they decided to call it a day and left.

As they walked across the yard toward their car, they saw a pretty girl heading toward the frat house.

Fiona stopped her. "Hi. Mind if I ask you a few questions?"

The girl, who had blond hair and big blue eyes, stopped, a sad and slightly weary expression on her face.

"Are you undercover cops here to ask about Abigail?" she asked. "Sorry, I don't mean to be rude, but I've been asked the same questions over and over again, and it just…hurts. Abigail was a friend. A bit of an airhead, but a friend."

"Did you see her with anyone at the party?" Fiona asked.

"No one in particular. She was just mingling, talking to people, having fun. You know how, when you start out in college, every boy is a mystery waiting to be explored? But then after a while the boys are just boys, except maybe for one you really like."

"Right," Fiona said. "And Abigail really liked Billy Harrington."

"Yes, exactly," the girl said, then frowned suddenly.

"What is it?"

"I had a weird dream that night. Maybe I was worried about her."

"What was your dream?" Fiona asked.

The girl laughed, looking a little embarrassed. "I dreamed that I saw her walking down the steps and out toward the street, looking tired—but happy, too." She shook her head, as if to clear it.

"I could see the veins in the leaves on the trees. It was

really freaky. And then...there was some boy, hurrying to catch up to her."

"Did you tell that to the police?" Fiona asked.

The girl laughed again. "Hell no! You don't tell the police about a *dream*."

"Did you recognize the boy who was about to catch up with her?"

"Yes, of course."

"And who was it?" Fiona asked.

"Billy Harrington."

Chapter 10

The staff had been apprised that Underworld would be closing early that night, with last call being given soon after 2:00 a.m. The ostensible reason was that the place was set for a massive cleaning. Since David was known for the high standards he applied to the place, it wasn't a stretch.

Earlier, Jagger had left most of the conversations with the cult members to Tony Miro and the other officers, and moved on to the frat house.

He'd been irritated to discover that Fiona and Shauna had been there ahead of him. And he'd been genuinely disturbed to learn how many people thought they might have seen Billy Harrington that night.

No doubt Fiona and Shauna had heard the same information—and maybe more. He could certainly see how a bunch of hormone-addled teenage boys might have opened up to a pair of gorgeous sisters who were so concerned for the safety of the community, and who were ignoring the fact that people shouldn't have been opening up to them at all. They didn't have any right to question anyone.

At 10:00 p.m. he'd called Tony and told him to go home at last. His partner was going above and beyond, and he was sorry that, to maintain appearances, he was causing his partner to waste hours of work that he knew would bring them no closer to finding the killer.

He rationalized the situation by telling himself that at least now they had a lot of information on record that might be of use in the future.

He was heading back to the French Quarter, planning to arrive at Underworld well ahead of time when he picked up a sound, some kind of a thud, coming from the cemetery off Canal.

Jerking his car to a halt, he looked around carefully. Seeing no one, he got out of the car and leaped effortlessly to the top of the wall, where he hunkered down, searching the rows of mausoleums and monuments in the darkened city of the dead.

Another thud.

His eyes quickly darted in that direction, and then he jumped down and started running toward the location of the sound.

Suddenly he crashed into someone hidden in the shadow of a massive—and armless—weeping angel.

Instantly on the alert, he drew back, reaching for the gun in his shoulder holster.

"*Stop*," came a woman's urgent whisper. "Please."

He was startled by her near hysteria, but even so, he recognized the voice. It was Sue Preston, a shapeshifter friend of Jennie Mahoney's.

He caught her hand as he hunkered down by her. "What is it? What's going on?" he asked.

"They're fighting—and it's terrible," Sue said. She was a pretty young thing, but right now she had giant tears in her eyes. "I saw Georgio Tremont on Chartres Street when I was having dinner, and then Ossie Blane. We started talking, decided to kill some time before the assembly, so we came out here to go walking, and the next thing I knew, they were tearing into each other."

Georgio Tremont was a vampire.

Ossie Blane was a werewolf.

This could be trouble.

"Stay here," he told Sue quietly.

He rose and slipped around the side of the small family vault where he'd found Sue. Another thud. Someone—or some*thing*—had crashed hard into the wall right beside him.

He didn't let who—or whatever it was—rise. He shot out an arm and reached, and found himself grabbing the scruff of a furry neck.

It was Ossie Blane. He'd changed, and was in rare, snarling form.

Werewolves were very powerful. Their teeth were merciless.

Jagger knew he would have one chance before winding up in a literal fight for his life.

He kept his grip hard and shook Ossie with all his strength. "Ossie! It's Jagger, Jagger DeFarge. Stop this now!"

Ossie was, at heart, a decent guy, and to Jagger's relief, that guy hadn't sunk too far beneath the surface. Ossie went still. Slowly the snout became a face. Hair dissolved.

Claws and fangs retracted.

The sleek shape of the wolf elongated and straightened into an erect position.

Gasping for breath, Ossie stared at him.

A wing of perfect, menacing darkness came gliding toward them both. Jagger stepped forward, using the full brunt of his body as a bulwark. The vampire came flying into him with so much force that Jagger had to take a step back to absorb the blow.

Bend and you'll never break.

He didn't think his martial arts teacher had been thinking vampires when he'd said it, but it had turned out to be true nonetheless.

Georgio dropped to the ground after slamming into him. For a moment Jagger was reminded of a commercial he'd seen, in which two birds laughed at a man who hit the ground after walking right into a newly cleaned and completely see-through glass door.

With a stunned cry, Georgio started to make his way to his feet.

Jagger helped him up. "What are you two idiots up to?" he demanded.

"DeFarge, what are you doing here?" Georgio asked. "That walking furball attacked me!"

"I didn't attack you!" Ossie protested, stepping forward belligerently. "I said that it was obvious that the killer's a vampire, and that no one should be attacking innocent college students."

Jagger interposed himself between them. "Look, we're all in a bad situation right now, and we have to keep calm. The last thing we need, if you'll pardon the pun, is some kind of witch hunt."

To Jagger's amusement, the other two pointed fingers

at each other at the same time and said in unison, "He started it!"

Most of the time they were both average citizens, interesting conversationalists over a meal or a drink. Ossie loved animals and worked at the zoo, and Georgio was a middle-school teacher.

"Both of you," Jagger said quietly. "Look at what you're doing. Myths and movies call us monsters. This is why."

Sue emerged from behind the angel-topped mausoleum at last.

"You scared me," she accused them. "I thought you were my friends."

They might have been a comedy act when they spoke in unison again.

"I'm so sorry, Sue."

Jagger leaned back, crossing his arms over his chest. "All right, time to kiss and make up. I ought to knock your heads together. Damn it! We need to get through this together or the whole city's going to turn on us. We need to find a killer—and I don't give a damn what race he is. To do that, I need help, not a couple of hotheads trying to rip each other to shreds."

Ossie hung his head. "I'm sorry, Jagger—Georgio. And Sue. Really."

"Maybe we could keep from mentioning this?" Georgio asked, looking across the darkened cemetery, worry creasing his brow. He turned back to Jagger. "All the Keepers will be at the assembly, right?"

"Just about everyone will be at the assembly. There are a few people working in emergency services or other jobs where their absences would be noted, but

I'm expecting a showing of at least two hundred," Jagger said.

"I'm planning to get there early. In fact, I was on my way when I got sidetracked by your fight. Speaking of... You all need to clean up and get there on time, and you had both better do something really nice for Sue." He turned his attention to her. "You okay?"

She nodded, linking arms with the two men. "Thank you. We're fine," she assured him.

He left them making their apologies, making it back to his car in time to see two thugs were trying to break in.

They were wearing ski masks.

In New Orleans.

"Hey!" he shouted.

One of the men looked at him, and then they both took off.

He could have caught them. Maybe he should have.

But he was looking for a killer who was going to take more victims if he wasn't stopped.

Soon.

"I'm sure of it. Billy is the killer," Caitlin said. She, Shauna and Fiona were in their communal living room, watching the clock, discussing the events of the day.

"I just don't believe that," Fiona said. She was pacing, she realized. Arms crossed over her chest, walking back and forth in front of the fireplace like the depressed polar bear in the Central Park Zoo that had needed therapy, because all it did was swim back and forth, back and forth....

She stopped pacing and realized both her sisters were staring at her, waiting for her to speak.

"Are you even listening? I said if Jagger won't put him down, you'll have to," Caitlin said.

"We don't have any proof that it was Billy," Fiona said. "Look, for one thing, we're all concentrating on the second murder and forgetting about the first. Billy has no connection to Tina Lawrence, who was last seen at a strip club. The police have a sketch of a man who was there that night, and not a single person has come forward to say they recognize him, *think* they recognize him, or even know anyone who even slightly resembles him."

"Could there have been two separate killers?" Shauna wondered aloud.

"I don't think so. Too many similarities," Fiona said, and took a deep breath. "Here's where we are right now. Tina Lawrence, last seen at the strip club. A man was watching her—he's never been seen again. We've actually questioned Abigail, but she doesn't remember anything. She was at a party, she was drinking beer. Someone might have slipped something in her drink— frat boys have been known to do that—but we don't actually know, since there was obviously no autopsy. No one from the party remembers actually talking to Billy, though a lot of people got the impression he was there. They all knew he had plans in the Quarter—which he did. He was at the meeting with the three of us."

Caitlin had been curled up on the sofa. Now she stood, walked up to Fiona and placed a hand gently on her shoulder. "Look, I know I've been a bitch. It's just that I can't forget that vampires caused all our problems—caused Mom and Dad their lives. But I want to help you, want to be a good sister and a good Keeper. And I don't want to upset you, but I do need to point out two things. First, both victims were drained of blood, vampire style. And this wasn't the act of a human being. A human being might have pulled off the blood draining, but both victims woke at dark. Only a vampire can create a vampire."

"Or a shapeshifter—posing as a vampire," Shauna pointed out.

"I think you're forgetting one thing. Shapeshifters can take on many forms, but when it comes to masquerading as another supernatural, they don't have the strength of the real thing," Caitlin said.

"That's true," Fiona agreed. "But," she asked quietly, "how much strength would a shapeshifter have needed to attack two women? Tina Lawrence had a violent streak, true, but she was still only human. A shapeshifter might not be as strong as a vampire or werewolf, but he would still be more powerful than a human being."

"You just don't want to accept that it was a vampire," Caitlin told her.

"*You* just don't want to accept the possibility that it might have been a shapeshifter," Fiona countered.

They stared at each other. Then they both started to smile at the same time.

"All right—it was most likely a vampire," Fiona said.

"And, I admit, there's a possibility it was a shape-shifter," Caitlin said.

"What a relief," Shauna said. "Now we can go to the meeting and present a united front."

"We have to," Fiona said. "We have to make the entire paranormal community understand completely that we're not only judicious but strong—and we *will* keep the peace."

Shauna jumped up from the sofa.

"Group hug!" she cried.

Laughing, Fiona let herself be dragged into her youngest sister's exuberant embrace.

"All right—enough," she said finally, taking a step back. "One for all, and all for one. Now, let's get over to that meeting."

Despite the time it had taken to break up the altercation, Jagger arrived at David's early. A little while later, from his seat in the front row, he watched the attendees filing in and realized everyone seemed to naturally group together with the other members of their own race.

Ossie and Georgio had made up, but even so, they split up when they entered, Ossie to sit with the werewolves and Georgio with the vampires. Even the Keepers separated on arrival and sat with the races they were charged to protect.

Jagger was grateful when August Gaudin came down the aisle and sat next to him, breaking up the divisions.

He thought back to the war—and the peace. The peace motivated by the deaths of the elder MacDonalds had forced them all to learn patience and tolerance, and to obey the unwritten laws that allowed them to maintain their place in society. Their laws, like the Constitution of the United States, mandated equal rights for all.

But laws didn't always end old hatreds or prejudices.

Even Caitlin MacDonald couldn't let go of her belief that the vampires alone had caused the deaths of her parents. But the vampires hadn't caused the war all by themselves.

It took two to fight. And once two were fighting, everyone wanted in on the brawl, or so it seemed.

He found it especially sad that the war had been started on behalf of perhaps the finest emotion of all: love.

"Shall I open?" August asked Jagger.

"That would be fine," Jagger said, taking another look around the room. It was filling up. It was almost like a wedding where no one got along with anyone else. Vampires to the left, shapeshifters to the right, werewolves in between, the others finding space where they could.

Sean O'Casey came in, nodded to him and took a seat between the vampires and the werewolves. Leprechauns were not in large supply in New Orleans, but as far as he was concerned, they were as welcome as anyone else. Sure, they tended to drink and get in bar brawls now and then, but most of the time they were cheerful, and a big presence in the local art and culture scene.

A well-respected voodoo priestess known as Granny Caldwell, one of the few human beings welcome at a major assembly, came in, greeting friends, and chose to sit next to Sean O'Casey.

Granny Caldwell had to be about eighty, but she had the bearing of a young woman. Her skin was a beautiful copper hue, and she wore a blue turban that emphasized the aristocratic bone structure of her face. She wore a dress in shades of green and the same blue as the turban.

She nodded at Jagger, and he smiled in return. Her eyes sparkled, but she wasn't going to smile back.

"Are we about ready?" David said.

Jagger turned to see their host at his side.

"Yeah, thanks, looks like we're about set to go. You'll introduce us, then August will speak first, and Jennie Mahoney is here—she'll want her turn at the microphone." He turned to August. "Let's make that the order—David, you, Jennie, then me. I have a feeling I'll be trying to hold the peace together by then."

David must have seen Jagger's frown of concern and known what unspoken question lurked behind the expression. He bent down to whisper, "It's okay. Abigail is here—and safe." Then he nodded and went to the podium, where he cleared his throat and tapped the microphone. "Welcome, everyone, to this emergency meeting of our peoples. We all know that we have a dire and escalating situation not only in our community but in our beloved city as a whole. We're here for two reasons. First, to discuss what has happened, all the possible explanations and how we proceed. Second, to see to it that we remain strong among ourselves. To that end, we'll have three speakers, one for each of the most populous, but we're not attempting to exclude anyone, so if…anyone else…wants a say, they're more than welcome to come to the podium."

He paused, looking around the room. When no one seemed inclined to comment or object, he went on.

"First let us welcome August Gaudin."

August was greeted with massive applause.

He flushed and began to speak.

"First, I'd like to sincerely thank all of you for your commitment to keeping the peace between the races.

Some of us are young and don't remember what it was like when war broke out among us. The death toll was excruciating, and if two of the finest Keepers I've ever known, the MacDonalds, hadn't used their last strength—indeed, their very last breaths—to subdue the violence, things might have escalated to a point where we became visible and the human population not only felt threatened by our very existence, but determined to erase us from the face of the earth. The MacDonalds have left us their daughters, fine young women in their own right. We *must* take our grievances to them—not fight each other in the streets."

His words were greeted with more applause.

"I'm calling out now to my own people, the were-wolves and all the were-creatures. Thankfully, due to our very nature and powers, we're not suspects in these heinous crimes, but that doesn't change the fact that we're called upon to remember that we are all brothers in a special and tight-knit society that demands we respect one another. I ask you, my brethren, to keep the peace at all times and no matter the costs. Shauna MacDonald is here tonight, not only our Keeper but our mentor and our guide. If one of you has any problem at all, please come to me or to Shauna. Whatever you do, don't let a petty squabble lead to teeth and fangs and more bloodshed."

Shauna nodded gravely to him from her seat in the audience as more applause greeted his final words.

When the applause died down, he said, "And now I give you Jennie Mahoney."

Jennie, as regal as ever, rose and walked to the stage. The shapeshifters applauded her loudly, and the rest of the room politely followed suit.

"I, like my dear friend August Gaudin, am here to ask

that we remain calm and rational in these trying times. These are the facts. Two human women were murdered and drained of blood. We are all aware that they rose as vampire, and we are all also aware that only the bite of a vampire—or a shapeshifter in vampire form—could be the cause. Therefore we must take great care not to look at each other with suspicion, or let our fears lead us to violence. We must put our faith in our own Keeper, Caitlin MacDonald, along with her sister Fiona, Keeper for the vampire community, and Jagger DeFarge, not only one of this city's most respected vampires but an upstanding officer of the law. I hope you'll all join me in being grateful that Jagger DeFarge was put in charge of the investigation into these murders, because we know he won't let personal bias get in the way of his search for the truth. He's lucky, because he'll have the help of the entire New Orleans Police Department, including several members of the underworld who also carry a badge. I want to finish by asking all of you to be open minded, to recognize the fact that we all have weaknesses and emotions but can't let ourselves act on them. In particular, I'd like to ask my fellow shapeshifters to understand that we may fall under suspicion. We must not let ourselves fall back on resentment, but instead answer any questions willingly and honestly, out of our desire to end this horror as quickly as possible."

After the applause that followed her speech, she said, "And now Jagger DeFarge would like to speak."

Jagger stood, grateful to realize that the explosion of applause came in equal amounts from all the races.

He looked around the room when he reached the podium, then started to speak.

"Like you, I've listened to my colleagues' words, and

they've spoken the same truth that I see. We have to take the high road now. We can't be afraid of each other, and we can't blindly attack each other. However, I believe we have to go even further. I would bet that every one of you can say with complete honesty that you have at least one friend whose race is different from yours. But what hasn't happened since the war is a real combining of the communities, and I think that's going to prove crucial now. We need to mix, to mingle, to merge into one whole with the same goal in mind: apprehending the killer whose viciousness has put all our lives in jeopardy. And the easiest way to become a community is simply to act like one. Vampires, go to werewolf restaurants. Werewolves, I charge you to shop at shapeshifter-run stores. We need to get past looking at one another for what we are biologically and embrace one another as if we were all the same."

He was pleased to see the attendees start looking around, to see realization on their faces as they noticed that they had come into the room and automatically segregated themselves by race.

"At the same time, feel free to just dislike someone now and then. We have to get past the idea that somebody doesn't like so and so, it has to be because of what they are. Sometimes you just think someone is a jerk—and maybe the rest of us have to learn that you just might be right."

He was glad to hear the rise of real laughter at his words. Their situation was serious, but that only made laughter more necessary.

After that he went on to recap what little the police knew about the two murders, with the additional information that, as all those in attendance already knew, both women had risen from the dead, and the revelation—greeted with a gasp—of the real fate of Abigail's corpse.

"Now I'm going to open the floor to questions and comments," he said when he was done, wincing inwardly at what he knew was to come.

Jennie Mahoney stood immediately. "Jagger?"

"Yes, Jennie?"

"Frankly I can tell by looking around that most of us are disturbed about your decision not to stake Abigail. Would you care to explain yourself?"

He took a deep breath. "When Abigail rose at the morgue, I was faced with a swift decision. She was a student, bright, sweet—raised by nuns. I chose not to end her existence."

"And what does Miss MacDonald say to that?" Jennie asked primly.

Fiona stood. "I was there," she said. "And I approved the decision."

"Really?" Jennie said, sounding doubtful. "I don't mean to find fault—"

"Then don't," Fiona said pleasantly.

Mateas Grenard stood up, and Jagger wondered what was coming next.

"I'm new to this community, so I don't know most of you yet," he said, addressing the room. "But the longer I'm here, the more amazed I am at how much a part of the city you are, not just as businesspeople, but in government and, of course—" he nodded toward Jagger "—in the police force. Which does make me wonder, Detective DeFarge, since you're in charge of the investigation, doesn't it concern you that you have to make a show of searching for a corpse you know doesn't exist when you should be searching for a murderer?"

"Of course. Obviously that's made my workload more difficult," Jagger said.

"Aren't you worried about bringing the city's suspicions down on us?" Grenard asked.

"I'm up to the challenge, I assure you. My top priority is finding the killer, not the corpse."

"What about Billy Harrington?" Jennie demanded.

"What about him?" Jagger asked.

"First, why isn't he here?"

"Because he's doing what I told him to do. He's staying in his room at the frat house and acting like a teenager who's depressed over losing a friend," Jagger said.

August Gaudin stood, clearing his throat apologetically. "Jagger, I believe that Jennie is hedging around something that must be said. We're suspicious. It's evident that Billy was very fond of this young woman. I believe that the natural question—question, not accusation—is whether the young man might have been fond enough of the young woman to want to make her his for eternity, whether she agreed or not."

The room fell silent, and Jagger was certain everyone was waiting for him to deny the possibility.

He didn't.

"We have certainly considered that theory," he said.

There was a murmur in the crowd.

"However..." Jagger lifted a hand and waited for the noise to die down. "However, in my position, I've learned to consider all the facts. Have we forgotten Tina

Lawrence already? Billy was at the frat house, with witnesses, when Tina was murdered."

"He could have moved quickly, could have left and returned before anyone noticed he was gone," Mateas Grenard said quietly.

"Yes, he could have," Jagger conceded. "But he has no history of frequenting strip clubs, and he did—does—feel a fondness for Abigail. It's doubtful that a man in love—human or vampire—would suddenly start spending time in a strip club. Additionally, as you all know, we found a witness who gave us a good description of a man who talked to Tina that night, though we have yet to find that man."

Jennie gasped indignantly. "Are you implying that he was a shapeshifter?"

Jagger spoke quickly and loudly before her words could sow dissension. "No, Jennie, I'm doing no such thing. I'm simply saying that all the evidence isn't in yet. And in fact, I expect help from this community that no one else can provide, because the rest of the world doesn't even know that we exist, much less what to look for. But I've also been a cop long enough to know that what we see is not always what it seems. Therefore, as we've all made a point of saying tonight, I'm not casting suspicion in any specific direction. We know the killer wasn't a human being, because both women rose. So yes, I'm saying the killer had to be either a vampire or a shapeshifter. An *individual* shapeshifter or vampire. And we *all* want that person apprehended—don't we, Jennie?"

Jennie opened her mouth, but she had to agree—she had just given a speech about doing exactly what he was asking—and after a moment of hesitation, she finally did.

Sean O'Casey suddenly stood.

"Sean?" Jagger said.

"I just want to add that peace is the most precious thing in the world. I come from a land that spent hundreds of years in battle. To this day we still fight prejudice—and the hatreds of the past. It's ugly. Innocents get hurt, and the good die with the bad. I pledge my support to you, Jagger. And so will everyone who's seeking the truth and wants to see this murderer caught."

Sean spoke softly, but the Old Country lilt in his voice commanded attention. When he finished, spontaneous applause broke out.

Beside him, Granny Caldwell stood. She was a tall woman, nearly as tall as Sean.

"This city of ours, it has magic. To this day it bears traces of both the shame and the beauty of the past, and life here is a mix of the old ways with the new. But we love our city and hold it dear in our hearts. We come from different places, and different histories run in our veins. I have prayed at the altar of my beliefs, and I'm here to say that I believe in the man who stands before us. The readings say he is a good man, a man who will seek the truth. The father of lies is at work among us now, and we need to learn to see through the forest of his deceptions. In your hearts, don't be angry. Be strong, and look for the truth and goodness that surround you."

She fell silent and looked around at the crowd, as if to emphasize her point.

"Thank you, as always, Granny Caldwell, for your support," Jagger said. He wanted to run over and kiss the old woman. She was as strong as an oak.

She nodded and pointed a finger at him. "There are many paths that lead to God. but the important thing to know is that God exists. And in this, as in so many things, He will have his say. I have seen things while in a trance, and I know that the day will come when the murderer is caught."

The room was eerily silent.

The killer is here among us, in this room, Jagger thought.

He could feel it. Feel the truth as if it were a palpable thing. He wished that he could see *who* with the same certainty, but he knew the killer was there, smiling, nodding, speaking to his neighbors, watching....

Laughing.

And maybe feeling the slightest hint of trepidation after Granny Caldwell's words.

It was time to end the assembly, he decided, but before he could speak, that option was taken away from him.

"Where is the young lady who's the newest addition to vampire society?" Mateas Grenard asked.

Jagger was surprised when David Du Lac rose from his chair to reply. "Why, she is here, of course. I am grooming her for her new role in life."

"How can we be sure that she will understand and obey the laws of our community?" August Gaudin asked quietly.

"Would you like to ask her that yourself?"

"Of course," Mateas Grenard said smoothly.

David looked at Jagger, who shrugged.

Fiona was still standing. She smiled and walked over to David, who took her arm. They went out together.

"What about this witness at the strip club?" a shapeshifter who was also a reporter called out. "Is she reliable?"

"I'm going on instinct here, but I believe she is," Jagger said. "What concerns me is that no one has admitted seeing the man she described."

"I hate to say it, but in the interest of being open-minded and catching the killer, that suggests a shapeshifter to me," shapeshifting cop Michael Shrine said. "The problem is, a shapeshifter can be anything or anyone, then choose never to appear in that guise again."

Jennie looked as if she was about to object when a sudden hush fell over the room, for the first time that night making it feel like the consecrated church it had once been.

David and Fiona were back, escorting Abigail, and the three of them were walking down what had once been an aisle toward the podium. Jagger backed away, staring at Abigail.

She had undergone a complete transformation. Her long blond hair was now short and curly and red, her blue eyes were hazel, and she was dressed in the kind of suit a new MBA graduate would wear to look for a job in a bank. With heels, she appeared taller. The overall look was both cute—and oddly sophisticated, half gamine and half urban sophisticate.

"Ladies and gentlemen, I'd like to introduce Annie Du Lac, my niece, who will now be living in New Orleans and working at the club," David said.

"Hello," Annie, nee Abigail, said to the crowd. Though she appeared to be a little bit overwhelmed, she had a beautiful smile, and despite the touch of sophistication, there was still something—naive and sweet about her.

Someone in the crowd suddenly stood.

Valentina.

"Annie, is it?" Valentina said. Jagger was surprised to realize that David Du Lac had been keeping his plan for Abigail a secret from everyone, even his hostess. "Annie, how do we know that we can trust you? You'll be working with me. How do I know that you won't look at my throat—and decide you're hungry?"

"Oh, there's absolutely no fear of that," Annie said. "David has been a wonderful teacher. I know how to find nourishment when I'm hungry."

"Right," Valentina snapped. "Because kids are always such models of self-control."

Fiona stepped up to the microphone. "David and I have complete faith in Annie. She will still need day-to-day help and guidance in negotiating our world, of course, and, Valentina, she'll be looking to you, especially, since you'll be working together. I have no fear whatsoever that Annie will be violent. On the contrary—I worry that her soft heart may be her undoing, if she sees her former friends mourning her death and feels tempted to reassure them."

"I have a question," Mateas Grenard said.

"Yes?" Fiona asked.

"Abigail—Annie, did Billy Harrington kill you?" he asked bluntly.

Annie stepped to the microphone. "No. He most certainly did not."

"How do you know that?" Valentina demanded. "Did you see your killer?"

"No, I didn't," Annie admitted.

"Then how do you *know?*" Jennie Mahoney demanded.

"Because I know Billy," Annie said. "I know in my heart." She put a hand on her chest. "And the heart is more than an organ. It's a part of the soul, and I have a soul, and I know Billy does, too."

"You can't know any such thing," Mateas said with a sniff.

Fiona took back the microphone. "I think we should leave the solution of these murders to the police and move on to the purpose of this meeting, which is that every one of us needs to work, and work hard, to keep the peace. My parents died for the peace we've enjoyed for so many years. Why do you think they did that? Because they believed. They knew in their hearts that peace could exist. And now it's up to all of you to keep the peace, and I know you'll do it. My sisters and I learned well from our parents. They taught us about strength, about wisdom and mercy and most of all, they taught us about acceptance. And no, I'm not talking about being blind or naive and just ignoring problems and differences. I'm talking about working together. About relying on instinct, the instinct that lets us distinguish between good and evil—even in one of our own—and believe love. Trust me. My sisters and I *will* keep the peace."

Caitlin and Shauna stood, walked to the podium, joined Fiona.

The three of them joined hands.

"There *will* be peace," Fiona announced. "Prejudice and intolerance killed our parents, and we're not going to let those attitudes win. We can promise you two things. The killer will be found. And the peace will not be broken. As Granny Caldwell said, our city is magic. And we intend to keep it that way."

Chapter 11

Jagger was exhausted. He'd joined David after the meeting, staying to speak with those who wanted a word, and he felt disheartened.

One of the werewolves was certain the killer was the vampire down the street.

A vampire was certain it was his shapeshifter hairdresser.

He stayed, he listened, he carefully noted every complaint and tried each time to remind the accuser not to cast suspicion unless they had evidence. Because of course none of the accusers had anything approaching proof.

Of course, he realized he had his own suspicions. While he believed in Billy Harrington, the nagging knowledge that Billy did have a motive in the second slaying kept him in the picture as a suspect.

Mateas Grenard was a newcomer and seemed to have a hidden agenda.

And then…any shapeshifter out there.

It was nearly light when he made his way to the MacDonald house, and he realized he was so tired he could barely make the shift into the mist that would allow him to enter unnoticed.

He slipped into Fiona's bedroom and discovered that he was not the only one who was exhausted.

She was sound asleep, lying on one side of the bed, as if she'd been waiting for him but been unable to stay awake until he arrived.

He watched her sleep. Not even Abigail, as young and innocent as she was, had ever looked so beautiful, he thought. Fiona's hair was splayed out in a glorious golden halo around her perfect face. Her lips were slightly parted, moist, and so tempting that he was drawn to touch them with his own.

But he didn't.

He didn't want to disturb her.

She was lying on her side, her arms around a pillow, partially covered by the drape of the sheet, the beauty of one long leg bared to his view.

He sat carefully on the side of the bed and shed his shoes and socks, jacket, gun and holster, then stood to discard the rest of his clothing. He lay quietly down beside her but kept his distance, propped on his elbow to watch her.

Just to watch her.

He was hopelessly infatuated, he realized.

No, this was far more than infatuation.

He took pleasure in watching her sleep, in watching her breathe.

A sudden chill shook him.

She was blonde, with immense blue eyes. She was beyond beautiful.

She was the exact type the killer seemed to like.

He'd been so busy debating the possibility of vampire vs. shapeshifter that he'd somehow managed to miss making that basic connection until now.

He moved closer to her, taking her gently into his arms. She stirred, and a murmur escaped her, but she didn't waken, though she seemed to know, in the depths of sleep, that he was there.

And she was content to be in his arms.

He suddenly knew that if she was ever threatened, he would not be a cop. He wouldn't even be a vampire. He would be a man who would defend her in any way he could, with his very last ounce of strength and being. He would die a thousand times for her, or follow her into eternity, if that was where she chose to lead.

Holding her close, he felt the beat of her heart.

He was afraid, and he was renewed.

And he knew he would move heaven and hell to end the evil that had entered their world.

Fiona awoke slowly, aware that she wasn't alone, and basking in the comfort of being exactly where she was, in the comfort of her bed.

And in the sheer heaven of Jagger's arms.

She had thought that he would come. She had waited.

But the day had been too long, and sleep had won out over her determination to stay awake.

She felt his arms tighten around her, and she opened her eyes slowly to find that he was watching her. She smiled slowly.

"You certainly make me hope I don't snore," she said.

He laughed. "If you snored, I'm sure the sound would be pure music."

She felt a surge of vitality fill her, and she rolled, casting off the covers, to straddle him. "Tell me it's still early," she whispered.

Without answering, he slid his hands up her torso. He cradled her nape, drawing her down to him, and their lips met in a liquid kiss. Before she knew it, he had shifted just slightly, arched, lifted her, and brought her slowly back down over his erection, drawing her closer, filling her completely and igniting a wild and abandoned desire in her.

His whisper touched her ear. "I'm not sure if it's early or late, so…"

Then he moved.

And she moved.

And the world moved with them.

In minutes, the earth itself seemed to explode, and she fell against him, awed and dazzled, and wondering how she had lived without this, without the sound of his voice, without him so solidly in her world.

Her sheets felt softer, the sun shone brighter, than ever before.…

He kissed her quickly and rose.

"Another day, and another reason to work quickly," he said huskily, then started toward the bathroom.

"Oh, no! I get the shower first…or too," she said, racing after him.

It was a mistake—or would have been, if she'd had any interest in getting an early start on the day.

She loved to shower.

She loved it so much more when he was there.

They made love again, slick with soap, luxuriating in the suds and water and steam.

But as he held her, steam rising around them like a cocoon, the spell was broken by a pounding on the door to the bedroom.

Fiona swore softly.

"It's Caitlin, I'm sure of it, and she doesn't accept the fact that we're together," Fiona told him, angry. Then she left Jagger in the bathroom and, wrapped in her towel, hurried to open her bedroom door.

It wasn't Caitlin. It was Shauna.

Her face was white, her expression tense.

"It's on the news. There's been another murder."

Once again, the corpse had been found in a cemetery just outside the French Quarter, no ID anywhere to be found.

The dead woman was wearing a long white nightgown, blond hair streaming around her face. Her flesh was cold, her skin as white as snow.

She was lying on a tomb in the middle of a family vault—the Taussant vault, this time. Her hands were folded over her chest.

She looked like an angel.

Jagger managed to get his team out of the vault long enough to find the telltale pricks, so small that not even Craig Dewey would notice. This time the killer had gone for the throat.

The jugular vein.

The kill had probably been quick; that might have been the only mercy.

He was standing there, staring at the corpse, when

Dewey walked in. The M.E. was silent for a minute, staring at the corpse.

"Another angel," he said softly.

"Well, I'm not sure Tina Lawrence was an angel," Jagger said, shaking his head. "And we don't know anything about this woman yet," he added wearily. "She could be a nun or the biggest bitch in the city, for all we know."

"I haven't touched her yet, but I can tell you the cause of death is going to be the same as the other two," Dewey said. "I'll get this one straight into autopsy."

Jagger nodded, feeling ill. Another death. It was on his head. He should have caught the killer by now.

"Thanks, Dewey," he said. "The sooner we check her prints, compare dental records, the sooner we'll know who she is."

"I'll get right on it," Dewey said. "I won't leave her for a minute."

"Think you can give me a time of death?" Jagger asked.

"Sure."

The girl was dead, but even so, Jagger turned away while the medical examiner opened her eyes, checked her limbs, gave the body a cursory examination and checked the corpse's temperature.

"She hasn't been dead long. I'd say she was killed around five this morning. Just before light," Dewey told him. "I think someone is really trying to make this vampire thing look real."

"So it seems," Jagger said. "Thanks, Dewey."

"I'll be opening her up in about two hours, if you want to meet me at the morgue."

"Thanks."

Jagger walked outside.

He'd searched the tomb and the cordoned-off area around it. The killer hadn't left behind a single clue.

He looked across the cemetery. Celia Larson and her crew were coming to comb the cemetery for footprints, for any small piece of trace evidence the killer might have left behind.

He already knew they weren't going to find anything.

"DeFarge, I would have thought you'd have put a stop to this by now," she said. "You know, the city will rise up in a panic soon. Maybe they already are."

"Thank you, Celia. I'm glad to be aware of your thoughts," he said flatly. He started to walk by her, but then returned.

"It would be helpful if I were getting more from my technical support team," he said.

Her eyes narrowed. "We've gone over everything with a magnifying glass," she snapped.

"No, you haven't."

"The killer hasn't left any clues! Not so much as a drop of blood, nothing with DNA, nothing anywhere! Not a single victim scratched her assailant or—"

"Celia, there *is* a clue."

"What?"

"The nightgowns."

She looked at him blankly.

"Celia, they've all been wearing white nightgowns, different, but basically the same. Or did you think they all went to bed in white nightgowns? Where's my report on the gowns?"

She turned away, her face red. "They were killed at night. We didn't think—"

"I need to know where those nightgowns were purchased. Can you get on that?"

"You should have asked before," she pointed out.

She was right. He should have.

He didn't reply but headed over to the cemetery gates. The press was gathering outside. He saw Gina, and gave her a nod, assuring her that he was coming out to speak.

First, though, he walked over to where Tony was talking with the "City of the Dead" tour guide who'd found the body. The man was about fifty, dressed in an official uniform and obviously shaken.

"I…I suppose I shouldn't have been so shocked. Not after the other two murders," the man was saying to Tony.

Tony saw Jagger and interrupted the guide to say, "Jagger, this is Arnie Offenbach. He found the corpse. He had five people in his tour group, but when he saw the open doorway to the tomb, he made them wait while he went to check. The door is solid brass, so he knew it hadn't just blown open."

"Mr. Offenbach, thank you for calling us in so quickly. And thank you for keeping the tourists away," Jagger said, feeling unutterably weary.

Offenbach nodded.

"Did you see anyone in the cemetery?" Jagger asked.

Offenbach shook his head. "No, another group was coming in, but they were behind me."

"Where is your group now?" Jagger asked.

Offenbach turned and pointed. There were two men—retirees, from the look of them, one white-haired, the other balding. Two older women, probably their wives, were sticking close to them. The heavier of the two women had seated herself on the low stone wall around another family vault. She was fanning herself vigorously with a guidebook. The fifth member of the party looked to be around twenty-five, and was carrying a camera and a notepad.

"Thank you, Mr. Offenbach," Jagger said, and walked over to join the tour group. He introduced himself, and met the Winstons and the Smiths from Calgary, Canada, and Sophie Preston, from New York City.

"Did any of you notice anyone in the cemetery when you got here, or maybe somebody leaving?" he asked.

"The officers already asked us that," Mr. Winston said. "I'm sorry, I didn't see anyone."

His wife shook her head. The Smiths solemnly did the same.

"I didn't see anyone in the cemetery," Sophie Preston said. "But there was a man walking down the sidewalk, heading toward Canal, when we arrived."

"Can you describe him for me?" Jagger asked.

She was thoughtful. "He was wearing a short-sleeved, tailored blue shirt and blue jeans. Dark hair. He was walking fast, like he was hurrying, and he was good-looking, I'd say thirty-five or forty."

"Muscular?"

"Um, tall. Yes, broad-shoulders, and…yes, I'd say he was muscular," she said.

The description could fit half the men in the city.

It certainly fit Mateas Grenard.

"Could you possibly come to the station and work with a sketch artist for me?" he asked her. "I realize that we're asking for your time, and that it will be an inconvenience, but we need your help."

"Of course, I'm more than happy to help," she assured him.

"Come to think of it, I noticed him, too. And she's right. He did seem to be in a hurry," Mr. Winston said.

"Perhaps you could help with the sketch," Jagger said.

"I'm willing, yes, sir, I'm willing, but I didn't see his face. All I can say is that he was tall, and that he had dark hair. Honest to God, sir, I'd love to help you, but all I can say is tall and dark haired."

Fiona was with her sisters in the shop when more news started to flow in about the most recent murder.

Shauna was their Internet expert, and she had been Web surfing all morning, looking for information.

"No ID yet," she told her sisters. "Another blonde. Like us." She grimaced. "I wonder if the brunettes in the city are feeling safe?"

Fiona felt sick.

Of course every paranormal who'd stopped by that morning suspected a vampire. And that made her, as the vampires' Keeper, at fault. She had to find out what was happening. She had to stop this. It wasn't that she didn't have faith in Jagger, it was just that…

She suddenly realized that both of her sisters were staring at her. She was the oldest and the vampires' Keeper. She was supposed to have the answers.

As her parents had always had all the answers.

"If anyone asks for me, I'm heading back to the frat house to talk to Billy," she said.

Just as she grabbed her purse and started for the door, the little bells above it began to ring.

They had a customer.

"Thank God, child," Granny Caldwell said as she spotted Fiona and hurried over. "Thank God you're here."

"What is it?" Fiona asked, tempted to help the old woman over to a chair at one of the tea tables by the counter.

But Granny Caldwell was strong and proud—and she didn't like being helped. She had told them all often enough that when she was ready for help, she would certainly ask for it.

"I just had to see you, Fiona. All of you, really," Granny Caldwell said.

"I just came from Papa Joe's House of Voodoo—you know, down toward the CBD?"

They all knew Papa Joe. He was as beloved as Granny Caldwell, and he was as old as she was, too. He catered to the people who lived on the other side of Canal Street, near the Central Business District.

"Papa Joe is a brilliant man," Fiona said.

"Yes, that he is," Granny said. "Well, he put together a mojo sack, and he went into a trance, and he saw many of his ancestors there."

"And what did his ancestors tell him, Granny?" Fiona asked, as her sisters came closer to listen.

"They told him that we all have to keep thinking beyond what we see. The day can be beautiful—and then a storm strikes by night. He wants to be sure that you know this, Fiona. We are not of the underworld, we are among this world, Papa Joe and I, and you three straddle the two. Papa Joe says that he prays you will pay him heed. His ancestors have told him that you must look beyond the gloss of the picture to the substance beneath. He prays that you will believe in faith—that all paths lead to God—and that you will listen to an old man who knows that the world is not black and white, but many shades of gray."

Fiona gave the old woman a warm hug. "I will always pay heed to you and Papa Joe, as will my sisters. You are goodness made flesh, and we listen to goodness, no matter how it comes to us."

"Of course," Caitlin echoed passionately.

"You bet," Shauna assured the old woman.

"Now you must go," Granny Caldwell told Fiona. "You must listen, and you must look beneath. You must also remember that God sees the soul in all living things, though it is invisible to us. And one more thing. Remember that you know what you must do."

Fiona nodded. Because suddenly she *did* know what she had to do.

"There is nothing that fills me with greater sadness than to have to tell you that yes, we have another victim," Jagger said, meeting with the press that had gathered at the cemetery gates. "I can only beg the public again for help, and assure everyone that we will not rest until the killer is caught."

"There isn't anything you can tell us? No profile of the type of guy we should be looking out for?" a reporter called from the back of the pack.

"We have been in contact with profilers at the FBI," Jagger assured him.

"So what does the Blood Sucker profile look like?" another reporter called out.

"He wants to be a vampire," Jagger said, groaning inwardly at the nickname the press had given the killer. "And, most importantly, he wants the world to think he really is a vampire—to believe that he actually feeds on blood."

He had heard that just minutes before the press briefing, in a call from Jarrett Gilfoy, a senior agent at Quantico.

"How exactly are the victims killed?" Gina asked, thrusting a microphone toward him.

She had her job, he thought.

He had his.

And there was no way to avoid her questions or the answers they required.

"First, Gina—and all of you—right now this is an active investigation, and we all know that it's imperative that we catch the killer as quickly as possible. It would only encourage copycats if we were to tell you everything we know about the killer's methods."

Someone else called out a question about rape.

"No, none of the victims has been sexually molested," Jagger said.

"Why would a killer want people to think he's a vampire?" a reporter from an overseas news station asked next.

"Perhaps he wants the power credited to vampires," Jagger suggested. "That's really all I can give you at this minute."

"Apparently not!" a woman from a local radio station called shrilly. "The police haven't done a thing—and this is the third murder."

"I can only repeat that the police force is working overtime, because all of us are committed to finding the killer. As I've said before, we need your help and that of the public. We will continue combing the area for witnesses, and we need any clue, any sighting, *anything*, you can give us. What we don't need are crank calls, because every second of manpower is necessary if we're going to find this killer before he strikes again."

"What about the man at the strip club before the first murder?" a woman in the back called out.

Jagger craned his neck, but he couldn't see who had spoken. "I'm afraid we've had no reports from anyone who might have seen him," Jagger said. "We *are* still looking, however."

"Is it possible that there are two killers?" someone else asked.

"Possible—but I sincerely doubt it," Jagger said.

He noticed Tony watching him from the edge of the crowd, looking irritated by the tone of the continuing questions.

But one thing Jagger had learned over the years was to keep his temper firmly in check and answer every question as calmly as he possibly could.

Finally he excused himself, and saw Tony snap to attention and run to get the car. Sophie Preston had already been taken to the police station to start working with a sketch artist.

When Jagger arrived at the station he discovered that they had already come up with a picture of the man she had seen outside the cemetery.

Mateas Grenard.

Chapter 12

Fiona loved going to church. She loved ritual and ceremony, and deeply believed in one God, though she also believed that there were indeed many paths that led to Him.

Her beliefs had never been put to a test up to this point, but the time had come.

She didn't head toward the cathedral on Jackson Square. Although it was a beautiful church and a place of worship despite its location in one of the city's most popular tourist destinations, she didn't want to be seen on her mission, and there were always too many people there.

Instead she headed across Frenchman Street, toward the small church she had attended with her parents—and last visited after her parents had died.

Their funeral services had been performed there.

As she walked in, she wondered if she was crazy.

No, this would be fine, she told herself. She would see Father Maybury. He'd been close to her parents, and he must have known…something.

And if he wasn't there, then she hoped to manage a few moments alone so she could fill up several vials of holy water without being stopped.

Oh, God, what she wanted to do probably *was* crazy. Admittedly, she wasn't sure it would work, so she might be risking harm to an innocent, but something in her somehow knew that holy water could be the key.

Jagger knew how to deal with vampires. A stiletto-style stake, straight to the heart.

But she didn't want to start indiscriminately killing vampires.

She simply wanted to know the truth.

When she arrived, she found that the church was quiet. The lowering sun was shining gently through the gorgeous stained-glass windows portraying various saints and key events in the history of the Church.

She walked down the aisle, heading toward the center of the room, where a large stone vessel stood, holding the blessed water.

So far, so good. She was safe, and she was alone.

But as she neared the holy water, she noticed a young priest come in from the apse. He crossed himself and genuflected as he faced the altar, then walked up to her, his smile welcoming. He appeared to be about thirty-five, a handsome man with dark hair and dark eyes. His demeanor was friendly, easy—it seemed to say that he was comfortable in his beliefs and comfortable in himself—and calming.

Which was good—she had begun to feel a sense of panic stealing over her. She'd wanted to get quickly in and out of the church, and if not, at least a visit with a man who might have understood…something.

Where was Father Maybury?

"Hello, and welcome," the young priest said to her. "Can I help you? You appear to be at a loss."

"I'm sorry. Is Father Maybury here?"

"I'm afraid that I'm the one who is sorry. Father Maybury died last fall," he told her.

She must have appeared stricken, she realized.

"May I get you some water? Would you like to sit down?" he asked.

"No, I just needed to see him," she said quietly. "And—well, obviously, I can't."

"Perhaps I can help you," he told her.

"I'm afraid it's an unusual problem," she said.

"Try me," he suggested.

"Father Maybury was…he was a personal friend," she explained. "He was close with my parents before their deaths."

"I see. I am so sorry. I'm Father DiCarlo, by the way."

"It's a pleasure, Father," she said, shaking his hand. He was watching her with eyes that seemed at ease, knowing eyes. She wasn't sure if she felt comforted or wary.

"You're Fiona MacDonald," he said.

She started, almost yanking her hand from his.

"I haven't been here since my parents died," she said. "And I don't believe you were here then."

"No, I wasn't. But Father Maybury was my mentor," he said.

She nodded, not sure what to say.

"It seems that you have questions," he said very quietly.

Fiona noticed that an elderly woman had entered the church. She knelt down at one of the back pews and was quickly immersed in prayer.

"Well…" Fiona murmured uncomfortably, looking in the direction of the newcomer.

He smiled. "That's Mrs. Sienna. She's quite deaf. But we can talk elsewhere, if you prefer."

She flushed. "Father, you do believe in good and in evil, don't you?"

"I am a priest," he said, smiling, his expression friendly and open.

"Those of good heart, no matter what their circumstance, are always welcome in church, isn't that right, Father?"

"Absolutely. All are welcome in God's house," he said. "But you know that."

I need to take several vials of holy water. Is that all right with you?

She just couldn't manage to spit out such words.

"I'm getting the feeling that you might want to be alone in God's house," he said. "You don't know me, and you don't trust me."

"Oh, no, I don't mistrust you," she said.

Though of course she did, she realized. There was no guarantee that everyone who came into God's house was good. History had proven that evil men were perfectly capable of using religion as a cover for their misdeeds.

He laughed, and she had the uneasy feeling that he was reading her mind.

But he was definitely human. She would have known, would have sensed it, if he belonged in the underworld.

"I think I'll go and say a word to Mrs. Sienna," he said. "Please, say whatever prayers you intended, in your own way."

"Thank you."

She smiled awkwardly at him and started to turn away.

"Fiona MacDonald," he said softly.

"Yes, Father?"

"Sometimes," he said, "it seems that no goodness exists in the world at all. We question why terrible things happen. And none of us has the answers. Then again, sometimes, when we think we're alone, we realize that we're not, and we're filled with tremendous strength when we suddenly discover the help that can come from opening ourselves to a greater power. I believe that we are given only the tasks we can manage—and that, if we ask, we will receive the help of good to vanquish evil. I'll leave you now, so you may do what you must. The city needs you, and I know you'll rise to whatever task is asked of you. Goodness is in the heart, and in the soul, and those who are evil are afraid of all that is good. Belief, not just in God but in one's self, can be one of the most powerful weapons known to man. Even the angels learned the importance of faith and belief."

She stared at him, a tremor rippling through her.

He knew. He would never admit that he knew, but he did. He was a man of faith, and his faith led to the belief that things existed that the eyes couldn't always see.

"Thank you," she whispered.

"Bless you, my child," he said softly, and turned away.

He knew, she was sure, that she had come for holy

water. Was he telling her that it would work for the project that she had in mind?

"Thank you," she told him again.

"I'm always here," he assured her.

Somehow those words managed to impart some of his confidence to her. She had been afraid, she realized. She had never really been challenged—until now, when she was being challenged in so many ways. But now she realized that she could indeed take her place in the world, just as he would take his and be there for her.

As he smiled and moved away to speak with the elderly woman at the back of the church, she hurried forward with her vials to collect holy water.

"I think I've seen this guy," Tony Miro said, tapping a copy of the picture of a man's face, which had been copied and passed around. "Maybe in the market… maybe the Square. Somewhere."

Jagger, with the support of his chief and other key members of the task force, had decided against handing the likeness out to the media just yet. Witnesses had seen Grenard in the area where the latest body had been found, possibly leaving the cemetery, but there was no proof that the man had actually been *in* the cemetery, or that, if he had, he was guilty of murder.

Of course, Jagger, along with a few other members of the force, knew there was the best reason in the world that Mateas Grenard might have been guilty of behaving like a vampire.

Jagger wanted to find Grenard himself. If he *was* guilty, Grenard would never be willing to go to trial. If someone else attempted to arrest Grenard, they might find himself with at least one dead police officer, along with the three dead women.

"Listen," Jagger told Tony, "I'd like to start walking through the tourist sections, see if I spot him. I need you to go talk to Celia Lawson."

Tony frowned at him. "Hey, two of us walking the streets would be better."

Jagger shook his head. "I want you to hound Celia until we find out where those white nightgowns were bought. And then I want you to take a trip back over to the college and check on everything there, find out if anyone has remembered anything about the night Abigail was killed. When you're done there, we'll meet back at that strip club—Barely, Barely, Barely. What I'm worried about is panic in the streets, so be careful when you're questioning people. Make sure it's clear that all we're looking for are witnesses. Oh, and if you find anyone resembling the sketch, call me immediately. Don't go after the man alone. I told everyone that when we handed out the sketch, and I mean it."

"All right. But don't run around thinking you have to protect me, Jagger. I'm a good cop," Tony told him.

"I never thought you were anything but," Jagger said.

Tony studied him, nodded and offered a tight smile. "I'm on it, then."

Jagger nodded. "I'm going to check in on the autopsy of the newest victim, and then I'll hit the streets."

It was the truth.

Almost.

He meant to be at the autopsy.

And he would be out on the streets.

Because he intended to find Mateas Grenard.

* * *

"It's Fiona. I need to talk to you," Fiona said, as soon as Billy answered his phone.

"I'm in class. Out in an hour," he said in return, his voice low.

"All right. Where?"

"Wait a minute! Is this about Abigail? She's all right, isn't she?" he asked anxiously.

She was officially dead, and now she was a vampire. If "all right" could be defined in such a way, then Abigail was all right.

"There's nothing wrong with Abigail. I just need to speak with you. I'm hoping you can help me, that's all," she said.

"Where?"

"The cemetery where they found the first body," Fiona said.

"Fiona, if there were any clues there that Jagger DeFarge missed, we won't find them," Billy said solemnly.

So innocent. But they had to look past what they saw on the surface. Or did they? Maybe everything was all exactly what it seemed. A vampire was committing the murders. Perhaps that vampire appeared to be honest and aboveboard, and *that* was the surface she needed to see past. There was still good reason to believe Billy was guilty, and that good reason even had a name: Abigail.

"Please, this is getting worse by the day. I'm afraid we'll have riots in the streets soon. And we all know that no matter how good a detective Jagger may be, we're not looking for a normal murderer, so normal police procedures don't apply," Fiona stressed.

"You *are* the Keeper," he said softly. "If you tell me to be somewhere, I'll be there."

They'd taken the dead girl's prints but so far there was no match on record.

She had died in the same manner as the others: exsanguination, though the manner was eluding everyone—except Jagger.

Eventually, of course, the marks would be found. But Jagger wasn't really afraid that the city would instantly start believing in vampires. Instead they would start looking even more closely at the cults and the self-proclaimed vampires.

That day, feeling dread and pain unlike anything he had experienced in a very long time, Jagger watched while the beautiful blonde victim was autopsied on the sterile table in the sterile room, the scent of chemicals rising around them, barely hiding the natural release of body gases.

But none of those scents meant anything to him. Nor did it particularly bother him to watch the M.E. make the Y cut on the body, or listen to him drone on into the overhead voice recorder as he listed facts and figures on the healthy young organs, pristine liver—she hadn't been a drinker—clean lungs—she hadn't been a smoker—and perfect heart. Life had stretched ahead of her. She shouldn't have been dead. She should have been joining friends for coffee after work, or attending classes, meeting a lover...*living*. Somehow, this girl seemed to epitomize the tragedy and the loss present whenever life was stolen from one so young. He knew that professionally he should be keeping his emotions in check. Still, this hurt, almost as much as if he had known her. Or maybe she reminded him of Fiona, and that was why he felt the pain of her death more deeply.

He waited until Craig Dewey had finished, leaving his assistant to sew up the beautiful young woman who would never have a husband or children, never laugh or love again.

Craig shook his head. He had nothing new to offer.

Jagger knew that she was still a mystery woman, and that somewhere, a mother, father, lover, brother or friend was missing her, praying for her safe return.

Not knowing yet that she would never come home.

By day, New Orleans' cities of the dead were unusual places. They were sites of strange and twisted beauty, filled with unique vaults and monuments, their walls often lined with "oven" style graves. Over the years, many tombs had collapsed, and on occasion neglect had interrupted the normal process of natural cremation in "a year and a day," leaving bleached pieces of bone lying atop crumbling masonry.

Not these days, of course. This was the modern world. Care was taken so that the living would not be offended by the dead.

And still...when the day came to an end, when the heat of the sun died away and the great orb began to fall toward the western horizon, the cemeteries were transformed by shadows from something spiritual into— something frightening.

Certainly some of the danger came from the living— those who prowled behind closed gates in to deal drugs—and worse.

Some originated in the mind, because in the darkness and the mist that came when rain and heat collided, monsters rose from the depths of the subconscious to haunt the night.

And some monsters were real.

Fiona arrived just before the gates were closed, and she knew where to hide when the guides urged the last of the day's visitors to leave.

She stood near the Grigsby tomb, watching as twilight came. At first the light was gentle and beautiful. Soft pink rays falling on the serene faces of angels, wrenching the heart as the light darkened to mauve over a monument for a child, an infant sleeping peacefully by a lamb. Then the shadows came in earnest, transforming the mausoleums stretched out in awkward rows, here a grand vault from the eighteenth century, there a more modern mausoleum with touches of bronze. Some had broken windows, as if the dead had sought a way out, and some were still whole, with stained or etched glass windows, opaque, so no one could look in, and—more importantly—no one could look out.

As she was watching the light and the colors fade, she heard someone nearby. It was just a touch against stone, a whisper of movement in the air.

"Billy?" she said quietly, but no one responded. She decided she must have imagined it, so on edge that she was hearing things.

She slipped around the Grigsby tomb and hurried silently along a path that led toward a monument to the Italian workers in the city. She skirted the rusty ironwork fence and paused behind the monument, listening.

Nothing.

She checked her watch, certain that Billy was due any minute. Perhaps the noise *had* been Billy.

Perhaps he hadn't heard her call his name.

But then she heard something again, and this time it was like the rush of giant wings.

She headed for a grand marble mausoleum owned by a family named Tricliere. She saw that the door—which should have been tightly closed—was open, and she held very still, listening.

The sound of wings slicing the air came again.

Nearer.

She slipped past the slightly open gate in the rusting fence surrounding the small stone building, then into the mausoleum itself, steeling herself to see a corpse lying on a stone coffin in the center of the room.

There was no corpse. No newly deceased victim lying bloodless and still. The vault was old, probably one of the earliest in the cemetery. The mortar used to seal the vaults in the walls had long since crumbled away, and there were gaping dark holes where the bodies of the deceased had lain, and might lie again.

But now, in the darkness, she felt surrounded by the scent of the damp earth. Not death, just the smell of the earth itself, and the dust of the ages. And it *was* dark. Not a silent or complete darkness, for she could distantly hear the street sounds, unintelligible messages from the world of the living, and a tiny trickle of gray light seeped in through the broken, barred window at the rear of the vault.

Gray dust motes fell in gray air.

She heard the wings again, flapping just outside the mausoleum.

She didn't speak.

She slid into a broken vault, lying on the ash and bone shards of the last Triclieres to be buried there.

And then, just as she pressed herself more tightly

against the wall, her hand falling on a broken skull, she heard a sound, and she winced.

The gate.

Creaking farther open.

And then she knew.

It had been a trap.

The city had changed so much over the decades, and yet in so many ways it had stayed the same.

Street names and numbers, old houses, awkwardly slanted second-story balconies, filigree and decoration… these were the same as they had always been. Modern storefronts punctuated rows of houses that, by night, looked no different from when they had been built, nearly two hundred years before.

Jagger hardly even noticed all that history as he walked quiet streets where frightened residents had holed up for the night, afraid of a killer who'd already claimed three victims. It had been easy for most residents to feel safe when the first victim had turned out to be a prostitute, but Abigail's death had ruined that illusion of safety. Still, he was certain that plenty of people were feeling safe for different reasons—they weren't female, for one. Or they weren't young. Or blonde.

Some might even have been happy, perhaps for the first time, not to be considered beautiful.

Still, most of the residents of the city were frightened. The most common theory was that some psycho who thought he was a vampire was on a killing spree, so what if he decided that he just desperately needed some blood? He might strike anyone then.

Even Bourbon Street was quiet—though far from shut down.

Walking along, Jagger tried calling Fiona's cell phone for the third time that night.

Once again, it went straight to voice mail.

He headed down toward Esplanade and David Du Lac's club, Underworld.

Walking the streets had done nothing. He had not seen Mateas Grenard, Billy—or any other vampires, who might have fallen under suspicion simply by being out and about. The only vampires he saw at all were those on the force, who were searching as diligently for the truth as he was himself.

Calling the morgue—where there was still no word on an identity for their latest victim—also brought him nothing but frustration. Tests for toxins, for semen, for fibers on the body, threads in the hair—had all revealed nothing of any use.

He was glad, at least, that he hadn't needed to worry about *being* at the morgue.

Sinner or saint, the latest victim was really, truly dead, not *undead*, thanks to the fact that all her organs—particularly the heart—had been removed in the course of the autopsy.

He was about to head toward the shop to talk to Fiona's sisters when his phone rang.

It was Tony Miro.

"I'm having trouble with the nightgowns. Celia told me that they're a cotton polyester blend—available at major department stores all around the parish and beyond. Even some of the boutiques carry them. I realized I couldn't cover the city by myself, so I have some of the men questioning sales people, too. It's like finding a needle in a haystack. Just at the mall across from Harrah's, they've sold twenty similar gowns in the last week, eighteen through credit card sales, and two for cash. Lord, Jagger, we don't even know how long ago the murderer bought them. He could have been planning ahead for these killings for months."

"I know, Tony, but you and the guys need to stick with it. It's all we've got, and those officers have to be on the streets no matter what."

After the call, Jagger turned and headed toward the sisters' shop, but it was closed. He wasn't thrilled about heading to the house to talk to Caitlin and Shauna, but he had no choice. He could still see the beautiful blonde woman on the autopsy table, and he was growing edgier by the minute, even as he tried to tell himself that Fiona was a Keeper—that she had the power to keep herself safe.

The power to change.

The house was just down the street from the shop, but even as he started in that direction, his phone rang.

He was expecting Tony again.

But his hello was greeted with a second's silence.

"Hello?" he said again impatiently, and checked the caller ID.

The number was listed as "Unknown."

"Who is this?" he demanded.

"Good evening. Such impatience, Detective." The voice was hoarse and raspy, making it impossible for him to tell whether his caller was male or female. Someone was playing him.

And doing it well.

"May I help you?" he demanded.

"I was just wondering if you had noticed…how blonde and beautiful they are. I read the papers, and they're all blonde and beautiful."

"We're aware of that fact," he said, turning back toward Bourbon Street, searching for another officer—or anyone—whose phone he could nab and call in to the station to get a trace put on his phone.

But the caller was smart and knew what he was doing.

"Don't bother trying to trace this call, by the way. We won't be talking long enough. Just remember...blonde, beautiful—and dead. Just like Miss Fiona MacDonald may be at this very moment. Just as she soon *will* be, I promise."

Jagger fought desperately to keep from throwing the phone away in denial, to keep from screaming at the speaker.

He didn't know if he had a quack on the phone—or the killer. If it was the killer, then he was talking either to a vampire or a shapeshifter. But Fiona was a Keeper. She had power...if she got the chance to use it.

If she didn't...

She was as vulnerable as any other beautiful young woman.

And if she trusted the killer, she wouldn't think to use her power until it was too late.

"Do you know something about the killings?" he asked, keeping his voice as low as possible.

He'd reached Bourbon Street and searched the crowd, knowing that a mounted patrolman should be within quick reach. All he needed was time, a minute, seconds...

Sean O'Casey, uniformed and on foot, was standing on the corner across the street. Jagger waved him over, and Sean instantly sprinted across the street.

The caller was chuckling softly.

Jagger covered the mouthpiece of his cell and silently mouthed the words, "Get a trace on my phone."

O'Casey nodded.

"Look, we've asked the public for help on these killings," Jagger said conversationally. "If you're willing to help us, if you know something, we'll be grateful for anything you can give us."

From the corner of his eye, Jagger could see that Sean was already on his phone, calling the station, asking them for a satellite trace.

"Oh, Detective, please. I can almost hear her screaming now." Then the chuckling started again, and before Jagger could respond, the phone went dead.

Chapter 13

The old rusty iron gates were impossible to open, no matter how slowly and stealthily, without squealing.

The noise was like nails—talons!—against a black board.

Fiona held her position, praying she was hidden in the darkness, planning her next move and praying it would work.

She was certain the killer had found her, had known exactly where she would be and then had driven her into this dead end.

Because the killer was Billy?

She swallowed hard, waiting.

She was startled to hear shouting from out near the street. Someone calling her name.

The voice was far away, but thunderous.

The squeaking of the gate stopped.

"Fiona?" A different voice, closer, the tone quizzical. She must have made a noise, because she heard the gate open noisily, and then the door swung wide.

"Fiona?"

It was Billy.

He homed in on her position, hidden in the vault, and came closer.

She was ready. She tossed the holy water into his face.…

"What the hell did you do that for?" Billy demanded, wiping his face and obviously completely puzzled. "It's me—Billy. Hey, I just heard Jagger out there. What's going on?"

She stared at him from her hiding place, still hidden in darkness, incredulous that he hadn't screamed in pain, hadn't blistered hideously or turned to ash.

"Billy, did you see anyone out there?" she asked.

"No—I didn't even know you were in here—until I heard the gate creaking a minute ago. I was over by the Grigsby mausoleum, waiting for you."

"Fiona!"

Jagger's voice was closer, and he sounded frantic.

"We're in here, Jagger!" Billy called, stepping out of the tomb.

The next thing Fiona knew, Jagger, as impressive as any action hero in the movies, was suddenly slamming open the door to the tomb. "Fiona!"

"I'm here. I'm fine."

Jagger turned to Billy, who lifted his arms in confusion. "What the hell is going on?"

Jagger turned to Fiona, puzzled himself. "What are you doing here? In that vault?"

Before she could reply, Jagger reached for her. She was glad that her remaining vials of holy water were shoved deep into the pockets of her jacket. He took her arms, and she slid to the floor, a plume of ash and dust coming with her.

He stared at her, searching her eyes, then he drew her close against him, shaking for a moment.

Then, suddenly angry, he pushed her away. "What were you doing in there?" he demanded.

"I was meeting Billy here," she murmured.

"Why were you meeting him? And in a tomb?"

"Just in the cemetery."

"And what are *you* doing here?"

He was silent for a long moment.

"Jagger?"

"I asked you a question you've yet to answer," he said firmly.

"I was meeting Billy because..."

Billy suddenly gasped. "You asked me to come here because you didn't believe me! You thought—oh my God! You really thought I killed those girls. That I wanted Abigail so badly that I would not only kill her and make her a vampire so she could be with me for all eternity, but I'd kill two other women just to make it look like some demented serial killer was on the loose! And then...then you threw holy water on me."

"You threw holy water on him?" Jagger asked.

"Yes," she admitted. "But it didn't do anything." She smoothed back her hair, trying for dignity. It was difficult when she was covered in the ash of a long dead Grigsby. "Don't you see? If it didn't burn him, he's not evil. He's not the killer. I don't know how I knew it would work that way, but I did."

"Fiona, do you know what kind of danger you could have been getting into?" Jagger demanded.

"I know how to take care of myself," she said. "I'm a Keeper, remember?"

"You're also human," Jagger reminded her.

She inhaled. "It made sense. Billy was a suspect. Now he's cleared."

Billy stared at her incredulously. "I can't believe you really thought I could be a murderer."

"You *are* a vampire," Fiona reminded him.

"I'm a civilized vampire," Billy said. "I'm—I'm a student. I'm American as apple pie."

"Billy, I'm sorry, but I had to know. It's—it's my job. I'm the Keeper," Fiona said.

"You may be the Keeper," Jagger said softly, "but you're in danger.

"Someone—and I think it was the killer—called me to make sure I know he intends to kill you."

"What?" Fiona and Billy asked in unison.

"Billy, give me your cell phone," Jagger said.

"Hey! It wasn't me. I'm a good guy, remember? She just proved it," Billy said.

"Billy, your phone," Jagger said.

Billy shook his head, reached into his pocket and produced his phone. Jagger took it and checked the call history.

"That the only phone you're carrying?" he demanded.

"Search me," Billy said, lifting his arms, then looked indignant when Jagger took him up on the offer and patted him down.

"I didn't call you," Billy said.

"All right. And neither of you saw anyone else in the cemetery?" Jagger demanded.

"No," Billy said.

"Someone else was here," Fiona admitted.

"What? And when were you going to tell me this? Who was it?" Jagger demanded.

"I don't know—I heard…noises, so I ran in here. And then I heard the gate creaking, but then you and Billy showed up, and whoever it was ran away," she said.

"It was the killer," Jagger said.

"How can you know that?" Fiona asked him, feeling even more uneasy than she had before, because instinct told her he was right.

The killer had been close. But she hadn't been helpless; she had been ready to fight. Even if the holy water had only been enough to wound but not kill, it would have bought her the time to turn, and that would have given her the strength to fight.

She shuddered, spooked by the knowledge that she was a target. She was the vampires' Keeper, and yet a creature was out there, ready, willing—no, eager—to kill her.

"I found Sean O'Casey on Bourbon Street, and we put a satellite trace on my phone. The killer hung up before we could pinpoint his location, but we were able to target this part of town, and given this case, I was sure he had to be in the cemetery." He took her by the shoulders and stared into her eyes. "Look, you've got to get out of here. Now. I don't want to have to explain your presence to the police. I'll just say it was a lead that didn't pan out, that if he was here, he got away. Fiona, please, go home and stay there. Billy, stay with her."

Fiona steeled herself mentally and drew herself up with all the dignity she could muster. "I am the Keeper," she reminded him. "This is my business as much as it's yours."

"Fiona," Jagger said, "I'm begging you, for everyone's sake, to take care, now more than ever. Please. Go home, and let Billy stay with you and your sisters until I can get there. This killer is after you. Somehow he knew you were meeting Billy here. He intended to catch you unaware. Please. You are responsible not only for us but *to* us—and in turn, *we* are responsible for *you*. I balance dangerously between a police force that has no idea we exist and the reality of what we are. I have to be here when backup arrives—and I have to be here alone."

With the situation put in that perspective, she felt like a fool, but she had no intention of betraying that fact.

"All right. Billy, let's go," she said.

"Of course," he agreed, nodding earnestly.

Together, they hurried out the door, and she and Billy headed away from the main gate. They could already hear sirens, and with the police arriving soon, they would have to scale a wall to get out.

A minute later, after leaping gently to the pavement, they hurried back into the French Quarter.

Looking at her, Billy laughed.

"What?"

"You look like a corpse."

"Thank you."

"No, you're all gray and dirty from hiding in that vault."

"Oh, that makes it so much better."

"I'm just hoping we don't meet anyone on the way back."

"Me, too. When we get there, you explain to my sisters while I hop in the shower, okay?"

"They won't suspect me, will they?" Billy asked.

She shook her head. "Not when you're with me,"

she promised, even though she was all too aware that Caitlin certainly seemed to hate Jagger. Maybe she just felt threatened by his close relationship with Fiona.

"It'll be fine—you'll explain, and I'll shower and try not to look like a corpse."

"Okay, deal. And then, perhaps…" Billy murmured as they walked.

"Perhaps what?" Fiona asked.

"Perhaps I could see her tonight?" he asked wistfully. "Abigail, I mean."

"Billy, David is working with her on her new identity," she reminded him.

He swallowed. "But her memorial is tomorrow. It will be a tough day for her. She might need a friend tonight," he said.

"Perhaps," she said softly, feeling suddenly very fond of Billy.

Someone out there was planning to kill her.

It wasn't Billy, and there were very few others she could be so certain about.

Tony Miro arrived in the first of the screeching police cars.

Jagger met him at the front gate, which had been opened by a representative of the church, as a number of other officers spilled from their cars.

"We need to get some floodlights and search the entire cemetery," Jagger said. "Someone was in here tonight, and we need to find him or at least whatever traces he left behind."

Police with portable floodlights went marching grimly into the cemetery. With three bodies so far, no one complained that it was a tedious task that would probably lead to nothing, as the other cemetery searches had.

But it didn't lead to nothing. They hadn't been there long before Sean O'Casey, who'd been among the first arrivals, shouted, drawing Jagger and a half dozen others to where he stood.

He was over by the Grigsby vault, hunched down by a gargoyle that guarded the family gates.

"What?" Jagger demanded.

"I haven't touched it," Sean said, pointing. "There!"

Jagger knelt down and saw that something was stuffed behind the stone monster.

Celia Larson and several of the crime scene techs ran up just then. She pushed her way through the cluster of officers, shouting, "Damn it, don't go touching anything without gloves on!"

Jagger didn't have gloves, so he waited for Celia, who immediately reached behind the gargoyle.

"Damn," she said, looking at him, her eyes wide.

"What the hell is it?" Sean demanded.

"A nightgown. A white nightgown. Just like the others," Jagger said, and stood. He felt sick, thinking how close Fiona had come to being a victim tonight, but he had to remain stoic. It was his job to keep the balance.

He was suddenly nothing less than desperate to be with Fiona.

But he was the lead investigator; he had to supervise the search for clues that was going on with such grim determination.

While the officers and techs continued to comb the

cemetery, he put through a call to Fiona. When she answered her phone, his relief was limitless.

She and Billy were both at her house, and he spoke to Billy for a few minutes before hanging up, glad to hear that both Caitlin and Shauna were being courteous. They were all watching a comedy Shauna had rented, Billy reported. Yes, Fiona seemed ready to crawl the walls, but they had gone through the house, closing and locking windows and doors, and they were armed and ready in case of attack.

There wasn't going to be an attack on the house, Jagger was certain. But it didn't hurt that they were on the alert.

He thanked Billy and hung up, then called David Du Lac. It took a while to get him. Valentina answered the phone, her voice low and sultry as she questioned him, then explained that she would have to find David, implying that it could take some time.

Jagger suggested that he really needed her to hurry up.

Finally David came to the phone.

"David, have you seen Mateas Grenard?" Jagger asked without preamble.

"Grenard? No," David said. "He hasn't been around at all today. Pretty much no one has. The place is more than half empty. People are getting scared."

"Yes," Jagger agreed. "And things will get worse if we don't find this guy."

"Why are you looking for Grenard? Do you actually suspect him? Personally I think the guy is all mouth," David said. "Mouth, not teeth."

"A witness gave the police artist a description of someone seen in the vicinity of the cemetery after the last murder. And that someone looked pretty much identical to Mateas Grenard," Jagger said. "So keep an eye out for him. And if you see him, call me. Immediately. All right?"

"Of course," David agreed. "Of course."

Jagger closed his phone and began to pace in front of the Grigsby tomb. It seemed forever ago that they had found the first victim.

Forever…and yet the murders had taken place in almost no time. If the killer kept up this pace, they were in serious trouble.

The nightgowns…The nightgowns were his only real clue.

And they had found one here tonight.

One intended for Fiona.

He could barely restrain himself while the team went through the cemetery. Finally they determined that they weren't going to discover anything else that night, so he said his goodbyes and left.

Forgetting his car, heedless of those around him, he slipped out the gate, around the corner of wall, turned to shadow and flew—like a bat out of hell—to Fiona's.

The mood was, beyond a doubt, tense.

When they heard someone knocking on the front door, all three sisters and Billy Harrington leaped from their chairs. Fiona wanted to kick herself for overreacting, then wondered why she cared, when the whole evening hadn't gone well. Caitlin and Shauna had been horrified by her appearance when she and Billy had walked into the house, and it had only gotten worse when they'd heard the story.

She had told them about her trip to the church, and the

holy water, and that Billy had passed the test. After that they had tried to relax, watching a movie, even laughing on occasion.

They were still as tense as taut wire.

"It's just the door," Caitlin said.

"It's Jagger," Fiona said, and hurried to answer.

"Don't open it without checking!" Caitlin warned, running after her.

Fiona paused, looking back at her reproachfully. "No, of course not," she said.

"Jagger doesn't need to knock, does he? He's been invited in," Caitlin reminded her.

"He would knock anyway," Fiona said. "He's polite, okay?"

She looked through the peephole, and it was indeed Jagger. She quickly let him in.

He didn't care about Caitlin standing there staring at him with ill-concealed hostility, as he pulled Fiona into his arms. He didn't do anything, though; he just held her. She could feel him trembling again, and she realized she'd been angry earlier when she should have been gratified.

He was afraid for her. Afraid as she had been in the tomb, hiding in the vault, hearing the gate creaking as it opened.

Afraid as she was now, because her parents had seemed all powerful to her, and they'd had to use all that power and give up their lives to stop the violence that had broken out before, and now it was all up to her.

She held Jagger in return, drawing strength from him. She wasn't alone. She had her sisters…and she had Jagger.

Caitlin cleared her throat. "So now the killer is threatening my sister. What's taking so long? Why haven't you found this monster?"

Jagger was still holding Fiona close, but she could tell from the sudden tension in him that he was staring at Caitlin.

Just as Billy and Shauna came running up, Jagger said, "I will find the killer, Caitlin."

Fiona looked up at him. "*We* will find the killer." She turned to Caitlin. "We'll find him. I swear it."

"Before the next victim dies?" Caitlin asked. Without waiting for an answer, she turned and headed for her own apartment.

"She's just scared," Shauna said, when Caitlin was gone.

Not to mention that she hated vampires and always had, Fiona thought.

Billy ignored the tension and turned to Jagger. "I'm so glad you're here and I can go. Jagger, please, I need to see Abigail. I mean, come on. It's not like I haven't been to Underworld often enough before. And there's going to be a memorial service for her tomorrow. She needs me," Billy said.

"I think it would be fine," Fiona said.

Jagger looked at her, and a small smile just barely lifted his lips.

"Fiona is the Keeper," he said. "If it's all right with her, it's all right with me. I'll call David and arrange it. Just make sure you're back in your room by morning."

"Of course," Billy assured him. "Of course."

"Just make sure everything is locked up, okay?" Shauna said. "I'm going to try to get some sleep."

"Good night," Fiona said.

"Good night. And don't worry. I'll make sure the door is locked and the house is safe," Jagger promised.

Shauna nodded and headed up the stairs. Jagger pulled out his phone and called David Du Lac, and in moments Billy was on his way out, a happy man.

When the house was locked, Fiona said, "I was afraid you weren't going to let Billy see Abigail."

"I couldn't stop him tonight," Jagger said.

"Because—you were going to defer power to me?" she asked.

"I never even had to think about it," Jagger said. "I knew how desperate I was to see you tonight, Fiona. And I couldn't deny Billy."

She walked back into his arms.

She wasn't sure how they made it up to her bedroom.

She only knew that in minutes her flesh was against his, and his hands were on her, drawing her close. There were intense moments in which he just held her, drawing her closer and closer, as if he could pull her underneath his skin and into his very being.

Then there were moments when all that was separate and distinct between them was erotically enhanced, when his lips found the most erogenous zones of her body, when his tongue teased. And then he thrust into her, and they came together in a flood of passion and urgency, writhed and arched together with a wild and abandoned need, then climaxed ecstatically, shuddering, holding on, holding in, cradling one another as they drifted down to the coolness of the sheets and the air around them.

That night Jagger didn't sleep. He lay, staring up at the ceiling, cradling her against him in the darkness.

"I have to find the killer," he said.

"*We* have to find the killer," she told him. "I told you that."

He shook his head. "Not anymore. I have to find the killer—before he finds you."

Jagger was awakened by his cell phone.

It was Tony Miro.

"Jagger, I think we know the store," Tony said excitedly.

Jagger frowned, still trying to blink sleep from his eyes. He seldom needed much sleep, but when he did sleep, it was deeply.

"The store?" he murmured now.

"Where the killer bought the nightgowns. Hey, where are you?"

"On my way in. What time is it?" Jagger asked.

"Ten-fifteen," Tony told him.

Jagger tried not to groan aloud. He'd overslept.

"Where are you—that's the question. I'll be right there."

"Ooh La La," Tony told him.

"What?"

"It's the name of a shop over on Royal Street. I'm not a hundred percent certain, but…just come on down here. You'll see what I mean."

"On my way."

Jagger leaped out of bed. Fiona was still sound asleep. Apparently her sisters had decided not to interrupt the two of them.

Maybe Shauna had said a good word, because Caitlin certainly wouldn't cut him any slack. She hated the fact that he was in the house.

He showered and dressed quickly, and looked down at Fiona.

She made him tremble inwardly, constantly. He watched her sleeping, the gentle rise and fall of her breasts, the pulse at her throat. Her lips were slightly open as she hugged a pillow.

Her back was sleek and long, and every inch of her arresting and arousing. The golden spill of her hair would have stopped his heart if it still beat. He was ridiculously in love.

He pressed his lips against the gold of her hair, but she didn't waken.

He slipped out.

Afraid that if he waited longer, he would remember the killer's threat and be afraid to leave her side.

The sound of the phone was shattering, but Fiona tried to ignore it. She wanted to sleep and dream. She wanted to think of the future—of a vacation.

Time away.

Long days on a beach…

Mexico, the Caribbean. Texas or Florida. Anywhere… away.

Finally she gave in and answered. David Du Lac was on the other end of the line.

"Hey," he said tensely.

"Hey what?" she asked.

"He's here," David said.

"Um—who?" Fiona asked.

"Mateas. Mateas Grenard. Jagger thinks he may be involved in all this somehow, and he wanted to know if he showed up here. Well, he's here."

"Jagger isn't with me. Did you try his phone?" she asked.

"Yes. I don't know why he isn't answering," David said, sounding worried. "I'm not sure what to do."

"David, I'm on my way over," Fiona told him.

"Wait! If he's the killer..."

"It's daytime, I'm forewarned and you'll be there. And I'll try to get hold of Jagger myself, so he can join us."

"All right," David said, sounding uncertain. "No, I'll try calling him again. You just get over here as quickly as you can. I don't like this."

Fiona said firmly, "Call Jagger's partner, and call the leprechaun—Sean O'Casey. One of them will find Jagger soon enough if he's not answering his own phone. And have some faith in me, okay? I am your Keeper, after all."

"I just don't want to lose you, kid," he said.

She smiled, though of course he couldn't see it. "Thanks. I'm going to call August Gaudin, too. It will look like friends meeting by chance for lunch. Oh, you should call Jennie Mahoney, too. All right?"

David agreed and hung up.

Fiona bounded out of bed and into the shower. As soon as she was dressed she hurried downstairs. She found a note on the door from her sisters.

We're at the store. You stay home.

They had each signed it individually.

She left a note in return.

Love you two so much. Gone to David's.

After taping it on the door, she headed out.

Tony Miro was an excellent cop, even when given a tedious task. Jagger started off at a quick pace to meet him at Ooh La La.

The owner and shopkeeper, a woman of about thirty-five with the improbable name of Misty Mystique, was charming and determined to be helpful.

She was slim, blonde, pretty—and worriedly talking to Tony when Jagger arrived, leaving her assistant to help the customers.

Tony introduced Misty and Jagger, explained that she carried all four nightgown styles they'd found so far, and let Jagger take it from there.

"Did you sell the nightgowns yourself?" he asked. When she nodded, he said, "All to one person, or were they sold to several people?"

"Each one was sold to a different person," Misty told him, her dark brown eyes huge. "They were all men, though. Do you really think I sold one of those nightgowns to the killer?"

Jagger showed her the artist's renderings of Mateas Grenard and the unknown man from the strip club.

Her eyes widened further.

"Yes! I sold one of the nightgowns to each of these men."

"What about the others? Please, this is very important. Can you remember what they looked like? Did they pay cash, or do you have the credit card receipts?" Jagger asked.

"How odd. Every one was sold for cash," Misty told him.

"Is it possible for you to leave the store?" he asked her. "I know I'm asking a lot, but perhaps you could help our artist create sketches of the other two customers."

"Yes, of course. Except that I'm afraid to leave Lilly alone these days," she said quietly, nodding toward her assistant.

The girl was perhaps twenty-five, pretty.

And blonde.

"We'll call in an officer to keep an eye on her," Jagger promised.

"But if a cop just hangs around in here, I'm not sure I'll get any customers," she said, then sighed. "This is so terrible. Everyone is afraid and tourism is down—and I want to be smart, but I don't want to go out of business."

"Don't worry—he'll just be out on the street, in plain clothes, watching the store but not getting in the way or drawing any attention himself," Jagger assured her.

Misty agreed, so Jagger put through a call and arranged for Michael Shrine, one of the best cops and most trustworthy shapeshifters of Jagger's acquaintance, to take the assignment—and use a few of his "talents" while he was at it.

Michael could stand guard all day—and no one would ever know he was out there the whole time, much less that he was a cop.

As soon as Michael got there, Jagger, Tony and Misty headed down to the station.

It took about a couple of hours, but at the end he had a very curious bunch of sketches.

First there were the two they already had: Mateas Grenard and the unknown man from the strip club.

The third drawing was of Billy Harrington.

The fourth was of David Du Lac.

Chapter 14

Valentina was standing at the hostess desk. The luncheon courtyard had only just opened when Fiona arrived, but already Valentina was guarding her stand with buxom majesty.

"Good morning," Fiona told her. "David is expecting me."

Valentina arched a brow with royal disdain. "I don't believe so."

"I spoke to him earlier. I assure you, he's expecting me," Fiona said, and stared hard at the other woman.

Valentina's eyes fell. "Look, maybe he *was* expecting you, but if so, he didn't tell me. And he left around half an hour ago, muttering something under his breath."

Had something happened? If so, Fiona wondered, why hadn't he called her? She checked her cell phone for missed calls. Damn! His number was listed.

"What about Mateas Grenard?" she asked.

Valentina waved a hand in the air. "I don't know. He comes here...sometimes."

"What about now?" Fiona asked. "Is he here now?"

Valentina wrinkled her nose. "So good-looking," she murmured. "But...a vampire. The vampires come and go as they please."

"All right, I'll try again. Have you seen him since you got here today?" Fiona asked.

Valentina gave it some thought. "No, I do not believe I have. But the vampires often go straight into the main room." Suddenly Valentina smiled sunnily.

"August Gaudin is here—with Jennie Mahoney," she offered.

Fiona decided that maybe Valentina was more than a shapeshifter.

She had to be a schizophrenic, as well. She was nice one minute, haughty the next.

Fiona looked out toward the courtyard and saw Jennie Mahoney and August Gaudin chatting away.

"Thanks. I'll join them," Fiona said, deciding that would be safer than checking the main room of the club, the massive core of the old church, on her own. "Did you catch anything David was saying? Do you have any idea where he went?"

Valentina shrugged. "No, but I'm sure he'll be back. I think August and Jennie were expecting him, too."

Fiona walked past Valentina and headed for the small table where the werewolf and the shapeshifter were sitting, deep in conversation.

"Morning," she said.

They both looked up.

"Ah, Fiona!" August said, and, ever the gentleman, he rose.

Jennie offered her a smile that wasn't much warmer than Valentina's usual attitude.

Fiona accepted the chair August drew out for her. "Lovely to see you both."

"We're a bit perplexed, but now that you're here, maybe you can clear things up. You and David called us, asking us to lunch, but he isn't here," August told her.

"Something needs to be done," Jennie said firmly. "Three murders now. One corpse missing. And the police still don't have an ID on the last victim."

"They're doing everything possible," Fiona said, knowing she sounded defensive. Too bad. She *was* defensive. Jagger DeFarge was working nonstop—as a vampire *and* as a policeman. She found herself leaning forward. "Jennie, you know that the police don't have a prayer of solving this case, but Jagger is doing everything he can. As to not putting a name to the latest victim, that's…that's not that unusual. Her prints aren't in any system. She doesn't match the description of any missing women. And you know damned well where that 'missing' corpse is."

"Yes," Jennie said primly, wrinkling her nose. "She is another vampire—despite all our unspoken agreements."

"Abigail will be an asset to our community and…you know it," Fiona said.

Jennie shook her head and sighed. "I'm sorry, Fiona. It's a terrible situation, and even I can't help but be afraid. And please forgive me for saying this, but it does seem as if vampire society is having trouble managing its own."

"We're managing just fine," Fiona said, deciding not

to argue the point that no one had yet ruled out the possibility of the killer being a shapeshifter. She rose.

"Aren't you going to wait for David?" August asked her.

"I'm going to find David," she said.

And Mateas Grenard, she added silently. There was no reason to tell Jennie and August her suspicions. The lynch mob mentality could take root as easily among the inhabitants of the underworld as among the humans.

"All right," August told her. He pulled out his old pocket watch and checked the time. "I'll wait awhile longer—might as well have lunch while I'm here—so call me if you find him. I have a meeting with the tourism board this afternoon," he said, grimacing. "Anything positive to tell them will be most welcome."

"I'll stay for lunch, as well, and then my poetry group is meeting," Jennie said. "So please call me, too, if you find out anything—if you find David."

"Yes, of course," Fiona said, and smiled.

She left the courtyard and the club, and started down the street, then found a dark alley and…changed.

She was mist, had substance but not. She could move with the air, with the breeze. She was a cloud, she was a shadow and, like both, she could become an illusion that teased at the senses but passed otherwise unnoticed.

She reentered the club and slipped unseen into the body of the church.

By day it was an oddly haunted place, even more Gothic than it seemed by night. In the evening and into the wee hours, music throbbed in the air, and the beat itself could be felt in the walls. Patrons danced, drank and laughed. Men and women flirted—and more—with each other, or with their own sex. Everyone was welcome, everyone was accepted. Colors, religions, sexes, sexual orientations, old and young. Everybody came to play. Laughter was a melody that complemented the melody of the music.

Now the huge room was empty.

The massive stained-glass windows let in a whisper of light broken into a myriad of colors.

Medieval and Victorian art lined the walls.

St. George regally sat his horse and stared down at the dragon in its death throes.

The old stone of the deconsecrated church kept the heat of the city at bay and created an aura of time gone by. The place had an atmosphere all its own.

Bodies had once been buried beneath the floor, and some of the headstones that were set between the marble pavers were still legible. All the bodies should have been removed and taken to one of the local cemeteries, but politics and money were always a factor, and some had been left behind. Now the place was silent and steeped in a potent brew made up of the combined energies of the living and the dead.

Fiona stood still, *feeling* the space. She looked around and saw no one, but there were side altars, and nooks and crannies, a choir loft behind what had once been the high altar.

She sensed that she was not alone. But she was ready, waiting and wary.

"Fiona?"

It was Billy Harrington's voice, calling to her softly from the shadows surrounding the choir loft.

She didn't answer, and he stepped out, holding hands with Abigail.

He looked even more afraid than she had felt, and she let out a silent sigh of relief.

"Billy, are you alone here—you and Abigail?"

"Yes."

"Do you know where David is?" she asked.

"No," Billy said, puzzled. "He isn't here?"

"No, and he was supposed to meet me," Fiona told him.

Billy looked at Abigail. "We saw him at breakfast," she said.

"Do you think he might have gone to my memorial service?"

"Abigail wanted to go. I convinced her that she couldn't," Billy said.

"You definitely shouldn't be there," Fiona said. "I'm sorry."

"I—I suppose it's better this way," Abigail said. She wore a look of indelible sadness. "I'd want to comfort the nuns. I'd want to tell them that I was really all right, that things would be okay."

"Precisely," Fiona said softly. "Won't people be surprised that you're not there?" she asked Billy.

"They'll understand that I couldn't bear it," he said, looking at Abigail with such adoration that Fiona wondered how she had ever doubted the boy. He would have died a thousand times over rather than do the slightest harm to her.

"I think I'll go over to your memorial, though," Fiona said. "Where is it being held?"

When Billy told her, she realized that it was the same church where the service for her parents had been held, and where she had just gotten the holy water.

She imagined that she knew just which priest was reading the service.

David might have gone—but if so, why hadn't he left her a message about his change of plans?

"All right, you two stay low—and I mean low," Fiona said.

"We're staying right here—we're not budging," Billy assured her.

Fiona changed, drawing a little gasp from Abigail, who whispered to Billy, "She's so good. She's a human being, but she has such power…."

"Well, of course," Billy replied. "She's the Keeper."

Fiona wished she felt as powerful as Abigail thought she was.

Still, it was good that others saw her that way. In fact, it was crucial that they did.

She slipped away from the deconsecrated church.

In an alley, she found her substance again.

She decided to hail a cab and get to the memorial as quickly as she could. On the way, she tried calling David again, but he didn't answer.

The driver let her off right in front of the church. Mourners were walking in slowly, some chatting softly, others quiet and thoughtful.

She saw a number of the students she had interviewed, along with what could have passed for a flock of very tall penguins. Every nun in the city must be attending, she thought.

She started to head in herself, but as she did so, her cell phone rang. Quickly, without even looking at caller ID, she answered, "David?"

There was silence, then a husky laugh.

"Is it true that blondes have more fun?" a raspy voice asked.

She froze, certain that the murderer was on the phone.

"I *will* find you. And I *will* destroy you," she said.

"This city was founded by the French, ruled by the Spanish, and peopled by those of all colors and faiths—along with all kinds of creatures, of course. Like vampires. Drinkers of blood. Killers."

"Men kill, too, but they don't have to, and neither do vampires."

"Ah, that's where you're terribly wrong! Man loves to kill. And vampires long not only to kill but to possess, to capture a beauty and watch her eyes as they consume her blood and her life drifts away."

"You're sick," she said, realizing with a nauseous feeling that the killer was a vampire. One of hers gone over to the side of darkness and death.

That husky laughter that seemed to slip right beneath her skin sounded in her ear again.

"Then there were three. Three little Keepers, and all of them blonde. I'm watching you right now. And you should know—I have a little blonde beauty. She's not you, but she's so like you. She isn't dead yet, but she will be soon. When we hang up, you will close your phone. You will start walking back toward the French Quarter, and you will keep walking. If anyone calls, you will not answer your phone, because I will be watching you all the way. Will it be a long walk, you ask. Yes, it will. But if I see you reach for your phone, if I see you so much as say hello to a stranger, I will kill your sister before you can reach your destination. Do you understand?"

Fiona felt as if she had been stabbed through the heart with an icicle.

Caitlin.

Shauna.

Oh, God.

Who did he have?

How could he possibly have gotten to either one of them?

Maybe he didn't have one of her sisters. Maybe it was a bluff.

How could she take that chance?

She looked at the church. David might well be there.

Jagger, too. So close, and yet…

"Do you understand?"

"Where am I going?"

"I'll call you when you're closer."

"I thought I wasn't supposed to answer my phone."

"I can see you. I will see you all the way there. It will ring once, stop, and then start to ring again. Then, only then, do you answer your phone."

"If you're following me, you can't be holding one of my sisters hostage," she said.

The laughter sounded again.

"Whatever made you think I was working alone?"

Fiona wasn't answering her phone again, but today Jagger had no intention of wasting any time. A storm was rolling in, bringing early winter darkness and rain. He wanted to be back with her before the darkness came.

He called the shop. "This is Jagger. Where is Fiona?" he asked without even trying to figure out which sister he was talking to.

"We left her sleeping at home."

"She's not answering her phone," Jagger said.

"Oh, Lord, I'll have to close up shop."

"I'm sorry," he said flatly, "but is this Shauna or Caitlin?"

"Shauna. Caitlin went out. August Gaudin called, something about a meeting with the tourism board. Said he was looking for Fiona, too, and Caitlin said she'd go talk to him. Personally I think it was my place to go. I'm the Keeper for the werewolves, after all."

"You're alone at the shop, and Caitlin is out?" he asked.

He wasn't sure why that worried him so much. He trusted August Gaudin. Or did he? Did he trust anyone anymore?

"You stay where you are—and while you're at it, stay up front, where people can see you. I'm not far, just at the station, and I'm on my way. I'll go to the house with you," Jagger said.

"All right. But…Fiona's probably just sleeping and didn't hear the phone. What do you think is the matter?"

"I don't know. Maybe nothing. Just wait for me."

"I'll be here, Jagger," Shauna said. "For whatever it's worth, I believe in you. I know you're doing your best."

"Thanks," he said, and hung up.

He hit the street and started walking, but by the time he hit Royal Street, he was running.

It was a long walk. Visitors to New Orleans had a tendency to stay in the French Quarter, where they could walk to anything. If they were headed to the Garden

District or Uptown, they were usually bright enough to drive, grab a streetcar or take a taxi, options that were forbidden to her.

Her phone rang half a dozen times.

She didn't touch it.

He had said, *Whatever made you think I was working alone?*

He could have a partner. And his partner could have one of her sisters while he was watching her.

Or he could be lying.

She didn't know which.

She looked up at the sky. Clouds were roiling above her, and it was growing darker by the minute. A breeze had picked up, and as she walked, the trees were being stripped of leaves. In the wind, they seemed to reach down for her as if they had boney, skeletal arms and fingers. The sound of the rustling leaves was like the laughter of the man who had called her.

Darkness was coming.

The killer wanted darkness. The false darkness of a storm, fading to the ebony blackness of a moonless night.

Her fingers twitched on her phone.

He might be bluffing.

But he might not be.

Caitlin…Shauna…

She couldn't take a chance.

As she got closer and closer to the French Quarter, she felt the shadows darkening around her and began to imagine she heard the whoosh of wings.

Giant wings.

Shadow wings.

Following her.

She had to come up with a plan.

And she had to save her sister.

Those two thoughts kept her moving.

And all the while, the shadows were darkening.

Shauna was standing right inside the doorway of the shop, waiting for him. She was ready with a sign for the door—*Must close early—our deepest apologies. Please come back*.

He nodded to her as she locked up and they started down the street.

"Thanks for coming with me," he said.

She glanced at him sidewise. "Are you kidding? I'm losing my mind. Neither one of them is answering her cell phone!"

"Caitlin isn't answering, either?"

"No," Shauna said. Her face was white with worry.

He pulled out his cell phone and called August Gaudin. A secretary answered.

"May I speak with August, please. This is Jagger DeFarge."

"Oh, Detective. I'm so sorry. He left—he said something about lunch, and then he had a meeting to attend."

"This is his cell phone, isn't it?" Jagger asked, perplexed.

"Yes, yes—he's a brilliant man, but forgetful. He left it on his desk. I just heard it ringing because I was dropping off some papers that needed to be signed," the secretary said.

"I see. Well, if he comes in, please ask him to call me," Jagger said.

Shauna looked worried. "He's not there?"

"It's all right. We'll get to the house, see if we can find out where Fiona went and then I'll get my men looking for both of them," he promised her.

She stared at him with huge eyes. "But they won't know what they're looking for."

"Shauna, there are...*others*—on the force. We'll find them."

They reached the house. As soon as they went in and closed the door, they found the note Fiona had left.

Jagger swore softly.

As he did, his phone rang.

He answered it crisply, praying it was Fiona.

It was Sean O'Casey, and his voice was excited.

"I've been going through the FBI database, and I got a hit, Jagger. I just got a hit."

"On what? The last victim?"

"No, the sketch of the man at the strip club. The guy no one has been able to find. And you're never going to believe who he is."

The rain was just waiting to fall.

The clouds were growing oppressive, and Fiona knew it would be sweltering if not for the strange breeze blowing through the trees.

Street lamps, whose sensors told them to turn on when darkness fell, began to light up, but their illumination seemed oddly weak, creating only small pools of brightness against the shadows.

She could change, she reminded herself.

And she was still armed. She felt surreptitiously for the holy water in her pocket.

It didn't matter if a creature was Jewish, Hindu, Christian or worshipped aliens, any touch of the one true goodness that ruled all religions would work against any personification of evil.

Or so she believed...

She had to trust in that belief. Power lay in belief, and most of all, she knew, she had to believe in herself.

Leaves rustled.

And the growing darkness seemed to become one massive shadow, hovering over her.

Her phone rang once. Stopped. And rang again.

She answered.

"Know where you're going yet?"

"No."

"Then I'll tell you. There's a cemetery near the Quarter where they haven't yet found a beautiful blonde. I'm sure you know which one. There is a mausoleum there, one I know you know—well."

Her heart seemed to stop.

She knew exactly what he was referring to.

"It's quite a glorious memorial, large and magnificent, with rows of crypts, and a massive sarcophagus right in the middle holding two Keepers not long gone. Have you figured out what I'm talking about yet?"

"Of course I have," she said, praying that she could keep her tone flat and dry. "Obviously."

That wretched laughter sounded again.

"Where else to find a beautiful blonde MacDonald than atop a MacDonald tomb? Move quickly," the voice added harshly. "Time is everything now."

"Thomas Anderson," Sean O'Casey said.

Jagger blinked and waited. When Sean didn't explain Jagger asked, "Am I supposed to recognize the name?"

"Yes. Well, maybe. He was a serial killer who preyed on women here—in the 1940s."

"The 1940s? He'd be way too old," Jagger said. "Can't be the same man."

"Get this—he was killed in 1949, hanged by the neck until dead," Sean said.

So a ghost had been haunting the strip club.

Or the man had been hanged by the neck until dead—but bitten by a vampire while no one was looking?

Or…the man in the strip club had been a shapeshifter. But was he also their killer?

"Okay, Sean, thank you. I need you to get over here to the MacDonald house and stay with Shauna MacDonald."

"I'm on it."

"What?" Shauna protested. "Wherever you're going, I'm going with you."

"No," he told her.

"Hey, I'm not a damsel in distress—I'm a Keeper. I can turn into a wolf with massive teeth and long, long claws whenever I desire."

"Shauna, if anything happens, you have to survive. Do you understand? One of us has to be here to—to be the one to pick up the pieces if I don't manage to…"

"Don't you dare say it! My sisters have to be all right."

"Shauna, I'm begging you—it's imperative that we all think logically right now, and I need you here. What if I need help? I need to know there's someone I can reach."

"You better not be patronizing me," Shauna told him.

"I'm not. Sean O'Casey is coming over and—"

"I don't need police protection."

"He's a leprechaun—" Jagger began.

"A leprechaun?" Shauna asked, frowning fiercely. "You have a *leprechaun* coming to watch over me?"

"He's one of my best, trust me," Jagger said.

"A *leprechaun?*" she said again.

Just then there was a pounding on the door. He checked the peephole, then threw the door open and let Sean in.

Shauna stared at Sean O'Casey, then at Jagger.

"He's a *leprechaun?*" she demanded.

"It's the hormones in the milk," Sean said wearily. "Shauna, I know who you are—I saw you at the assembly. Please, I know your capabilities, have some faith in mine."

She turned back to Jagger, shaking her head. "At least he's a very good-looking leprechaun."

"We're all good-looking. We just don't tend to be tall," Sean assured her.

They would be fine together, Jagger decided, as he paused in the doorway. "Hang onto your cell phones, and be ready to go wherever I send you whenever you get a call."

"Whatever you say, sir," Sean promised.

Shauna nodded, and Jagger was on his way.

The gates to the cemetery were still open.

Fiona walked in, aware of the chill tendrils of the growing breeze at her nape, aware of the shadows taking shapes between the monuments and mausoleums.

The family vault was toward the far end, where once things had been pristine and beautiful, but where time and the elements had led to corrosion and decay. She and her sisters kept up the MacDonald tomb, but many of the surrounding families were long gone, and the three of them couldn't maintain everything that should have been maintained.

She walked over weeds and stones, and wove through broken bits of funerary art, past a row of fine vaults and toward a towering angel.

Past the angel, she reached an expanse of grass that led toward the family tomb.

And someone was standing there, waiting.

David Du Lac.

Jagger headed straight to Underworld.

Valentina was at the hostess stand, but he didn't bother to stop and speak with her. He strode straight into the courtyard, looking around. When he didn't see David, he turned and headed for the main room, bursting through the double doors.

Valentina came running up behind him. "What are you doing, Jagger?"

"Where's Fiona?"

Valentina shook her head. "She was here around lunchtime, but she left hours ago."

"I want to see David. Or Mateas Grenard. Is either of them here?"

"Mateas Grenard is here right now," a voice boomed.

The man rose from a shadowed table against the wall and strode toward Jagger. "What is it? Why are you looking for me?"

Jagger drew a copy of the sketch artist's rendering from his pocket.

"You were seen leaving the cemetery immediately

before the third murder was discovered. And now I can't find Fiona MacDonald—or her sister. So you will talk to me, and talk quickly, or—"

"I was never anywhere near that cemetery!" Grenard interrupted in protest.

"You also purchased a nightgown like the ones worn by the victims in all three murders," Jagger said.

"I've *never* bought a nightgown," Mateas protested.

Jagger reached into the lining of his jacket for the stake he carried at all times.

"You've spoken against our ways," Jagger said softly.

"So what? I'm innocent!" Mateas cried. He started to bare his teeth, his fangs growing, saliva dripping from them. "Where is your law?" he asked. "I'm innocent."

Jagger felt his own fangs growing, felt the fury begin to ripple through him.

Fury born of fear. Fear for Fiona.

"Stop, please!" a voice interrupted.

It was Abigail. Or Anne, as she was now called. She rushed forward, holding Billy's hand and dragging him with her. "Please, stop!" she said. "I don't know what's been going on today, but Mateas has been here with us for hours. He's been teaching me all kinds of history, and how to behave and things I need to know."

"She's telling the truth," Billy said.

Jagger's phone rang. This time it was Tony Miro.

Apparently Tony had taken over the database search when Sean left to stay with Shauna.

"Hey, boss. I went further on that dead guy thing— you know, the murderer who died in the forties. He wasn't just hanged. Folks in the city were crazy. They dug him up right after he was buried and chopped him into pieces. He wasn't walking around this city in any way, shape or form—not unless he had a doppelganger of some kind. Sorry, boss, wish I could be more helpful. Says he died without children, so this has to be some kind of a fluke. I'm sorry."

"Don't be sorry, Tony. You might just have given me exactly what I need."

Jagger snapped the phone shut and headed straight to the hostess station. He didn't see Valentina, but he did see her friend Sue.

He walked up to Sue and took her by the arm. "That was you before, wasn't it?" he said.

She flushed. "So what? Valentina just wanted some time off, so she asked me to cover for her. But there's this really cute guy over there, so…I wanted to see if he would like *me*."

He didn't reply. He was already halfway back to the church.

"Billy, you stay put with Abigail. Mateas, you come with me."

"Where are we going?"

"Where are the bodies found?" Jagger asked.

"In cemeteries," Mateas said. "But…which cemetery?"

"I think he's taken at least one MacDonald, so we're heading to the MacDonald vault."

"David," Fiona said. "It was you? I don't believe it."

"You don't believe what?" he asked. "That one of your precious vampires was a murderer? That you weren't in control? Well, believe it. Now it's up to you. Pick. I can kill you—or I can kill your sister."

"Or I can kill you," she said.

David shrugged. "Caitlin is not alone. She has supposedly been out all afternoon—with August Gaudin. But August is really in a meeting, and Caitlin—well, one bump on the head and...let's just say she's a bit tied up right now. So here, you see, is the problem. Either Caitlin goes free or you do. Either way, it's such a beautiful ending. Your precious sainted parents expended the last of their strength to stop the fighting. Now one of you will die on their tomb, and the races will go to war again over the evil of the vampires."

"Take me to Caitlin," Fiona said.

"Lift your arms," David said.

"I have no stakes on me," she said, lifting her arms as directed. She had to pray he wouldn't notice the little vials in her pocket.

"Jagger will be here to save me," she said.

David Du Lac laughed. "Jagger will be too busy chasing Mateas and hunting for someone he'll never find."

"What are you talking about?"

"A long dead serial killer," David said with pleasure. "A will-o'-the-wisp he'll never find."

"Take me to my sister."

"Do you really think you can save your miserable lives?" David asked.

"Of course."

He laughed. "Fine. Follow me."

He turned, knowing full well that she wouldn't do anything with Caitlin at risk. But as she followed him, a shadow suddenly loomed up before her.

"Stop!"

The voice...

The shadow resolved itself into a man, stumbling as he tried to walk forward.

David Du Lac swore, striding toward him. "You're harder to kill than I thought."

"Wait!" Fiona cried out.

For a moment she felt a shiver of uncertainty wash over her, but then she knew.

David Du Lac was the man struggling to reach her. And David Du Lac was the one going over to finish off a murder. The murder of a man who had wanted peace, who had opened his heart and his club to all of them.

"You're not David," she said to her captor. "And if you kill the real David, I swear, you'll never get a chance to murder me or my sister. Touch him and you die."

"Fiona, watch out!" the real David Du Lac cried.

Too late. The blow caught her on the head. Her last thought was that she'd never even sensed the shapeshifter's accomplice coming up behind her.

And when she awoke, she was lying on her parents' sarcophagus, next to her unconscious sister.

"I don't understand," Mateas said.

"The killer wants a war. He wants all vampires destroyed. First he tried to turn us against each other, and then he wants to turn everyone else against us," Jagger explained. It was difficult to speak. They were traveling as night and shadow, flying through the tempest the breeze had become.

"So the serial killer from the past—how does he fit in?" Mateas said.

"When I learned he had been dismembered, I knew then. The killer's a shapeshifter. He allowed a witness to see him in the guise of a long dead killer just to confuse us, so if we ever identified the man in the sketch, we wouldn't know what to think. And he appeared outside the cemetery as you," Jagger explained. "Now he believes the deaths of the Keepers will give him the opportunity he wants to control the entire New Orleans underworld."

"God help us," Mateas said.

They had reached the cemetery. Jagger motioned to Mateas to stay dead quiet as they tried to see what was happening.

Silently they made their way to the MacDonald mausoleum.

It was large, adorned with cherubs and angels. It sat past a shrine to little children who had died of yellow fever, and a monument to fallen Confederate soldiers.

Jagger noted the stained-glass window in the back, which had been broken in a recent storm and not yet replaced.

He motioned to Mateas to follow him, then moved in that direction.

They must not have expected that she would regain consciousness so quickly, because she could hear her attackers whispering as they struggled to tie her ankles, making so many things clear. She looked at Caitlin, who still seemed to be unconscious. Then she saw Caitlin open one eye and mouthed two words.

"Holy water."

Caitlin tried to nod, but she was clearly very weak.

Fiona looked at her captors and wasn't surprised to see Valentina.

Bitchy shapeshifter? Oh, yeah. She was a bitch, all right. And a murderess.

It made sense that the victims hadn't been sexually molested. The killers weren't sexual predators; they simply loathed vampires, wanted power and were willing to do anything to create chaos and blame it on the race they despised.

"I should have expected you," Fiona said. "Really. I mean, you are a jealous bitch, so this is really no big shock."

Valentina laughed. "I'm a bitch—but so are you. And tonight you'll be a dead bitch."

She wasn't beautiful anymore; she looked furious and mottled. She was going to change into something, Fiona thought, something ferocious, to slap her, claw at her…kill her.

But she was stopped by the person behind her.

The *woman* behind her.

"Stop it, let's get this done. Don't touch her! If you wanted to hurt her, you should have hit her harder."

Fiona knew the voice. And as the woman stepped out of the shadows, she also knew the face.

It was Jennie. Jennie Mahoney. The brilliant, uncrowned queen of the shapeshifting community.

"I'll get it done," Jennie said, staring at Fiona.

And then she started to change—into a vampire. She took on Jagger DeFarge's face and form, laughing all the while.

Behind her, Valentina began to laugh, and she started to change, too, shifting into Billy Harrington.

There was no time. Fiona fought against the pain in her head as she began to change herself, at the same time reaching for one of the vials of holy water.

Valentina reached for her, and she threw the vial.

Valentina shrieked and fell, twitching, screaming, to the ground.

As she fell, the real Jagger DeFarge burst into the room, brandishing his stake. In a rage, Jennie Mahoney flew at him, already changing form.

But a shapeshifter's weakness was that she could never be as strong as the real thing. Even as Jennie ripped and tore at him, becoming a wolf, a tiger and finally herself, Jagger fought her, slowly but surely bearing her down.

Valentina was on the ground, twisting and turning, becoming an octopus and snaking out a suction-cupped arm to wrest Caitlin from the table. Caitlin was weak, but she became a mouse, escaping the attack.

Someone else was there.

Mateas Grenard.

Fiona didn't know who was who anymore, and she tossed holy water at Mateas, who stared at her blankly.

"Sorry!" she cried swiftly.

She dug in her pockets for another vial. Valentina was a tiger now, and she lunged at Fiona, who ducked behind her parents' tomb.

Jagger flew at the shapeshifter, tearing at her with his fangs.

"I need holy water!" Caitlin, back in her own form, cried.

Fiona freed the vial from her pocket and tossed the water over Jennie Mahoney, who screamed as she writhed. Fiona splashed the rest of the vial's contents over Valentina.

Then the smell of charred flesh filled the air, and thick smoke rose from the shifters' still forms.

Suddenly everything was silent.

Exhausted, the four of them looked at each other, Fiona and Caitlin started hugging, both of them gasping for breath.,

They all jumped as someone lunged through the doorway.

"Thank God," David Du Lac—the real David Du Lac—gasped out. "I've been out there waiting, hoping... Well, we were all fooled, weren't we?"

Epilogue

It wasn't quite Mexico or the Riviera, and Fiona wasn't on a beach yet.

But still…

Just being alive was quite enough for the moment.

The condition of the women's bodies meant things had to look as if they had died in a fire, and luckily they had brought a gas lantern into the mausoleum with them, so it had been easy to spill the gas and light it.

Easy to physically carry out the action, anyway, a lot harder mentally. But the stone-and-brick tomb would survive, and the MacDonalds had given up their lives for peace—they would understand a little charring in the family vault.

The five of them had stayed to greet the police and firemen. Fiona had explained how she had been tricked into the mausoleum in search of her sister, and then she and Caitlin recounted how the two dead women had conspired to put the city in a panic and throw suspicion on the vampire cult. The murders themselves had been so bizarre that no one questioned such a bizarre explanation. Then there had been all the annoying paperwork, the even more annoying problem of dealing with the press, and then...

Then it was over.

No one could believe that Jennie had been behind the killings, and everyone wondered what demon had lived inside her. Sometimes hatred and anger could fester unseen, and the general theory was that that was what had happened with Jennie.

As far as Valentina went...

Fiona kept her own counsel on that.

Valentina was simply a bitch, as far as she was concerned, and that was that. She was a woman who'd wanted everything, and killing had seemed like nothing to her.

Some of the men mourned her. Even Fiona had to admit she'd been a beautiful bitch.

But the important thing was that they had brought an end to the situation. Jagger was upset that it had taken him so long to figure out the truth, but then again, no one in the human world or the paranormal community had suspected Jennie. And, of the two, she had been the leader. She had hated the vampires—and the Keepers—since the war. She had bided her time.

And now...

Now they were celebrating, and naturally the party was at Underworld. People from all over the city came, and not just the paranormal races but regular people were welcome, too.

The band was fantastic. The food was delicious. Alcohol flowed.

Fiona and Jagger had danced and danced. With each other, with shapeshifters, werewolves, and even a leprechaun or two.

It was a party to end all parties.

Finally she and Jagger slipped out, and stood alone under the stars.

"What do you think made Jennie so hateful?" Fiona asked, as he held her and she leaned back against him, gazing up at the night sky.

"Sue told me that she'd been in love with a vampire once. He rejected her," Jagger said.

"Do you think that's true?"

"I don't know," he said.

"Do you think that a werewolf and a shapeshifter, or, say, a shapeshifter and a leprechaun, could ever find true happiness? Or," she asked, turning into his arms, "a vampire and a Keeper?"

"Ah," he said thoughtfully. "Well, I know that I'm very much in love," he said. "In fact, I was thinking of slipping away and exploring just what love can be. I'd like to forget all about hate and evil and cruelty… and there's no better way than looking deeply into the possibilities that love holds."

She laughed and rose on her toes, and they kissed.

And then she whispered against his lips, "I'm quite ready to explore."

So they held hands and slipped away.

And looked deeply into love and all its endless possibilities.

* * * * *

HARLEQUIN®

nocturne™

COMING NEXT MONTH

Available October 26, 2010

#99 THE SHIFTERS
The Keepers
Alexandra Sokoloff

#100 SHADOW OF THE SHEIKH
Immortal Sheikhs
Nina Bruhns

REQUEST YOUR FREE BOOKS!

2 FREE NOVELS PLUS 2 FREE GIFTS!

 HARLEQUIN®

n○cturne™

Dramatic and Sensual Tales of Paranormal Romance.

YES! Please send me 2 FREE Harlequin® Nocturne™ novels and my 2 FREE gifts (gifts are worth about $10). After receiving them, if I don't wish to receive any more books, I can return the shipping statement marked "cancel." If I don't cancel, I will receive 4 brand-new novels every other month and be billed just $4.47 per book in the U.S. or $4.99 per book in Canada. That's a saving of at least 15% off the cover price! It's quite a bargain! Shipping and handling is just 50¢ per book.* I understand that accepting the 2 free books and gifts places me under no obligation to buy anything. I can always return a shipment and cancel at any time. Even if I never buy another book from Harlequin, the two free books and gifts are mine to keep forever.

238/338 HDN E9M2

Name _____ (PLEASE PRINT)

Address _____ Apt. #

City _____ State/Prov. _____ Zip/Postal Code

Signature (if under 18, a parent or guardian must sign)

Mail to the **Reader Service:**
IN U.S.A.: P.O. Box 1867, Buffalo, NY 14240-1867
IN CANADA: P.O. Box 609, Fort Erie, Ontario L2A 5X3
Not valid for current subscribers to Harlequin Nocturne books.

Want to try two free books from another line?
Call 1-800-873-8635 or visit www.ReaderService.com.

* Terms and prices subject to change without notice. Prices do not include applicable taxes. N.Y. residents add applicable sales tax. Canadian residents will be charged applicable provincial taxes and GST. Offer not valid in Quebec. This offer is limited to one order per household. All orders subject to approval. Credit or debit balances in a customer's account(s) may be offset by any other outstanding balance owed by or to the customer. Please allow 4 to 6 weeks for delivery. Offer available while quantities last.

Your Privacy: Harlequin Books is committed to protecting your privacy. Our Privacy Policy is available online at www.ReaderService.com or upon request from the Reader Service. From time to time we make our lists of customers available to reputable third parties who may have a product or service of interest to you. If you would prefer we not share your name and address, please check here. ☐

Help us get it right—We strive for accurate, respectful and relevant communications. To clarify or modify your communication preferences, visit us at www.ReaderService.com/consumerschoice.

*See below for a sneak peek from
our inspirational line, Love Inspired® Suspense*

*Enjoy this heart-stopping excerpt from
RUNNING BLIND
by top author Shirlee McCoy,
available November 2010!*

**The mission trip to Mexico was supposed to be an
adventure. But the thrill turns sour when Jenna Dougherty
and her roommate Magdalena are kidnapped.**

"It's okay. I'm here to help." The voice was as deep as the
darkness, but Jenna Dougherty didn't believe the lie. She
could do nothing but lie still as hands slid down her arms,
felt the rope around her wrists.

"I'm going to use a knife to cut you free, Jenna. Hold
still."

The cold blade of a knife pressed close to her head before
her gag fell away.

"I—" she started, but her mouth was dry, and she could
do nothing but suck in air.

"Shhh. Whatever needs to be said can be said when
we're out of here." Nick spoke quietly, his hand gentle on
her cheek. There and gone as he sliced through the ropes on
her wrists and ankles.

He pulled her upright. "Come on. We may be on
borrowed time."

"I can't leave my friend," Jenna rasped out.

"There's no one here. Just us."

"She has to be here." Jenna took a step away.

"There's no one here. Let's go before that changes."

"It's dark. Maybe if we find a light…"

"What did you say?"

"We need to turn on the light. I can't leave until I know that—"

"What can you see, Jenna?"

"Nothing."

"No shadows? No light?"

"No."

"It's broad daylight. There's light spilling in from the window I climbed in through. You can't see it?"

She went cold at his words.

"I can't see anything."

"You've got a nasty bruise on your forehead. Maybe that has something to do with it." His fingers traced the tender flesh on her forehead.

"It doesn't matter *how* it happened. I'm blind!"

Can Nick help Jenna find her friend or will chasing this trail have Jenna running blindly again into danger?

Find out in RUNNING BLIND, available in November 2010 only from Love Inspired Suspense.

SHLISEXP.I.I 10